TIM EWINS had an eight-year stand-up career alongside his accidental career in finance, before turning to writing fiction. He has previously written for DNA Mumbai, had two short stories highly commended and published in Michael Terence Short Story Anthologies, and had a brief acting stint (he's in the film *Bronson*, somewhere in the background). He lives in Bristol. *We Are Animals* is his first novel.

Praise for *We Are Animals*

A warm, funny and original story about chance meetings, unlikely friendships and love lost and found. Beautifully written, it's been one of my favourite books of 2020
Frances Quinn – author of *The Smallest Man*

A heartwarming tale of lost love and unlikely friendships, featuring a menagerie of animals who each have their story to tell
Waitrose Weekend

Wonderful. A funny, heartwarming and craftily clever book
Matson Taylor – author of *The Miseducation of Evie Epworth*

A feel-good story about how sometimes the best thing to do is just have faith that everything will work out in the end. It's the story we all need right now
Popsugar

I loved the wacky situations that Manjan found himself in because of misunderstandings. His antics reminded me of any good episode of Seinfeld
Books Over Everything

Not just a funny book – it's a story with genuine heart. At times I was reminded of Jonas Jonasson's novels, but in truth it's hard to compare *We Are Animals* to other works: it is resolutely its own beast
Ellie Hawkes – Elspells

An amazingly inventive, funny book that deals with fate, love, teenagers and chance. It's like *Life of Pi* on its gap year. Utterly brilliant!
Victoria Dowd – author of *The Smart Woman's Guide to Murder* and *Body on the Island*

A witty, engaging, offbeat tale of a decades-spanning love, set in various locations across the world and co-starring several animals
Bristol 24/7

If you read one book this year, read this one. Seriously good stuff
Stewart Giles – author of *The Beekeeper*

So beautifully and cleverly written, a feel-good story that makes you think deeper about everything we want in life and what life offers us. The symbolism is so stunning, I'm in awe
The Book Confessions

A debut of magical charm, wit and humour. Echoing the spirit and the style of Jonas Jonasson, Ewins has a wondrous voice of his own
Lancashire Times

A tale that will warm your heart while breaking it a little
A Little Bright Corner

Quirky, thought-provoking and downright entertaining
Susan A. King – author of *Marrow Jam* and *Banana Devil Cake*

A most tender and endearing tale about friendship, love and heartbreak
Satabdi

Both amusing and profound, this book stands out from the crowd, and will stay with you long after the sounds of the silent disco fade
Bookshine and Readbows

Something quite special. Laugh-out-loud funny, quirky and with hidden depth
Laura Besley – author of *The Almost Mothers*

Seriously smart, heartfelt and original with a good dollop of humour thrown in
Well Read Cat

Poignant...astute...authentic and relatable... The hopeful ending encompasses the quirky nature of the story, whilst achieving a sense of completeness
Jane Hunt

We Are Animals spans decades and generations effortlessly, focusing on what it means to be human and to dream. A beautiful metaphor for how we should all approach life, with energy, gusto and passion
Hannah Persaud – author of *The Codes of Love*

What a funny, heart-warming and surprising book – the right mix of humour and emotion. The writing is so clever and witty
My Treasure in Books

A curious tale of love and fate, told with humour and insight
Gillian Harvey – author of *Everything is Fine*

Very different, witty, poignant, clever
Books are Cool

Funny, original and immensely cheering
Nicola Gill – author of *We Are Family* and *The Neighbours*

Written with great tenderness, truth and sprinkled throughout with some great comic one-liners...a truly joyful read
Babbage and Sweetcorn

Hilarious, heartbreaking, and absolutely entertaining
The Book Decoder

An unexpected and quixotic love story that had me hooked from the first page. Ewins somehow manages to be both hilarious and contemplative at the same time. If you've ever travelled, you will definitely 'find yourself' in these pages
Cat Walker – author of *The Scoop*

Very unique and whimsical
Coffey's Corner

A book you have to read if you want something special
Fany Goes English

If you trust my recommendations even a small amount, *please please please* pick this up...you will NOT be disappointed
Prdgread

WE
ARE
ANIMALS

TIM EWINS

Lightning Books

Published in 2021
by Lightning Books Ltd
Imprint of EyeStorm Media
312 Uxbridge Road
Rickmansworth
Hertfordshire
WD3 8YL

www.lightning-books.com

Copyright © Tim Ewins 2020
Cover by Ifan Bates
Typeset in Horley Old Style MT and Zona Pro

British Library Cataloguing in Publication Data
A catalogue record for this book is available from the British Library.

Printed by CPI Group (UK) Ltd, Croydon CR0 4YY

ISBN: 9781785632846

For Gemma and our own epic love story
And for Indy, the product of that story

PART ONE

PART ONE

1

A CRAB

Goa, India. 2016

The man looked to his right. Three Indian men walked along the sand holding hands, a French couple started to pack up their towels and put various beach objects into an oversized floral bag, and a cow looked out to sea, maybe dreaming of a life which involved grass.

He looked to his left. He could see the rocks where the beach ended. The sun was going down and there was an Israeli man setting up a tripod, holding his camera high to protect the lens from any stray grains of sand that might want to nestle in its cracks. A bit further down, an Indian family were playing in the water – the adults fully clothed, and the children fully not.

He saw no sign of her.

He looked right again. One of the Indian men was laughing and pushing one of the others, the French couple were halfway up the beach now, arms around each other, and the cow was still staring – or dreaming – whichever it was.

The man strained his eyes as hard as he could, but still he couldn't see her.

He looked again to his left. The men in the family were taking it in turns to hold their breath under the waves and the women were chatting among each other and watching their little ones. On the shore, predictably, the Israeli man was rubbing his camera's lens frantically with his t-shirt and grumbling to himself.

It was no good. She wasn't there. Just like she hadn't been there the day before, or the day before that. In fact, she hadn't been there any day for the past five years. But he always looked anyway. Just in case. Because, probably, one day, she would be there, and he'd hate to miss it.

Regardless of her persistent absence, the man always loved this time of day on Palolem Beach. It wasn't too hot, but it certainly wasn't cold, and everyone seemed relaxed. Even the lady who paced the length of the beach all day selling melons eased off on her selling at this time, and she would often find a tourist to sit and chat with. The tourist would always buy a melon afterwards of course, but that didn't seem to be her aim.

One more check, he thought. He looked to his right. This time he could only see the cow, who hadn't moved her holy self one inch. The men had gone, and the couple must have made it back to their beach hut. Then he looked to his left. The family continued to play, the cameraman was mounting his camera, seemingly content that he'd saved his lens from a sandy death, and a bar worker was bringing out a sign which read 'COCK-tails – buy one, get two free'.

The man scowled.

Three girls were climbing over the rocks where the beach ended, back onto Palolem, and the man wondered whether they'd enjoyed their day. He knew where they'd have gone because Palolem was the closest place he'd had to a home in forty-one years.

He knew that over the rocks they'd have found another smaller beach with rocks at both ends. Over the next set of rocks, they'd have found a much bigger beach which would've taken them about an hour and a half to walk down. And then, when they'd have reached the end, they'd have found more rocks. Some people would get bored of exploring at this point and turn back, but he'd noticed these girls leave early in the morning, so he guessed that they'd carried on to the next set of beaches and rocks. 'What an exciting day they must have had,' thought the man – he used to love exploring.

'That was awful,' said one of the girls, and the man sighed.

He was sitting four bars down the beach from the COCK-tail bar, but he still jumped when the DJ played the first thud of music. He wondered whether they'd started playing the music louder or whether it was the direction of the wind. It had definitely been getting earlier – it never used to start thudding until after dark. He sipped his red wine and closed his eyes.

'Silent disco tonight, ladies?' The man opened one of his eyes to see a young male with ginger hair, an insanely wide smile and a hint of crazy in his eyes next to the three girls. The boy was luminous from the waist up.

'Another poxy vest,' the man mumbled under his breath and then re-shut his open eye.

Even with his eyes closed, he knew that the vest would be

bending his knees in time to the thudding. His neck would be bobbing along too, and he'd probably have his mouth slightly open. They always have their mouths slightly open, he thought.

The man exhaled loudly and opened both eyes lazily.

'Yin?' the vest asked the girls. It was amazing, thought the man, how only when he was speaking, did the vest's mouth appear to close. What did he mean, yin? The man knew a few languages, but he had never heard 'yin' used in this context before. He'd heard of yin, as in the yin usually followed by yang. And he'd heard of yen, the currency. He even knew the meaning of yìn (a Chinese verb, meaning 'to print'), but it seemed such an unlikely verb for a vest to be using to sell a silent disco in South India.

'Yeah, we're in,' answered one of the girls, and the man felt silly – 'Y'in?' – of course.

The vest, bending his knees in time to the thudding, neck bobbing, and with his mouth slightly open, handed the girls some flyers and watched the three of them walk off.

If the man ignored the music, as he had grown used to doing each night, he could hear the gentle lapping of the waves on the beach, the quiet natter of the melon-selling lady with her chosen tourist, and the sounds of a few birds communicating in their bird way ('Cacaaa?' one bird would ask, and another would reply 'Cacaaa!' in agreement, and then they would steal some fish from the fishermen). It was getting cooler now and he pushed his toes into the sand below his chair as he drifted off into a blissful sleep.

'Silent disco tonight, old-timer?'

The man awoke and saw a boy with ginger hair, an insanely wide smile and a hint of crazy in his eyes peering down at him. He was bending his knees in time to a different, quicker-paced, thudding. His neck was bobbing along, and his mouth was slightly open.

The man stood up and walked towards the shore, ignoring the intrusive vest completely.

He looked to his right. The cow was now wandering up the beach by herself, gently waving her tail and probably looking for grass. The melon-selling lady was finishing her conversation with her chosen tourist and exchanging her last melon for a few rupees.

Then he looked to his left. He could see the rocks where the beach ended. The Indian family were now out of the water – the adults fully clothed and the children fully not – and the Israeli man was packing away his tripod, holding the camera high to protect the lens from any further stray grains of sand.

In both directions, he saw several gatherings of bubbler crabs, all rolling the sand into tiny balls behind them. That's what bubbler crabs do.

Still, the man saw no signs of her.

He made his way back to his chair, past the vest, who, amazingly, hadn't moved at all and was still staring at the spot where the man had been sitting originally, as if the man had remained sitting there the whole time. The man sat down, took a sip of his red wine, looked at the vest, and paused.

'Pardon?'

'Silent disco tonight, old timer?'

'Old timer?'

'Old timer. Y'know. Not like, old timer. But, old-timer.'

'I'm sixty-four!' said the man, as a small wave washed

away hundreds of the bubbler crabs' small balls of sand.

'I said, not like, old timer, but that's quite old...timer. Sorry. My boss says I've got to be friendly. You're a young man. Just not as young as me. But I'm youuung. Like, really young. Especially to you.'

The man stared at the vest, and the vest stared at the man. 'My name's Shakey,' said the vest, trying to be polite, and then they stared at each other for a few more seconds.

'Shakey,' said the man.

'Shakey,' said Shakey. 'Silent disco tonight old-t...?' His sentence trailed off.

The man was making things difficult for Shakey, who was, after all, just doing his job. Shakey had met people like this man before. Another stupid moustache, he thought. He hated moustaches.

2

ANOTHER POXY VEST

Goa, India. 2016.

You could be forgiven for thinking that vests can see in the dark. They're regularly found at night and they're often luminous. They congregate on small beaches in Thailand and India, or on large beaches in Australia for the high season. It's on these beaches that they successfully, quickly and loudly find themselves. They find that the country they're in is in actual fact their spiritual home, and they always seem to be holding a small plastic bucket of vodka and Red Bull.

The truth is that vests cannot see in the dark – not everything, anyway. They can only see other vests. They rarely see workers, restaurant owners, cleaners, the elderly or parts of the world without sand.

After dark, vests glow. This attracts other vests, and they discuss the ways in which the small particles of eroded rock beneath their feet have changed their outlook on life completely, and how they don't know if they could live in a Western society again. They discuss the blogs they've written (which are normally about small plastic buckets of vodka and Red Bull) and then later they find that they're both in the new spiritual home for two months, and that they're going to share the same flight home. Then they discuss the 'not even in the cinema yet' film it turns out they'd both watched on the flight out.

If you were to go through Shakey's backpack you would find one pair of shorts (he would be wearing the other pair), no less than eight luminous vests and three pairs of sunglasses. You might also find a small plastic bucket. Shakey was certainly a vest.

'Sleeves are heavy,' he would tell other travellers if they asked. 'I'm packing light.' But the truth was that he'd spent the past six months in a gym lifting dumbbells, and that he liked the look of his arms.

While on a fishing trip recently, a girl vest had asked Shakey what his best experience in India had been so far. He'd intentionally gone misty-eyed and looked slightly over her shoulder and into the distance. He'd been aiming for a 'man of the world' look, but he had actually been thinking 'can she see my bicep?' and 'is she looking at my bicep?' He tensed his bicep.

'I was sunbathing on Palolem beach, listening to my headphones and using my sarong as a pillow,' he'd said, 'when an Indian man took me in as one of his own.' At this point he rubbed the back of his red hair with his hand

and moved his gaze from the distance and directly into her eyes. He paused for an uncomfortable seven seconds before telling her how the Indian man had been dressed in beige, both on his top and on his bottom half, and how he had sat down next to Shakey, singling him out from everyone else on the beach.

'He must have seen me as some kind of a...a kindred spirit,' Shakey explained, still tensing his bicep even though it was beginning to hurt. He was beginning to burn from the sun, too.

The Indian man had asked Shakey if he wanted to join him and his family for a meal. Shakey had accepted, not through reasons of gratitude or intrigue, but in the hope that he would one day get to tell another vest about it – hopefully a girl, and maybe on a fishing trip.

Shakey told the girl how he had sat with the Indian man and several other people from all around the world and eaten naan, chapatti, samosas, dal, chana masala, and how it was all rounded off with several beers. Then he paused. 'I'm a vegetarian,' he said, while further raising one corner of his insanely wide smile, before looking into the distance again. 'It was quite spiritual,' he carried on. 'I mixed with the locals, ate local food and drank local beer.' He noticed that his bicep had become slightly limp so he tensed his other arm and turned his body so she could see. 'And it only cost me 2,500 rupees.'

The girl widened her mouth in awe. The boy she was with had immersed himself so entirely into the Indian culture that he had been eating in local family homes and meeting with kindred spirits. It was exactly the kind of thing that her guidebook had told her she should be doing.

Of course, what Shakey had actually done, was go to a

family-owned restaurant.

She smiled at Shakey and he smiled back. 'Wow,' she breathed, and then she touched his slowly burning bicep.

The fishing group had not really done much fishing up to this point. The boat owner had briefed them on some very basic safety points (don't jump off the boat, don't put the hook in your mouth/eyes/near your genitals, and don't forget to tip) and then he'd set up each fishing rod by himself. The tourists had spent the following hour just chatting as the boat chugged on, so it came as quite a surprise when the girl's fishing rod started violently jolting in its holder.

She moved her hand away from Shakey's arm and screamed. Shakey grabbed the fishing rod from its holder and pulled backwards, imitating a TV programme he'd seen. The rod pulled forward against him.

'Give me!' shouted the boat owner as he ran up behind Shakey, and Shakey thought that giving him the rod was probably a good idea. He looked back to the boat owner and tried to pass him the rod by letting go of it. The rod hit the inside wall of the boat, flipped overboard and landed in the sea.

He's such a hero, thought the girl vest as she skirted around the visibly distressed boat owner towards Shakey, and then they kissed. Somewhere, under the boat, a small milkfish celebrated its victory with a piece of bait and a rod.

Yes, Shakey was as vesty as a vest could be. If there was a hierarchy among the vests, Shakey would probably be the king. But there would be a good chance he wouldn't realise he was the king, and that's why there is no vest hierarchy.

Being a vest is only a temporary condition which is normally cured by the vest holding onto the material that's loosely hanging by its side and pulling its hands upwards and over its head. Once this process has been followed, the vest begins to realise that there is no spiritual home, it has crabs living in its flip flops and that it is in desperate need of a shower.

Often, later in life, a vest will become something useful like a doctor, a builder or a teacher. No one will know about its two months of being a vest, and an ex-vest will tend to lie about it. Lots of ex-vests will revisit the spiritual home some years later with their children and there will be new vests scattered around the beach.

Ex-vests don't usually like new vests, and they tend to mumble about them under their breath.

'Another poxy vest,' they mumble.

3

A COW

Goa, India. 2016.

The man was mumbling under his breath, and although Shakey couldn't make it out exactly, it sounded like he might be saying that the silent disco was going to be the poxy best... Or something like that.

The music from the COCK-tail bar was getting louder and ever more intrusive.

'How silent is a silent disco exactly?' the man asked. Shakey sat down on the chair next to the man but he didn't answer the question. This was good, thought the man, because now Shakey was at least being quiet, but it was also bad, because now they were sitting together, as if they knew each other... as if they were friends.

The sky turned to a dusty orange and the waves slowly

calmed to form a flat, open field of blue – it would have been a truly beautiful sight to have enjoyed alone.

The bar owner took away the man's empty glass and the man ordered the same again. Shakey, much to the man's surprise, ordered a vodka and Red Bull and requested that it be in one of those little plastic buckets.

'Why are you here?' asked the man a little too loudly.

'Initially? To find myself,' answered Shakey. 'Now? I think something bigger,' and then he rubbed the back of his head with his hand.

'No. Why are you here, now, sitting next to me?'

'Oh. I'm being as silent as a silent disco, if you don't put on the headphones, that is. If you put on the headphones they can be very loud. Would you like me to be as loud as a silent disco next?'

The man exhaled and frowned. 'I'm afraid I find even your presence loud. To me, your mere being here is like a thousand out-of-tune and out-of-time trumpets playing a symphony of bad hip-hop songs. Badly.' He put emphasis on the words 'hip' and 'hop' which made Shakey visibly cringe.

Shakey had met people like this man before. He called them moustaches and he didn't like them. He found them to be rude and stuck in their ways, but frankly he had been handing out silent disco flyers for two hours – he was hot and in need of a drink. He just wanted to enjoy the sunset and to sit next to someone, anyone, to whom he could pretend to be flyering, should his boss see him. This rude moustachioed man would have to do. Shakey did, however, try his best not to sound like a thousand out-of-tune and out-of-time trumpets playing bad hip-hop music, badly, but he found it difficult as he wasn't sure what it was that had made him sound like that in the first place.

'Did you say that you were finding yourself, initially?' asked the man, and Shakey confirmed that he did. 'So, are you telling me that you've succeeded? That you've found yourself now?' and Shakey confirmed that, yes, he had. The man, with one eyebrow down and one eyebrow up, enquired as to where it was that Shakey had found himself so easily.

'In the sand,' Shakey replied confidently and with a shrug, and then neither of them said anything for a few moments as the man took that in.

Four bars down, the DJ in the COCK-tail bar looked across the empty beach and out to sea. Then he turned and scanned the bar he was in. It was also empty. Where on earth was everybody? He set his laptop to loop, left the DJ booth and stepped onto the sand. Along the beach, about four bars down, he could see someone luminous sitting next to a man holding a glass of red wine. Beyond them, he could see a wistful-looking cow. The DJ, who was also quite luminous, thought for a second and then started off towards the man and the vest, having decided that cows probably don't like listening to music much. After a few steps he saw the vest turn its head.

'Shakey!' the DJ said to himself happily. The DJ liked Shakey because Shakey always really lost himself in the music.

He ran back to his booth – they must not be able to hear, he thought as he turned the thudding music up as loud as it would go.

'What an infernal racket,' said the man. Shakey wasn't sure what infernal meant, so he agreed happily that it was indeed an infernal racket, and quite a good one at that. The cow looked up from the sea and towards the COCK-tail bar. She shuffled her back legs, kicked up some of the sand behind her and then she turned her entire body to face the DJ.

'What were you doing in the sand?' the man asked, now resigned to a conversation with his new companion.

'I think I've always been in the sand, spiritually,' Shakey replied, 'but it's taken my physical self to travel the world to meet my spiritual self and now I've formed my whole self, y'know?' The man looked at Shakey in disbelief, which Shakey mistook for confusion, and so he continued, 'like when the Power Rangers come together to form Megazord,' as if to explain what he had meant. The man ignored this.

'Where exactly did you look for yourself, before the sand, that is?'

'Well. Just India so far.'

'India?'

'Goa.'

'Just Goa?'

'Just this beach really.' Shakey looked a little embarrassed. 'My parents met in India. Not Goa exactly, but I really like beaches, so...'

The man scoffed. 'It's lucky your spiritual self was in the sand on this beach then, isn't it?'

The cow had started walking towards the COCK-tail bar and was now standing directly in front of Shakey and the man, blocking their view of the sea. The waiter brought over the drinks and shouted 'shoo' at the cow, but she didn't move. Instead, she let out a rare, quiet and malnourished 'moo', leaving her mouth slightly open. Then she nodded her head slowly, repetitively, and maybe, just maybe, in time to the music.

'What's your deal anyway? What were you looking for on the beach earlier? When I came over you completely ignored me. That's pretty rude, yeah?'

'Jan,' said the man.

'What's that?' asked Shakey.

'A woman,' said the man, more in the direction of the cow than to Shakey.

Shakey asked where she was. He was hoping she would come back quickly so there would be three of them. Maybe she would dilute the man's rudeness, like polite water to his arrogant concentrated squash.

'When did you see her last? Maybe she's getting a drink before she meets you.'

'1978. I last saw her in 1978, and as to where she is, I don't know. That's why I was looking. If she is getting a drink before she meets me, she'll be pretty damn drunk when she does turn up.'

'Man,' said Shakey, and then, 'jeez,' and then, 'are you ill?' to which the man inhaled sharply.

'No, I'm not ill. I'm just waiting, that's all. You must believe in...' and then he trailed off, realising how silly what he was about to say would sound to the vest if he said it out loud. 'You talk some utter crap,' he said instead.

But then the man thought for a second, and he decided that he didn't mind sounding silly in front of this vest. Everything Shakey had said so far had been silly, even his name was silly, and if nothing else Shakey had been incredibly forthcoming himself.

'I'm waiting for fate,' he said. It did sound silly. It was true though – fate had, as far as the man understood it, always brought him and Jan together in the past. 'We never had to look for each other before. She was just there anytime I needed her. Until 1978, that is.'

'What happened in 1978?' asked Shakey.

'I don't know,' replied the man and then he took a long sip of his wine.

He explained how he'd always loved travelling, even before he had met Jan. 'People say it's a small world,' he said, 'but it's not. I've seen a lot of it and I promise you it's really very big. But we kept bumping into each other, Jan and I, and that had to be fate.' The man took another sip of his wine.

Shakey noticed the increased speed with which the man had started drinking, so he put all four of the straws from his bucket into his mouth and took a massive gulp to join in.

'The last thirty-eight years, however, fate must have found it hard getting us together because I've not seen her.'

'Man,' said Shakey again, and then, 'jeez.' No matter how many times he'd told other vests that he'd met his kindred spirit in that restaurant owner, he wasn't really feeling comfortable with the man opening up like this.

'Yes, well. Maybe I am ill then,' said the man under a stifled laugh. 'Anyway, I thought I'd give fate a hand this last five years, and I'm not getting any younger, so I've stayed here. Now fate just has to get Jan here, and when it does I'll be looking, just like I was earlier,' and then he apologised if he had seemed rude, even though he knew that he had and he didn't care.

'How long are you going to keep looking? I mean, you're living on a beach indefinitely like a hermit or something.' The man smiled at this. He still felt a bit silly for talking about Jan to the vest but at least Shakey had actually been listening.

He had no answer though. He didn't know how long he intended to stay on the beach and he didn't know how long he would keep looking. Maybe Jan would never turn up. He wasn't worried about recognising her – she was beautiful, and he was sure she would still be beautiful in her older age. But what if she, or indeed fate, had stopped trying? What if, out of the three of them, he was the only one still paying any attention?

'What's your name, old-timer?' Shakey asked.

'Jan,' replied the man.

'No. *Your* name,' Shakey asked again.

'Jan,' replied the man again. There was a pause.

'Because you're finding yourself, and when you look around the beach, you're really looking for you?' asked Shakey, looking like his head might explode with deepness.

'No. Jan is called Jan, and I am called Jan. We are both called Jan. She is a girl, and I am a man.' Jan the man really didn't enjoy saying this. It was hard to say without sounding like he was reciting a children's poem.

'Man-Jan?'

'Sure. If it makes it easier for you. Manjan,' said Manjan.

Four bars down, the DJ looked again across his empty bar. Where was Shakey? He normally loved this particular thudding song. He glanced towards the beach to see if Shakey was on his way, maybe with his wine-loving friend. He didn't see either of them, but he did see a cow with her mouth slightly open and her head nodding along in time to the music. The DJ put his hands in the air excitedly and pointed towards the cow.

'This song is for you,' he screamed with delight, dancing in time to both the music and the cow. The cow shuffled her back legs and once again mooed. 'Beach cow, this one is for you!'

Manjan watched this from his chair four bars down. Even the cows on this beach were adapting to suit the times. They've survived centuries with hardly any grass, and now, it seems, they'll survive the loud, thudding music too. This made Manjan feel slightly jealous. He wished that he could adapt to change quite so easily.

Manjan asked why Shakey was called Shakey, and Shakey laughed.

'Isn't it obvious?' he asked, and then he held onto one of Manjan's hands and shook it lightly, as a parent might do to a baby. Manjan had no idea why this was obvious, but he enjoyed it just the same.

Once Shakey had stopped, they both looked back out to the no-longer-obstructed sea view, one smiling more widely than the other, but both happy.

'Manjan,' started Shakey, still looking towards the sea, his smile slowly disappearing, 'what if Jan's dead?'

Manjan's smile quickly faded too and he took another sip of his wine. He thought about it for the first time ever, and then answered the only answer that was acceptable to him.

'She's not,' he said.

4

CLASSIC MOUSTACHE

Goa, India. 2016.

You can't always tell if someone is a moustache by the physical presence of hair on his top lip. What makes a moustache a moustache is his determined refusal to accept change in any way. Sometimes a moustache will have a face entirely void of hair, but there is a sure-fire test to find out if he is indeed a moustache. You just have to suggest that he grow a moustache. A true moustache would snort at you disapprovingly – 'I've never had a moustache before, why should I grow a moustache now?' he'd say. This is a typical moustache response. It's classic moustache.

Of course, if a moustache does possess an actual moustache, there is a good chance it will have been there ever since his adolescent face will have allowed it to be.

Millions of moustaches all over the world sit in their homes complaining that television programmes aren't what they used to be and that there are too many channels these days anyway. Don't even get them started on supermarkets. Most moustaches tend to stay indoors, shut off from the outside world, and they only communicate with the people they have direct contact with. A moustache will never check his emails. This is for the best though – have you seen the amount of spam emails supermarkets send these days?

A moustache living predominantly outdoors is a different breed of bristle altogether. Places change, and societies change. The world changes. In fact, the only things that don't change are the moustache's opinions and his upper lip (however decorated, or not decorated, it might be). A moustache outdoors is constantly outside of its comfort zone. As a result, these are the worst kind.

Manjan was one of those moustaches that did sport an actual moustache, and quite a moustache at that. It was long and grey, and it tickled the rim of his wine glass with every sip. He wouldn't have it any other way.

Over the past five years, he had established a comfortable routine on Palolem. In the morning he would scan the beach for Jan before enjoying a spot of yoga and a fruit salad in a nearby health restaurant. Then he would scan the beach for Jan, read a newspaper or chat with the melon-selling lady for a while. He would use the same health restaurant for lunch (but this time he would order a masala dosa), before scanning the beach for Jan. In the evening, after he had scanned the beach for Jan, he would sit in the very same bar he was sitting in now, with a glass of red wine, sometimes chatting to the bar owner and sometimes alone with his thoughts and memories. He would stay there until sundown, when he would have a quick look around in case Jan had turned up, and then he'd find his way back to bed. It was repetitive, and it was predictable.

Today had been a day like any other for Manjan, except today Shakey had sat next to him, and yesterday he had been called just Jan. They'd been sitting quietly for quite some time when Manjan said, 'I hate this beach,' flatly.

'Whoa!' exclaimed Shakey. 'I don't know if I mentioned at all, but this sand is me, man. You hate this beach and you hate me.'

After a few seconds of thought, Manjan replied.

'Sometimes. I hate this beach, sometimes.'

If Shakey truly believed he and the beach were one, then this statement rang true for both. Manjan did hate the beach sometimes, and, in the short time he had known Shakey, he also hated him sometimes. Only sometimes, mind, and that wasn't bad.

'What's wrong with the beach?' Shakey asked.

'It's changed,' Manjan explained, and Shakey remembered that Manjan, as interesting as he had first seemed, with his stories of a lady who was probably made-up (I mean, he couldn't even think of a name for her different to his own), was still a moustache. He decided not to listen to whatever Manjan had to say next. It would probably only serve to kill the buzz he was beginning to get from his vodka and Red Bull.

Manjan shuffled the back legs of his chair into the sand and then leant on them slowly to make himself comfortable.

He explained how he'd first come to Palolem with Jan, just for a week, when he was twenty-five. Travelling was still exciting then, and every new place he visited felt like an adventure, especially with Jan. Palolem had felt special. He'd fallen in love with the beach the moment the soles of his feet had touched the sand, and by the time they'd left, Jan seemed equally taken.

They'd visited a spice farm, learnt to ride motorcycles, and tried yoga for the first time. One day, they had climbed over the rocks at the end of the beach and found another beach with rocks at both ends. Over those rocks they'd found yet another beach, which they'd walked down for about an hour, and then, at the other end of that beach, they'd found more rocks. It had been a magical week. If fate had a plan to bring him and Jan together again, Manjan felt certain it would be on Palolem.

'Since then,' Manjan said, while Shakey nodded absently but politely, 'the beach has changed. It used to be quiet, peaceful and fun, but now it's loud and full of vests.' Shakey instinctively frowned when Manjan said 'vests'. It was the first word he'd really noticed, and he assumed he was being insulted. Then he realised that frowning was almost an admittance to being whatever it was that Manjan was accusing him of being, so he rubbed the back of his head with his hand and smiled his insanely wide smile. This annoyed Manjan more than the frown. Nothing he'd said had warranted an insanely wide smile.

'The good old days eh?' said Shakey, hoping this might end Manjan's monologue. Manjan sighed.

'I'm watching Goa fall apart around me,' he said 'and I'm talking about it to the source of the problem. To make it worse, you've not even been paying attention.'

'What are you doing here then? If you hate it so much, why not just move?'

Manjan flinched at the thought, and then sighed again.

He'd travelled the world – he'd spent most of his life doing it, in fact – but he couldn't leave Palolem now and he knew it. The beach had become his lottery ticket and he had the same numbers every week. If he stopped buying the ticket, Jan would turn up, he was sure. No, he was stuck on Palolem.

'Because there's nowhere better than Palolem,' he said, 'and I'm meeting Jan here. No no, I'll be staying on Palolem thank you very much,' and then he stuck out his bottom lip in a pout so that the very ends of his moustache hairs scraped the inside of his mouth.

'Classic moustache,' Shakey said to himself, but he actually found himself feeling sorry for Manjan. This grumpy moustache was living in the past – waiting for it to re-happen even – but he was completely lost in the present.

'Nowhere better than Palolem,' said Manjan again, matter-of-factly, resolutely and to himself, wondering if he meant it.

'Nowhere better than Palolem,' agreed Shakey quietly.

When a vest removes its vest, that vest becomes a person, but if a moustache removes its moustache, or indeed grows one, it just becomes even more grumpy. A moustache must escape a routine, and a frame of mind, to escape its true moustache.

Some moustaches have always been moustaches (often, these are the ones collecting football stickers in their childhood bedrooms at the age of fifty-five), and some moustaches gradually become moustaches as they grow older and begin to miss the good old days. Some moustaches – moustaches like Manjan in fact – used to be vests themselves.

That was back in the good old days though, and oh, how Manjan missed the good old days.

5

A FISH

Fishton, England.1965.

When Manjan was younger his family and friends had called him Jan, because back then he had not met Jan the girl, nor had he met Shakey the name creator, and, well, Jan was his name, so that's what they called him.

Jan lived with both of his parents in the small seaside town of Fishton, England. In the summer the town was alive with folk music, exciting pirate-themed arcades and restaurants with queues all the way down the street. Jan loved all these things (he was only human after all) but what he loved most about summer in Fishton were the tourists.

He would find tourists from exotic places like Hull or Milton Keynes and he'd ask them about their home towns. He learnt little titbits of information from them, such as: in

Hartlepool, people have something called a patty with their chips instead of fish; and in Birmingham some of the people do their shopping in a bull ring, which sounded dangerous, but fun.

Once he spoke to a man from Cornwall who ended everything he said with 'aar'. Jan thought this was fascinating, so he decided to copy the man and to follow him for what turned out to be an entire day. The man understandably found this annoying, but unfortunately he always punctuated his annoyance by saying 'aar'.

'Aar,' little Jan shouted back. By the time the man from Cornwall had climbed into his car to leave, he and Jan had attracted the attention of three dogs who wanted to play with them, and they'd both been offered jobs at the pirate-themed mini-golf.

In winter, though, when all the tourists had fled Fishton, Jan found it hard to pass time. There weren't any interesting people to talk to. Fishton, in the winter, was full of people from Fishton, and Jan already knew about people from Fishton. They were all either fish catchers, fish cleaners, fish sellers, or fish (and at the rate at which they were being caught, cleaned and sold, you didn't want to be a fish).

Jan's attention would always turn away from people, and instead he would stand at the harbour watching the boats coming in, fantasising about where they might have been or where they might be going next. Maybe one would be off to try a patty in Hull, or maybe they'd be going to Birmingham to do some extreme shopping. Mainly, Jan liked to fantasise that one of the boats might be going straight out across the North Sea to whichever country lay on the other side. Jan wanted nothing more than to cross the North Sea.

Once, when he was thirteen, his school had made him take a test to see what job he would be suited to when he grew up. Jan hadn't wanted to take the test because he thought he knew what the outcome would be. The test was funded by the Fishton fish factory and every year it turned out that nearly everyone who took the test was suited to a life of either catching, gutting, cleaning or selling fish. Jan didn't know exactly what he wanted to be when he grew up, but he knew it didn't involve fish. He thought it probable that whatever it was, it wouldn't be in Fishton.

He took the test. Jan, as it happened, was not suited to a life of catching fish. He was not suited to a life of gutting fish, cleaning fish or selling fish, either. Instead, Jan was told that he'd make an excellent 'box-packaging specialist and technician'.

At first Jan was relieved, but then, after he'd thought more about the words 'box' and 'packaging', and less about the words 'specialist' and 'technician', he felt like he had, himself, been gutted.

When he had got home and told his parents about the test they had been deeply proud of him. His father was a fisherman, and his mother sold fish in their own small fish-and-chip shop.

'You can carry on the family business,' his father had remarked gleefully, and when Jan had asked him what he meant, his father had said 'the business of fish!'

'Of boxes,' Jan replied.

'Boxes for fish!' his mother whooped, apparently not noticing Jan's lack of enthusiasm.

'Everything in Fishton is fish,' he answered, and then he

ran upstairs to sulk while his parents hugged each other and cheered. Jan loved his parents, but they certainly weren't dreamers.

Jan knew of course that the results of the test weren't written in the stars; they were written in the back page of his school exercise book and would probably never be seen again, but he also knew that unless he did something about it, he would become a specialist in packing boxes. This was something he wanted to be only slightly more than a regular box packer. He needed to leave Fishton. He wanted to get as far away from the fish factory as he possibly could, and maybe further still.

If he could just get to London – the land of British opportunity – or better still, if he made it to Hartlepool he could help to make patties, whatever they were. He felt certain that if he could make it all the way across the North Sea to a whole other country, he could be anything he wanted.

The day after the test, Jan spread his bedsheet out across the floor, and placed a pair of shoes in the middle of it. In one of those shoes he put five chocolate bars, and in the other he placed a small amount of money. Then, on top of these items, he threw three pairs of underwear and five single, un-matching socks. Then he tied the corners together around a stick.

On his way out of the house, his mother asked him where he was going.

'Nowhere,' he replied, and she believed him. She could see his makeshift bag, but Jan was only thirteen, so she assumed he was playing a game. There was no reason for him to run away – he'd just been told he could be a box packaging specialist and technician! Besides, if he was running away, surely he would have used his backpack.

But Jan was running away, and he hadn't used his backpack, because he was a dreamer, and dreamers keep their belongings in sheets tied to sticks.

Jan had previously noticed that one of the boat owners down at the harbour always wore a shirt that had 'England' written across the front of it, and he had decided to stow away on this man's boat. It made sense to a thirteen-year-old Jan that the only reason someone would have 'England' written on them would be if they were going to go somewhere other than England. Why would anyone wear a shirt with England written on it in England – unless they worked as a signpost?

Jan knew that England man's boat was the biggish white and blue one with Moondance painted on the side, so once he'd reached the harbour he went straight over to it, making sure that he could see the rest of the harbour clearly. Very few people were about, but he could see England man not far from Moondance the boat, chatting with one of the fish-sellers.

Jan watched them. He watched them discuss something presumably numerical because different amounts of England man's fingers kept going up, and the fish-seller kept shaking his head. He watched the fish-seller push down two of England man's fingers and then nod. He watched England man nod then too, and then he watched England man pat the fish-seller on the back and laugh. Finally, Jan watched them both walk into the fish shop, and he took this opportunity to jump aboard Moondance.

It was cold (Jan quietly thanked himself for packing those extra socks) but the sea seemed relatively smooth. This was a relief, as Jan had hidden himself under a bench on the wet floor at the back of the boat. He planned to remain there until they'd gone far enough out to sea for it to be unreasonable for England man to turn around back to Fishton. Then he would come out and introduce himself. Hopefully they would get on, and Jan could ask where it was they were going. To little Jan's innocent mind, it was a flawless plan.

He watched through the bars at the back of the bench as they pulled away from the harbour wall. He'd probably never see that harbour wall again, he thought. They passed the pirate-themed mini-golf that he saw every day on his way to school. He'd probably never see that again either. It seemed like a million fish-and-chip shops passed his view – he'd never see 'Dear Cod' again, nor would he see 'A Plaice to Remember'. He turned his head so that he was facing into the boat. He could see England man's big leather boots, one of which was tapping, and he could hear him singing a tune that Jan didn't know. England man was obviously completely oblivious to Jan's presence. He watched England man as quietly as he possibly could and waited for his heart to stop pounding.

Eventually, when Jan had relaxed a little he looked back through the bars for one last glance at his old home. Fishton was no longer recognisable to him; it was just a line on the horizon across the sea. He closed his eyes. I'll probably never see Fishton again he thought, before his body gave way to sleep.

'YES! COME ON!'

Jan came to, startled by England man's self-congratulatory

cheer, and was instantly splashed by what felt like a tidal wave. The deck became awash with fish, which were all flapping about with stupid and unmoving yet somehow clearly distressed faces. None of the fish formulated any kind of a plan and they didn't pull together in an attempt for survival, so, slowly, one by one, they stopped flapping about and lay still on the floor next to Jan in a puddle of water.

The fish closest to Jan was one of the last to stop flapping. One of its beady eyes seemed to be looking directly at Jan and Jan felt a sudden pang of guilt. Not for being human (the same species that had killed the fish) but for running away. He saw his mother looking at him. He hadn't even left a note, and this fish, with its perfectly circular eye and expressionless face, was judging him for it. 'I'm sorry,' Jan mouthed to his mother, through the fish, before it flapped its final flap and remained completely motionless on the deck.

Jan couldn't be sure how long he'd been unconscious, but he was relieved to see that he hadn't moved from his spot under the bench, and that England man didn't seem to be aware of his presence just yet. He could have been at sea for days, but equally he could have been at sea for minutes, so he resolved to remain hidden for a few hours longer. He daydreamed about where he might be going – what the people might sound like, what they might eat with their chips, where he would sleep when he got there. Would it be grassy, or would he be in a city? Would there be mountains? Come to think about it, where *would* he sleep when he got there? Would it be a hot country, or would it be cold like it was in Fishton? Crucially, though, where would he sleep when he got there? He kept coming back to that same question until, eventually, he decided to make use of his current position, and fell asleep under the bench again.

Jan's mother, still completely unaware of Jan's lack of presence in Fishton – and of his unauthorised presence on England man's boat – was washing the family's clothes.

Now, there are three types of clothes washers. There are those who don't use detergent and don't sort their socks (the slackers), there are those who do use detergent but don't sort their socks (the half-a-jobbers), and there are those who do use detergent and do sort their socks (the jobs-worths). Jan's Mother was of category number three, religiously. It was when she was sorting Jan's socks that she realised something must be wrong. There were seventeen in total, twelve of which she could match. She sat on her kitchen floor with the other five surrounding her. She'd had the odd odd sock before, and could handle that, but five? Something wasn't right. 'What a waste of detergent,' she thought. Then she worried about the five missing socks. She hadn't seen them when she'd been cleaning, and she prided herself on her housekeeping. Where were those socks?

Incidentally, you will notice that there are only three types of clothes washers – not four. No one has ever not used detergent but then sorted their socks. These people simply do not exist.

When Jan's father returned home with fish for their tea, he found Jan's mother sitting on the kitchen floor repeatedly tying the odd socks together and then untying them again.

'Look,' she said as he entered. Jan's father looked at the five socks and saw that none of them matched. He knew straight away that somewhere in the house there were five lost socks, and he knew what that would mean to his wife. He shook his head slowly, looked down and tutted.

'What a waste of detergent,' he said.

'What a waste,' Jan's mother agreed.

'Come on,' Jan's father perked up. 'They're only socks. At least we've not lost anything important.'

The very moment he said this…

…Jan woke up, still under the bench, freezing cold and wet, and without a clue where he was. One thing was for certain: they had hit land. The boat was no longer moving, and the fish had gone. The floor was cold, and Jan had never felt so uncomfortable in his life. He couldn't tell whether he was shivering because of the cold or whether it was through fear. He didn't want to leave the safety of the bench, but he knew he'd freeze if he didn't. He opened his mouth and tried to make a noise to see if he could hear any reaction from anyone who might be on the boat, but nothing came out. Just silence.

He tried again, and for a second he could feel only air escape his mouth. Then he heard a low rumbling noise which felt like it might be coming straight from his chest. He paused.

Nothing. No response from anyone. Jan wasn't sure whether this was good or not, but he wanted to check for life on the boat again. He parted his lips once again and let out a much louder rumbling grunt. This time a few seagulls reacted to the noise and flew off in a flutter. Then silence again. There was no one on the boat. Jan made what he thought to be the fairly safe assumption that England man must be selling his fish somewhere, and that he had the boat to himself.

He didn't want to get ahead of himself though, so he stuck one of his arms out from under the bench and waved it around. Still he heard no human voices, so he stuck a leg out and waved that around too. By this point half of his body was star-jumping without the health benefits of actually jumping. Still quite scared to completely leave the safety of the bench, Jan continued doing this for a whole twenty-two seconds, and just to make sure that there wasn't anyone there who might not be able to see him, he kept making his low but loud grumbling noise. Occasionally he would hit the floor with his hand too. If nothing else, he was beginning to warm up.

Eventually he stopped, feeling quite out of breath. Finally satisfied that he was alone, Jan started to emerge onto the deck.

'By the decks of the good ship Moondance,' said England man in a thick Fishton accent. Jan jumped so hard that he hit his head on the bench he had been so scared to leave. 'What was that? How long have you been under there? You haven't been there since we left Fishton have you?'

Jan didn't reply. He thought about running, but half of his body was still under a bench. He thought about answering England man's question, but what could he say? Sorry for hiding on your boat and acting like half a panicked, mad starfish? No. So Jan said, and did, nothing.

'Come on,' England man continued angrily, 'what are you doing on my boat?' He wanted answers and Jan didn't have any. Jan rose to his feet in silence, occasionally going to say something but then failing to at the last second. He looked straight at England man, who looked straight back.

'Where are we?' Jan asked eventually.

'Well, I'm not sure,' said England man, misreading the question, 'I'm not sure where we are. You tell me.' Jan was confused. 'But we're here now aren't we?' England man continued. 'That's where we are.' His nostrils were flaring, and bits of spit flew from his lips as he spoke.

'What?' asked Jan, somewhat pointlessly, more for something to say than anything else.

'What are you do...'

'GAZ!' came a high-pitched and shrill voice from somewhere off the boat, and England man's head turned.

'Wait here,' England Gaz said to Jan, 'and don't do anything weird like...whatever it was you were just doing.' England Gaz lurched forward at Jan, picked up a huge bag of dead fish from on top of the bench where Jan had been hiding, and left the boat.

Jan was scared, and he didn't know where he was – what country even – but he did know that he wasn't going to wait around for England Gaz to come back. He picked up the stick attached to a sheet that he was calling a bag, looked at England Gaz, who was now facing away from the boat and kissing a lady, and left the boat as quietly as he could.

As soon as his feet touched the land he ran.

'A box-packaging specialist and technician,' said Jan's father to his wife, his pride not yet faded. Then, after a pause, he said, 'do you think he's happy though? I mean, it's a good profession, but did he seem happy?'

'Of course he is,' replied Jan's mother, before jolting her head back towards the old writing cabinet in case a stray sock might have worked its way behind it. It hadn't. 'Our son, a specialist. Why wouldn't he be happy?'

'Aye,' agreed Jan's father, 'but did you notice that when we were celebrating, and we were all hugging and chatting about our Jan's future like we were, did you notice that Jan wasn't there? He'd gone upstairs.'

Jan's mother looked uncomfortable and thought for a minute. 'A lot of brain power is needed to be a box-packaging specialist and technician. He was probably resting his mind.' She said this firmly, and although she hadn't actually used the words, Jan's father knew that the sentence was meant to end with 'and let that be the end of it'.

'Aye,' agreed Jan's father, this time less convinced. 'Maybe he's scared of the responsibility,' he offered, as an alternative to his wife's frankly absurd suggestion. 'A lot of responsibility there. He might be scared of it. Running from it, as it were.'

'He's not a runner,' scowled Jan's mother sharply, shooting her husband a look. 'Jan is no runner.'

'I'm just saying, maybe he was hoping for something less important than box-packaging specialist and so on. Maybe he wanted to be a regular box-packer, less of the technician, none of the specialist.'

'Perhaps the socks are in one of the kitchen cupboards,' Jan's mother wondered out loud.

'We'll find them,' said Jan's father, reassuringly touching his wife's shoulder.

'I never lose anything,' she said to herself as she stood up and walked to the kitchen.

'I just worry about our Jan,' Jan's father mumbled, trying to steer the conversation back away from the missing socks.

'I'm telling you,' called Jan's mother from the kitchen, between the sounds of cupboard doors shutting and flour being knocked onto the floor, 'he's resting his specialist brain. He's not scared, and he's certainly not a runner.'

Jan ran away from the dock and away from the water. He ran through a small town he didn't recognise, past people he didn't know in a country he was yet to discover, and as soon as he was out of England Gaz's sight he started to enjoy himself. All his fear escaped into a flurry of excitement. He kept running – he had to keep running to release his joyous energy lest he explode with it. He ran straight into a large lady.

'I'm sorry!' Jan yelled behind him as he carried on running.

'No no, I'm sorry,' the lady shouted back, even though they both knew he had run into her. What lovely people, Jan thought.

The town was quaint and cobbled with bunting zig-zagging from one shop front to the next. It was still winter wherever he was, and he could see his every breath each time he exhaled into the white frosty air, before running into it. He could hear a folk song being played on banjos as he ran past one public house, and people were cheering and laughing in another. Wherever he was, Jan could tell it was a magical country, full of opportunity.

He ran past a fish shop and a small arcade, taking in everything he saw as best as he could, until the road started a steep incline and the buildings became fewer. He wanted – no, he needed – to know what would be at the top of the hill, but he noticed his pace was slowing and the white from his breath was becoming somewhat thinner. A man in a tracksuit casually walked passed him, and then so did the man's dog. Finally, Jan decided to stop.

He bent forward, put his hands on his knees and panted down at the floor. The town he'd run through was behind him, and had he looked, he would've seen past the rooftops of the houses and out to the most beautiful clear winter sea. But that's the thing with travelling; you always end up missing something.

Eventually, after he caught his breath, he started up the hill again, this time walking slowly so he could properly take in the first of what he decided would be many countries that he would visit. The trees were mainly bare with a frost tinted white on their few remaining leaves, and the road sort of disintegrated into soil at both sides. The scene wasn't a million miles from how the one and only road out of Fishton looked, but for a reason Jan couldn't quite put his finger on, this road was better. He'd earned it; it was his. It looked and it smelled like adventure. Crucially, it did not smell of fish.

It dawned on Jan at this point that he didn't know what people did when they were travelling. When he'd fantasised about it, he'd never really pictured himself; he'd always seen a muscular person (which little Jan was certainly not) with wavy red hair, because that's what true travellers looked like. They were brave, too. Jan couldn't gain muscles right now, and his hair was a dark brown, but he could be brave, so he turned off, away from the road, and walked between two trees. This was exploring. He was 'off-roading'.

He kept 'off-roading' until the trees stopped, and he found himself on top of a cliff. He couldn't see the town that he had just run through. In fact, he couldn't see a town at all. Along the coast there was nothing but white grass and the occasional short stone wall separating the land into fields. Every now and again there would be a flutter of movement from a squirrel or a fox, and at one point there was an eruption of birds taking off. It was mesmerising. Jan sat down, soaked up the scene and completely lost time. He thought of very little, except that it had all been worth it: leaving his parents' house; the fish; the not-really-a-tidal wave; even his fear of England Gaz. It had all been worth it, for this.

Jan was so lost in his own personal moment with nature that he barely noticed the large balding man who came and stood behind him, also admiring the view.

'Whacountryeh?'

Jan jumped, and then scrambled in the frosty ground, trying to stand up.

'Onlyplonearthtis. Onlyplonearth'. Jan looked at the man. He wore a thick brown cardigan and old jeans. He looked pudgy, but it was hard to tell because he was wrapped-up warm from his feet to his neck. His head was mainly hairless except for the insides of his ears and the grey halo connecting them around the back. Jan thought it curious, given the weather, that the man wasn't wearing a hat. He hadn't understood a word the man had said so he figured that he was in a non-English-speaking country. The man was smiling though, and he seemed friendly, so Jan decided to try to introduce himself. He spoke slowly.

'My...name...is...Jan. I...am...from...England.' The man frowned at Jan and nodded his head slowly. He grunted a grunt that universally means 'yes'.

'What...' Jan started again, 'country...is...this?' He waved his arm towards the cliff edge when he said 'this' to signify what 'this' referred to, and the man responded 'Aye, s'tinglan.'

'Icetingland,' Jan repeated.

'Aye,' said the man with a short pause. 'S'tinglan.'

'Icetingland,' Jan said again, and then bowed as a thank you.

The man put his hand on Jan's arm gently and turned him towards the cliff. In a soft and heavily accented, presumably

Icetinglandish language, the man started to talk at length to Jan, occasionally pointing at something on the horizon. Jan picked out words he understood from the man's speech here and there (wild, them hills, berries, eats, car), but for the most part he just enjoyed the gentle tones in his accent and his persistent attempts at communication.

The man was clearly proud of Icetingland, and Jan was more than happy to share the view with him. The fear of England Gaz had long vanished now, and Jan was feeling a lot more confident in his travelling abilities. He waited for the man's Icetinglandish monologue to end rather than interrupting.

'What's…your…name?'

'Hey lad? Name?'

'Hello Hylad. My…name…is…Jan.'

The man that Jan took to be Hylad laughed to himself but not in a rude way, and then said something else in his mother tongue. Once more Jan could only pick out a few words (mother, father, and car again) but he sort of got the gist from the man's movements. He was being invited for a lift in Hylad's car, presumably to meet his mother and father. Jan nodded gratefully.

'Thank…you,' he said, with another bow.

They walked to the car side-by-side in relative silence. The man had parked in the same place where Jan had started 'off-road travelling', and he had obviously just come to look at the view. They got in the car together and the man started the engine. Jan could barely put his feet down for all the crisp packets and old newspapers, and there was a surprisingly familiar smell of vinegar in the car.

'Ok,' said Hylad, and Jan was surprised to find that he understood. 'Thiyon wesson fesant?' And Jan was unsurprised to find that he had stopped understanding. He nodded anyway, as whatever Hylad had said had been a question, and happy with the nodded answer, Hylad turned the key, released the clutch and jerked the car forward.

Jan looked out of the window. The country he was in certainly was different to Fishton. Bunting adorned the streets, wildlife had the rule of the land for acres, and people offered lifts to people despite the fact that they couldn't even properly talk to each other. Jan wondered what Hylad's parents would be like, and what would he say to them? Presumably they wouldn't speak English either, and Jan definitely couldn't speak Icetinglandish (with the exception of maybe the words 'wild', 'mother', 'eats', 'them hills', 'father', 'berries' and 'car'). He started trying to make sentences out of these words in his head but found he couldn't get much further than 'wild mother eats berries'. He'd just smile and hope for the best.

Through the window he saw that the trees were beginning to clear, and there was a small ruined building made of stone that said, 'Bus Stop' on it. Well I understand that, Jan thought, and then he saw a sign that read, 'School – Slow Down'. He understood that too. He looked at Hylad, puzzled, and then back to the road. As it was getting more built-up around him, everything became more familiar. There were several fish shops and there was an arcade with pirates in the window. There was Dean. Jan knew Dean.

'Hi Jan,' shouted Dean as Jan and Hylad drove past. Jan sank into his chair as the familiar smell of fish filled his nostrils.

The doorbell rang at 31 Western Crescent and Jan's mother answered.

'Owsbeleib?' said Hylad. Jan's mother looked at Hylad, and then she looked at Jan, who was standing next to him. She put her hands on her hips.

'What have you been up to, eh?' she said.

'Pickimupfoooor,' answered Hylad on behalf of Jan. Jan's mother looked again at Hylad, and then she leaned her head backwards, still maintaining eye contact with Hylad, and called for Jan's father. They all stood in the doorway for a few seconds, quietly waiting for Jan's father to join them. When he came, Jan's mother whispered to him privately, although completely audibly to everyone present, that she's never understood why people still talk Old Fishton any more because no one understands it these days anyway, and that Jan's father would have to take over while she went to look for five single unmatching socks.

'Yusson,' said Hylad, who Jan's father recognised as Nigel from two towns across.

'Thank you,' said Jan's father. 'Jan, go upstairs.' Jan did as he was told while Nigel started another gentle monologue. Jan's father understood about half of it.

'I think I'm glad I'm home,' Jan said to his mother as he threw his stick-and-bed-sheet bag onto the kitchen table, 'I wanted to come home when I saw your face in a dying fish.' Jans mother sat down, feeling both offended and loved at the same time.

Upstairs in his room Jan realised that he really wasn't sad that he was back in Fishton. He looked at the ceiling, and at that moment, he didn't long for lands afar, and he didn't care about what was over the North Sea. Instead, he found himself dreaming of Fishton. The Old Fishton language, the town with the bunting that was about a mile down the road, and the wildlife that he never knew surrounded him. He dreamed of Nigel (but in his dream Nigel was called Hylad), and he knew then that he did want to travel one day, but first, he needed to travel Fishton, and for the next five years, that's exactly what he did.

Downstairs, Jan's mother picked up the makeshift bag to wash the bedsheet. Five single and unmatching socks fell out onto the table. She nearly fainted with relief. She sat down and checked that they were the right ones, twice.

Three times.

They were. Jan's dad came into the kitchen to find her leaning back exhausted on her chair.

'Are they the socks?' he asked, nodding towards the table, and Jan's mother gave him a proud smile.

'It's been an adventure,' she said.'

6

AN INSIGNIFICANT DOG

Goa. India. 2016.

The DJ had attracted a small crowd of vests. They were sitting in a circle on the sand with a little mongrel puppy jumping around between them, though none of the vests paid much attention to the puppy.

Some of the vests were bobbing their heads in time with the music and some had their mouths slightly open, but none of them were looking at the DJ and no one could be said to be truly dancing. Instead, they were discussing how they'd never really appreciated music until they'd come to Palolem, and how, actually, now that they thought about it, each thud sort of felt spiritual. They had all fully immersed themselves into the sound of India, they agreed.

One of the vests stood up, narrowly missing the puppy's

tail with her sandal.

'Bucket, anyone?'

She walked to the bar, passing the DJ (making the peace sign with two of her fingers for him, and he did the same back), ignoring a cow (which was still nodding its head in time to each spiritual thud) and up to the barman with the other three of her five fingers now held up.

'Five buckets and one COCK-tail,' she said, and then, 'namaste,' as a mistaken word of thanks.

Manjan watched all of this, still impressed with the cow's ability to adapt to her surroundings compared to his own. Shakey will leave in a couple of minutes, he thought, surprising himself to find that he was disappointed at this thought.

Shakey had also been watching, well aware that it was getting dark and he'd been selling a silent disco to the only person on the beach who would consider it too loud. He needed to get rid of some of these flyers and the group of vests did seem like the ideal takers. He looked at Manjan, shifted his legs as if to stand up, and then he settled again.

'Why don't I help you look for Jan?' he said. There was a brief silence between the two of them before Shakey's legs shifted themselves again. 'Ladyjan, I mean.'

Eventually Manjan replied, a little less than halfheartedly.

'Mm,' he said. Then he thought for a minute and told Shakey to look to his right. Shakey did. Next he told Shakey to look to his left. Shakey did that too. Then he asked, 'Did you see Jan?' before correcting himself for Shakey, 'Ladyjan.'

'I don't know what she looks like.'

'No,' Manjan responded, 'but that is not why you didn't see her.'

Shakey felt sad. He understood that his offer, as good-natured as it was, wasn't going to bring Ladyjan to Manjan. It was a hopeless situation and there was nothing he could do to help. In all honesty, he wasn't even sure why he cared, but he did.

'I have a bad neck,' Manjan said flatly. 'I find it hard to look behind me, towards the bar. Ladyjan, as you've dubbed her, could, I suppose be over there. It's unlikely, but it's possible.'

'Behind us?' Shakey asked, 'At the bar ?' He'd been talking to a madman. 'OK, sure, I'll check.' He stood up and looked behind him with an overly exaggerated twist of his hips. He raised one of his hands above his eyes and scanned into the distance of the small and very-easy-to-see-in-one-quick-glance bar. Next he took large, over-the-top steps towards the barman. He wasn't trying to be sarcastic, but he wanted Manjan's obviously senile mind to see that he was trying.

Manjan turned his neck to watch Shakey's performance. Sarcastic so-and-so, he thought.

As Shakey dramatically twisted his hips to come back he saw that Manjan was looking at him and tapping his empty glass.

'Might as well, while you're there.'

The barman down the beach had finished making the girl vest's order of drinks. She'd been telling the barman how in touch with nature she'd become since she'd been in India, although the barman made no response except to let her know the price of the drinks. She picked up the five buckets easily, using the handles, but she struggled with the COCK-tail, as it was presented in a long, tube-like glass, had off-looking cream on top and was served with two large, spherical biscuits either side. 'Namaste,' she called again as she tried her best not to drop the phallic masterpiece by clenching her elbows and – for some reason – her knees together.

'The next two COCK-tails are free,' muttered the barman, inaudibly.

On her way back to her fellow vests, the girl once again gave the peace sign to the DJ (who, once again, gave it back) and went out of her way to avoid the cow. The cow had now been joined by the puppy, who was repeatedly jumping up at the cow's nodding head, but finding himself just too little and insignificant to the cow to be noticed. It's a shame because the puppy had a lot to say to the cow, if only she would look down and listen.

'Drinks,' the girl said, and all the vests looked at her attentively while she handed them out. 'I've just been having the most amazing conversation with one of the locals,' she said, 'all about nature.' All the vests agreed that India had made them all very in touch with nature.

The puppy barked at the cow, the cow mooed to no one, and the vests started their mating ritual.

A few minutes later, Shakey returned to Manjan with a fresh glass of red wine and a new small bucket of vodka and Red Bull.

'I was only offering to help you,' Shakey said, emphasising the word 'you'.

'How would you have seen her, anyway?' Manjan mocked. 'You said yourself that you don't know what she looks like, but I thank you for the drink.'

'Is she fit?' Shakey asked, which Manjan decided to take to

mean the much more polite, 'what does she look like?'

He told Shakey at great length about the colour of Ladyjan's eyes and the shape of her face. He told Shakey about her numerous different hairstyles, before trying to rank them in order of his favourite and failing because, come to think about it, they were all perfect. Then he told Shakey in an even lengthier manner about her personality. How she used to laugh at the things he'd said, even though he didn't always understand why, and how the strength within her had left him awestruck. He told Shakey all of this in much greater detail and length in fact, than the pages of this book will allow. He could simply have said that she had very dark brown eyes, good cheekbones, ever-changing hair (sometimes short, sometimes long, often parted at the side and of varying colours) and an adventurous and caring personality. But he didn't just say that; he really didn't.

Finally, as Manjan was about to explain to Shakey how Ladyjan's shoulder sometimes smelt after sunbathing, Shakey asked his question again.

'Yeah,' he said, 'but is she fit?' Manjan thought about this. He'd never thought about it before because to him it didn't matter. Eventually, he concluded that she was, but he didn't say so.

Instead, sadly, he said, 'I guess I don't know what she looks like now.'

'That doesn't matter,' Shakey quickly replied, seeing Manjan's seemingly new realisation. 'How did you meet her? Why did you meet her? That matters. That might help us find her. What's your story?'

It wasn't that Manjan wanted to keep his and Ladyjan's story a secret – he'd told his story to lots of people before and for the most part they had been interested, entertained and often even compassionate. Sometimes they'd buy him a drink, and sometimes people had their own story to tell in return. People liked Manjan's story.

But Manjan had also told his story to a lot of vests. A couple of vests had laughed, some had stared blankly and not listened (although, to be fair, these vests were normally very intoxicated) and a few had simply wandered off, mid-story. Manjan now adopted a strict 'no vest' policy when it came to his story, but he had warmed somewhat to this particular vest. There was a chance that Shakey would listen. Manjan supposed that Shakey might laugh, but he doubted that he would wander off. In fact, he was beginning to doubt that Shakey would ever leave.

'Sorry, can you start again? I wasn't listening,' Shakey said.

'I hadn't begun,' Manjan replied.

'Perfect.'

There was a severe lack of intelligence in Shakey, but there certainly wasn't a lack of honesty.

Manjan sipped his wine and looked out to sea.

'For the purposes of the story,' he started, 'let's just assume that Ladyjan was fit.'

PART TWO

7

FOUR FOXES AND A MOUSE

Fishton to Norway. 1970.

Jan's mother helped Jan pack his bags. She would miss him, but he was only going to be away for a couple of weeks and at least he wouldn't be on his own.

'You'll have a full bag of clothes with you this time,' she said, 'and not just five socks.' Then she laughed.

'Mmm,' mumbled Jan, a little irritated. He'd had this from his parents on and off for the past five years. 'I took pants too,' he said defensively, and his mother laughed again.

'You'd have looked a sight in Norway.'

Although Jan hadn't properly gone travelling since his trip to, and indeed from, Fishton five years ago, he had learnt quite a lot about it. For starters, he had learnt that if you go out of Fishton via the sea and travel in a straight line, you get to Norway.

He'd also learnt the importance of planning. He'd learnt this after several nights camping in his parents' back garden staring at a bush and looking for wildlife. After four nights he still hadn't seen a thing. Sleepily, and smelling a little like wildlife himself, Jan went to Fishton library, where he researched what foxes ate and where they scavenged. The night after, he camped in his parents' front garden and stared at the bin all night. He saw three foxes and a mouse. Success! That same night a fourth fox had been in the back garden looking for a bin in the same smelly spot where Jan had previously camped. This doesn't negate the importance of planning though; it just emphasises another important lesson that Jan had learnt – the importance of washing.

Finally, Jan had learnt that to truly understand something, he must fully immerse himself into it. Since his last attempt at travelling, he had spent a long time learning the Old Fishton language. As a result, he found that the range of people to talk to in Fishton (and indeed the towns and villages down the road) had expanded. Everyone had a lot to say, but when you speak a different language, they had no way to say it. Recently Jan had been able to hear stories from perhaps hundreds of new and interesting people, not least Hylad.

It was thanks to Hylad that Jan was now packing. It had been five years since they had met on the cliff just outside the town two towns down from Fishton and now they were friends, although this friendship had started fairly one-sided. After their first meeting, Hylad (or Nigel as everyone else knew him) had found a thirteen-year-old Jan following him around everywhere, imitating the way he talked. Hylad found this more than a little annoying but because young Jan didn't yet understand the Old Fishton language, Hylad had no way of telling him to beat it.

'Oushna,' Hylad had said. This means 'beat it' in Old Fishton.

'Oushna,' Jan had shouted back, and an old lady who spoke fluent Old Fishton scarpered, not wanting to get in the middle of what she assumed would be a father-and-son fight.

Eventually Hylad had gone back to 31 Western Crescent to let Jan's father know, to let Jan know, to 'oushna'. Jan's father had let out a big sigh.

'I bet he's trying to learn Old Fishton,' he'd said apologetically. They had a long, slow and hard-to-understand conversation on the doorstep and at the end it was agreed that Jan would meet with Hylad each week to learn Old Fishton. In return, Jan had to help Hylad speak English and then, importantly, Jan must leave Hylad alone for the rest of the week. When they told Jan this he jumped with excitement.

'Yes, Hylad!' he shouted, before hugging Hylad.

'He's called Nigel,' Jan's father said, but Hylad didn't seem to mind.

Both Jan and Hylad kept their promise and over the following years they learnt how to understand one another. To begin with it hadn't been easy.

'How do we start?' Jan had asked. Without any clue of what Jan's question had meant, Hylad had scratched his large bald head and then asked the exact same question in Old Fishton. They looked at each other silently for some time after that. Then Hylad waved in greeting.

'Alloo,' he said slowly. Jan understood and replied with a very similar-sounding word.

After the fourth week they were both beginning to get somewhere. As it turned out English and Old Fishton were essentially the same language. Every word was accented and spelt differently, which made it difficult to learn, but when Jan and Hylad listened very closely to each other they could hear their own language lost in the heavily accented mist of the other.

By the time a year had passed Jan and Hylad were having full-on conversations in both languages. After the second year they realised that they were discussing things in a strange Old Fishton/English amalgamation that they had accidentally created themselves, and by the third year they were no longer teaching each other at all.

'What were you doing on that cliff?' Hylad had asked over a fish-and-chips lunch when Jan was seventeen. He'd often wondered but hadn't wanted to ask before in case the answer was...well, in case the answer was what the answer often is when people are found standing alone on cliffs. Jan was embarrassed.

'Don't laugh,' he had said, and Hylad feared the worst. 'I'd taken a test at school and the results...' Jan paused. Hylad worked quite high-up in the box-packaging department at Fishton's fish factory, and so Jan re-worded his sentence. 'The results...weren't what I'd been hoping for and – don't mock me when I say this but – I...was...unhappy.' Jan said this last bit slowly. Hylad felt himself well up inside but he wouldn't show it. He was a big man physically and he generally made a point of acting the part.

'Aye,' he said, without quiver or any outward show of

emotion.

'And, well, when you found me on the cliff...' Hylad prepared for the worst, forcing a stern face and holding back any visible sign of emotion by tensing his eyebrows.

'When you found me on the cliff I thought I was in Norway.' Hylad's face de-tensed and one side of his lips raised into a half-smile.

'Norway?'

'Yes, although I didn't know it was Norway then.'

'It wasn't Norway lad, not even close!' Hylad said this as the other side of his lips raised into a full smile.

'No, but I thought it was. I thought I'd travelled across the North Sea to the other side, to where I now know to be Norway. But obviously I hadn't.' Despite Jan's previous request, Hylad slammed his palms hard down on the table and let out a tremendous bellow of a laugh.

'You promised not to laugh,' Jan complained, even though Hylad had never actually made such a promise.

After some reassurance Jan told Hylad the whole story, from the moment he saw England Man to his first opinions of the town that wasn't Norway. Hylad had laughed at nearly every sentence, and by this point Jan had been laughing too.

Hylad had whooped when Jan was finished, slamming his hands down on the table again with joy.

'This is ridiculous, Jan. You are ridiculous.' But during Jan's story Hylad had made his mind up. This boy who had been inquisitive enough to annoy the hell out of him when they had first met, but who had then also been patient enough to teach him English, deserved not to be laughed at. Hylad wiped his now red face with his sleeve and cleared his throat to calm himself down. 'I'll have a word with your mother and father, and if they don't mind, and if you want to m'lad, I'll take you to Norway.'

The doorbell rang, and Jan rushed out of his room to escape the continuing ridicule he was getting from his mother.

'Every sock needs a friend!' Jan's father called out as Jan jumped down the last three steps to the hall, but Jan barely noticed – he was too excited to see Norway.

'Ready?' Hylad asked as Jan swung open the door.

'Nearly. Hang on, I'll just grab my bag,' answered Jan as he rushed back upstairs.

'Have you packed socks?' Hylad called after him, 'and then did you pack the same socks again? That's called a pair!' Then he and Jan's father enjoyed a good laugh and a chat at the door while Hylad waited.

Jan picked up his bag, hugged his mother and started his way back downstairs. Then, remembering the foxes and the importance of planning, he went back into his room and grabbed his already tattered and completely read *High-Tide Travel Guide to Norway*.

As Jan and Hylad turned away from Western Crescent and started on down to the harbour, Jan's mother walked downstairs, ready to enjoy a few days of peace with her husband, only to find that she wouldn't be able to relax at all. There, on the top step where Jan had turned to collect his travel book, were three individual odd socks.

8

HIGH-TIDE TRAVEL GUIDE

Fishton to Norway. 1970.

Three days is a long time to spend on a boat, especially one as minimal as Hylad's. It was solid enough for the task at hand, and indeed Hylad was a capable captain, but when it came to passing the time the boat offered little more than a view. Jan got bored of the view about five hours after they lost sight of land. He'd enjoyed watching Fishton become England and he'd enjoyed watching England become the sea. He'd even enjoyed the sea just remaining the sea for a full five hours, but then boredom set in. Hylad was busy navigating, steering and whistling, and Jan didn't want to distract him. Michael, the man that Hylad had bought along with them to drive through the night, was asleep in the single bed that Jan would be using later on. Even if Michael hadn't been sleeping, Jan didn't think he'd have made the best company. Michael had been incredibly nice to Hylad – very attentive and full of humour – but when Jan had tried to speak to him he had become defensive and short.

'How long have you known Hylad?' Jan had asked.

'Yeah, I've known NIGEL quite long.'

'How did you meet?'

'Well, you know,' Michael had started, as if he had more to say, and then didn't say anything for quite some time.

'Did you go to school together?'

'I just told you, it was quite a long time ago. I dunno, the details escape me,' but it was obvious that they didn't.

'But, vaguely...' Jan persisted in the way that he tended to do when he didn't sense that someone was annoyed with him.

'You really don't care, Jan. Look I appreciate you making the small talk but...'

'I really do care,' Jan interrupted, although by this point he wasn't sure that he did any more.

'Fine. Look, we met, and we tend not to talk about how, but if you must know it wasn't really a meeting at all, it was more like we crashed,' Michael said, somewhat cryptically. Then he'd got Hylad's attention by touching his arm and said, 'I'm going to bed,' softly.

'I'm going to bed,' he'd said to Jan harshly.

Jan was glad that they were to have alternating sleep patterns on the boat. He was also happy to hear that when they reached Norway, Michael was only planning on eating with Jan and Hylad in the evenings, so they would have the days to explore without him. Although when Michael had told them this, the source of Jan's relief also seemed to be the source of Hylad's disappointment.

Jan walked from one side of the boat to the other and saw

nothing but sea. He listened to Hylad's whistling and tried to guess what tune he was renditioning, but from what he could tell there was no tune – just high-pitched notes of different lengths and tone with no noticeable pattern. These three days are going to be long, he thought as he opened the first page of his worn and already repeatedly read *High-Tide Travel Guide to Norway*.

Top Ten Norwegian Experiences

1.

There is nothing like sailing around the fjords in the north of Norway. The water is crystal-clear, and the peaks of land are untouched spots of beauty. Make sure you hang around for sunset!

2.

Pulpit Rock offers one of the best views that the world has to offer. It's a gruelling hike but from the rock you'll experience nature in its truest form. With sunset cometh the best views from the rock.

3.

The city of Oslo offers a skyscape for score skies! Watch the sun set over the rooftops while enjoying a fiskesuppe *(fish soup) from one of many of Oslo's Kafeer.*

4.

The only way to explore a Norwegian city is by tram. Trams run through daylight hours and will offer you the experience of being a true Norwegian. The trams tend to stop just after sunset but it's worth putting your day trip on hold to experience this most magnificent of times to travel!

5.

The midnight sun is a truly Norwegian experience. The further north you travel the more nights of sun you can expect but an average year offers around seventy-five nights of the midnight sun from May. The midnight sun is best experienced at sunset!

Jan stopped reading. 'The midnight sun is best experienced at sunset,' he read again, this time out loud. 'Surely the point of the midnight sun is that there is no sunset for months. Then, when there is a sunset there isn't a midnight sun. How can I see the midnight sun at sunset when the sun sets the midnight sun? And when it sets, does it set at midnight, in which case, is that still the midnight sun or the just-before-midnight sun?' Jan's mind was baffled. Try to focus on the south of Norway, he thought. They wouldn't be going far north enough to see the midnight sun anyway.

6.

Why not visit one of Norway's stunning coastal villages? Grimstad, for example, is set around many small islands, with the harbour acting host to many maritime vessels. Why not make the most of your visit with a drink down by the water at sunset?

There it was again. That word. Everything seemed to be better at sunset. Jan had seen lots of sunsets in Fishton before, and there was no doubt that he liked them, but had the sunset enhanced the fish and chips he'd eaten next to the trolleys in the supermarket car park that time? He wasn't sure it had. And had he enjoyed lifting bricks onto his uncle's van more when the sun had been going down? No. It had hurt both his shoulders and his legs, regardless of the sun's position. Maybe the sunset was different in Norway.

Jan scanned the next page of the *High-Tide Travel Guide* and saw that numbers 7, 9 and 10 on the list of the top ten Norwegian experiences were all 'best experienced at sunset'. What were he and Hylad to do with the rest of their day? In fact, the only thing that wasn't best experienced at sunset in Norway was the Northern Lights. Jan put the book down next to him with a thump.

'But the sun doesn't even set for half the year,' Jan said to himself, a little indignant.

'Will you shut up?' came a sharp, barking noise from the single bed, 'I'll be up all night piloting this poxy boat, and I want to sleep now.'

'Sorry,' called Jan, genuinely apologetic for keeping Michael awake.

'Are you talking to yourself?' came another bark.

'Yes,' Jan answered, 'I am. Are you sure you only want to meet up with us in the evenings when we get to Norway? You can see us in the day instead if you'd prefer.'

Jan heard a grunt from the direction of the bed that sounded a bit like the word 'evening', and then some more grunts that might have meant 'thank you'.

'You won't miss out on much then. You'll be with us for all the best experiences. Don't worry.'

Another grunt, a shuffling sound and then nothing but the sounds of the sea, the boat and Hylad's whistling again.

9

A COCKROACH

Fishton to Norway. 1970.

It was about 4 am when Michael started to see the dim twinkle of lights in the distance. They weren't dead ahead of the boat as he had expected, but to the left.

'Nigel!' he shouted, but he received no response.

'Jan!' he called, this time slightly quieter, preferring to speak to Nigel, or Hylad, as Jan liked to call him. Again, he didn't get a response. The water was fairly calm, and they were all tired from the past two days at sea. It was going to take a lot for Michael to wake them.

He carried on forward, occasionally looking to the faint yellow glow on his left. 'Norway?' he thought, 'Surely not.' Both Hylad and himself had been checking the sextant repeatedly since they'd started the journey and it had always looked as if they were on course. Granted, they were aiming for the very south of Norway, but it seemed unlikely that they could have missed the whole country altogether.

'Jan!' Michael called again. It wasn't Jan he wanted, really, but he realised that if he could just wake up Jan, Jan could wake up Hylad. Hylad was an absolute nightmare to wake at the best of times, let alone at four in the morning.

Still there was no response.

Michael was aware he'd been hard on Jan when they'd set off. He'd been so happy to be having a trip away with Hylad, and then so disappointed to hear that this lad would be joining them. But that wasn't Jan's fault and he'd unfairly taken it out on him.

Michael rubbed the back of his nearly bald head and exhaled an extended 'h' sound, which he then watched linger in front of him in the cold air.

He was about to call for Jan again when he saw a dark oval run across the floor.

Fully under the impression that he was still in Fishton, but lost nonetheless, the cockroach lifted his front half to look at the large man who'd just been shouting. The man looked back at the cockroach, disgusted. People always look disgusted, thought the cockroach. What a terribly unhappy species they must be.

The man lifted one of his legs towards the cockroach with an angry expression. The cockroach knew that this meant it was time to scarper. He'd lost many of his friends to the feet of angry men and women. He ran to the side of the boat, banged into the wall and began to miss home – where was he? He walked to his right and banged into the same wall. He walked to his right and banged into the wall. He walked to his right and banged into the wall. It's not easy being a lost cockroach.

Michael grunted and put his foot back down. 'Jan!' he shouted, louder than before, keeping his eye on the little black dot that kept banging into the right side of the boat. After receiving no response yet again, he looked behind him towards the bedroom. 'HYLAD!'

He'd decided to make peace with Jan, who actually seemed quite nice, and calling Nigel Hylad seemed a good idea. There wasn't a response as such but he heard some movement from the bedroom, so he called again. 'HYLAD!'

Jan emerged from the bedroom sleepily.

'Why are you shouting for Hylad?'

'Why do you answer to Hylad and not your own name?'

Jan was confused. He hadn't heard Michael's other shouts, so this was a confusing question and he decided not to answer it.

'Just wake up Hylad for me, will you?'

'Hylad!' Jan shouted.

'Yeah, I tried that. Go and give him a prod.'

Jan wandered back down to the bedroom as Michael's thoughts turned back to the cockroach. 'Blasted thing, where is it?'

The cockroach turned right and banged into the wall.

'I see what you're saying,' Hylad pondered while rubbing his chin. 'It is definitely land.' Hylad and Jan were leaning on the left-hand side of the boat and looking at the row of dim twinkling lights in the distance.

'But is it Norway?' Michael asked from the helm.

If he was being honest with himself, Hylad didn't know whether it was Norway or not, but sometimes his confidence would portray a mere inkling as if it were fact.

'No,' he replied. 'No, it's definitely not Norway.'

'How can you tell?' Jan asked.

'Well, you see,' Hylad started, biding his time so he could work out himself how he could tell. 'Jan,' he started again, 'Michael and I have been using that sextant over there the whole time to navigate us to Norway. That,' he said, gesturing to the lights, 'is not Norway.' He could see in Jan's expression that this clearly wasn't going to be enough of an explanation. 'I certainly trust Michael's navigation, don't you?'

'I guess so,' Jan answered, acutely aware that he'd only met Michael two days ago. 'Although it was Michael who asked us whether the lights were Norway or not in the first place.'

'Hm,' said Hylad, and then he paused to think. 'Well I've been using the sextant too,' he said, 'and I certainly trust my navigation, don't you?' He smiled at Jan and raised one of his eyebrows.

Jan did trust Hylad. Hylad had proved himself to be very trustworthy and a good friend to Jan – the trip itself was proof of that. They both looked out to the lights again – Hylad puzzled and Jan wistful of the miscellaneous land that was laid out across the sea in front of them.

'So, if it's not Norway,' Jan asked slowly, 'where is it?'

'Just one of Norway's many islands, lad.'

'One of the many islands of Norway,' Jan repeated, now half in a dream. If just one of Norway's islands can be that big, he thought, and there can be that many of them, how will I ever manage to visit everywhere in the entire world?

How many people must live on that island? And yet the three of them weren't even going to stop; it was apparently that insignificant to them. There must be so much to see on this planet and so much to learn, an unfathomable number of people to meet and far too little time to do it all in.

A sharp wind blew across Jan's face, forcing him to squint his eyes. He didn't want to close them though. He wanted to watch just one of Norway's many islands pass them in the night.

For a while no one spoke. It was cold, but the night was calm enough to be peaceful and Hylad, Michael and Jan lost themselves in their own individual thoughts. Hylad wondered whether his assumptions about the land to the left of the boat were right, or whether they were all just watching Norway silently drift past them. If he was wrong, he would have a lot of explaining to do. Michael appeared to face the land, but he was actually looking at Hylad, quietly admiring his knowledge and assertiveness, and Jan… Well, Jan's thoughts and emotions were everywhere – wistful and longing, excited and calm, adventurous and sleepy. The early hours of the morning whistled a soft whistle and the chilled seawater rippled calmly behind the boat, creating a constant but gentle lapping sound. Michael sighed.

'So, we continue forward?' he asked.

Hylad turned around and he and Michael held eye contact for a couple of seconds. They both smiled.

'Continue forward,' he agreed.

The cockroach turned to his right and banged into a wall. He was tired of banging into the wall and he was beginning to get a headache. There had to be a gap somewhere, a way back to the familiarity of Fishton.

Since getting lost, the cockroach had drunk well. Water was plentiful and it kept splashing over him, he'd perhaps even drunk more than he'd wanted to, but he hadn't eaten a thing. He wanted to take a big fat bite out of one of the angry man's toenails, but the man was wearing cockroach-killing, life-threatening boots. There was plenty of decaying wood lying around but the cockroach didn't really like decaying wood. He was used to decent fish, moulted stray-dog hair and good, decent sewage from Fishton harbour.

He turned to his right and banged into a wall. He turned to his right and banged into a wall, and then he stopped.

He recognised this wall. He'd banged into this bit of the wall before. The poor cockroach moved backwards to examine the wall with his throbbing head, at which point Michael spied him from the wheel.

Hylad and Jan had gone back to bed for the last few hours of darkness and Michael had been left piloting again. He'd been looking for the cockroach unsuccessfully since he'd been on his own, and now here it was, in exactly the same place as he'd last seen it. But he still couldn't reach it to kill it.

The cockroach gave up. He'd been banging into a wall for over two hours and he simply couldn't understand how he'd ended up at the same piece of wall. Not many people know this, but cockroaches can't cry. This cockroach, however, at this moment, felt tears in his tiny cockroach heart.

It wasn't until the sun rose behind him that Michael saw the land in front of him. 'Norway!' he shouted, and this time both Jan and Hylad were on deck within minutes.

'Can we speed up?' Jan asked.

Seconds later the boat started kicking water violently out from behind it.

'Oh yes,' yelled Michael over the noise, and all three of them started shouting celebratory words that, out of context, would have had no meaning.

'Ooooh yes, come on!' Michael continued.

'This is it, lad!' Hylad bellowed, 'This is it!'

'Noooorway, Noorwaaaay, Nooorwaaay,' Jan chanted in a higher-pitched voice than he wanted and a little quieter than the other two. No one other than the three of them knew that at that very moment a calm sunrise over the east side of the North Sea was being disrupted by cheers, whoops, childish chants and a boat engine working overtime.

Michael slowed the engine again. 'Sorry,' he said, 'I don't want to ruin the party but it's quite a long way to go on that kind of power.' Jan and Hylad stopped cheering and once again the sunrise enjoyed a calm, cold sea to warm up.

In fact, the land was further away than it first appeared, and it took the best part of an hour for the three of them to reach it. Jan didn't mind. Of course, he was almost painfully excited to disembark and explore, but looking across the sea to the vast expanse of land in front of him he realised that he was seeing more of Norway than he would ever manage from the land. He soaked it up as best as he could, feeling almost scared to blink in case he missed something. The land was flat and green, with grey stone connecting it to the sea's horizon. A few buildings clumped together on the only yellow-looking section and the occasional light turned on in one of the windows. Whatever town he was looking at, it was just beginning to wake up.

'When we land, lad,' Hylad said, interrupting Jan's thoughts, 'I'm going to need you to jump off with this rope and tie us up, as solid as you can. Once the engine's off I'll come down and help you, and Michael can sort out the last bits on the boat.'

'Got it,' said Jan, still facing the land and not taking the rope from Hylad.

'You know how to tie a knot that'll hold the boat?' Hylad asked.

'Got it,' Jan answered again, vacantly.

'I'm going to need you to make me a sandwich, clean my boots and swim the rest of the way, lad.'

'Uh huh, got it.'

Hylad looked at Michael and shrugged his shoulders with a 'what are we going to do with him?' smile.

'Jan!' shouted Michael.

Jan jumped and stuttered 'S-s-sandwi... Yep. What?'

'No. No sandwich. Hylad's telling you what to do when we hit shore, and actually, while you're over there and you're listening, kill that cockroach for me, would you?'

Jan looked down by his feet to where Michael was pointing. There was a small brown cockroach next to the wall of the boat. He looked back at Michael, who was concentrating on the boat's wheel again, and then back at the cockroach. He put his foot hard down on the ground next to the cockroach and twisted it to simulate a killing.

'It's dead,' he said, as he bent down and tucked the live, confused but grateful cockroach into a small crevasse in the boat's floor. Then he stood up, holding his fingers together tightly and mimicked throwing it into the sea.

Another shout came from the wheel. 'Nice one, lad.'

The cockroach turned right and banged into the wall of the

crevasse, before deciding once again to just stand still.

The land was coming closer and they could clearly see the port that they were headed for. Jan was finally holding the rope and ready to hop off, eager for his first steps in Norway.

Hylad's boat was tiny compared to some of the large ships surrounding the port. *The High-Tide Travel Guide* had implied that the port would be fairly small, with a few fishing boats bobbing away (best seen at sunset), so Jan had been expecting a kind of Norwegian Fishton. Instead he found himself confronted with sea-liners, cranes and skyscrapers.

The boat bumped against the stone wall. Jan leapt to the land and wrapped the rope repeatedly around one of the bollards. He was full of excitement to see Norway, but he was also determined to tie the knot correctly for Hylad, so he concentrated hard on getting it right.

He was concentrating so hard, in fact, that he didn't notice the petite lady's hand slip inside his back-pocket. As he pulled the rope to tighten the knot he didn't notice the hand feel around for something to take, and as he looped one last loop of the rope around the bollard he didn't notice the hand leave his pocket with his passport.

He did notice the shrill blow of a whistle. He lost his concentration instantly and turned around to see the girl, one hand in her pocket, standing confusingly and uncomfortably close to him. A second later he saw two men, one little and one large, running along the docks towards Hylad's boat. The smaller of the two was blowing on a whistle with all his might repeatedly and the larger had his arm in the air and was shouting something in a language that Jan didn't understand. Jan looked back to the girl, who was now a more comfortable distance from him, and behind her he saw a uniformed man and woman casually getting out of a police car.

'*Hjälp, hjälp,*' shouted the girl, and she pointed at Jan. She had obviously seen them too.

The little whistle-blowing man and the large waving man were running at Jan up the docks and the policeman and -woman were running at him from the road.

On an impulse, Jan reached into his pocket – to find his passport missing. He shook his head from side to side in panic. Wait, where had the girl gone? He looked around for her whereabouts when – Slam! – he hit the floor with the full force of the policewoman's charge.

The policeman started talking into a big walkie-talkie while the policewoman adjusted Jan's position, so she could hold his right arm tightly behind his back.

The cockroach, having escaped the crevasse, ran to the side of the boat and banged into the wall. He walked to his right and banged into the wall. He walked to his right and then through a wide-open gap in the wall. He ran down the small wooden ramp to the port, expecting to see his Fishton cockroach friends. Whatever's happened these past few days, he thought, this is not Fishton. Sadly, but still with a great, panicked haste, he looked around in the only way he knew how – a full 360-degree rotation of his body. He scuttled over to the bare-handed uniformed woman holding Jan to the ground. He climbed up Jan's sleeve and paused by the woman's hand to make sure he could fully savour this moment. Then he bit down hard into the softest and tastiest fingernail he'd ever dined upon and the grip on Jan's right arm loosened.

10

ANNAN JÄVLA SJÄLVLYSANDE

Norway. 1970.

Jan couldn't understand what the policelady was saying
as she held him chest down on the cold harbour ground,
but he understood that he was being arrested. He couldn't
understand what the small man with the whistle and the
large man (who by now had stopped waving) were saying to
Hylad and Michael, but he understood that neither Hylad
nor Michael were allowed off the boat. Had he not been so
scared, Jan might have appreciated his ability to follow the
context without understanding any of the actual words. But
he was scared, so he didn't.

He watched from the floor as Hylad and Michael tried to
get off the boat. Hylad pushed the larger man out of the way

and the little man pushed Hylad back, preventing him from stepping onto the harbour. Both Hylad and Michael were shouting for Jan, but Jan couldn't reply through fear of the policelady who had plonked herself so forcibly on top of him.

He saw the little man hold Hylad and Michael back from the harbour with both of his little arms spread wide. It would have been impressive if it wasn't for the situation. Then the large man pushed the boat away from the wall with the use of his feet and an iron bollard.

Jan saw a cockroach fall from his shoulder and onto the harbour wall, and he focused on it as he began to realise that he was going to be left in a foreign country with no friends and no passport.

'They're saying we can't stop here, Jan, they won't let us get off,' Hylad shouted from the boat, and Jan's heart sank lower than his body. 'Don't worry, lad, we'll find somewhere we can stop, and then we'll find you. Hold tight.' Hylad continued shouting as the boat moved further and further away from the harbour, but Jan couldn't hear anything after 'hold tight'.

He didn't want to hold tight. He wanted to be on the boat with Hylad and Michael, or at home with his parents, or, well, anywhere but under the policelady in this unknown land. He didn't have much choice though; if he didn't want to 'hold tight', she would do it for him. He wasn't going anywhere. He watched the boat he'd spent the last three days travelling on move back out of Norway, with his travelling companions on it. Jan was left behind.

The policeman said something that Jan didn't understand to the policelady and she said something that Jan didn't understand back to the policeman. Had he understood, he would have heard the policeman tell the policelady that he recognised the girl who had accused Jan of theft, that she was nowhere to be seen and that maybe Jan was the victim here. Then he would have heard the policelady tell the policeman that he may well be right but this kid clearly didn't understand what they were saying anyway so they should probably take him to the station, so he can speak with an interpreter.

The policelady was right. Jan didn't understand any of their conversation, so when he was lifted backwards up off the floor and walked hastily to the police car he went numb with fear, dragged his legs behind him, and thus appeared instantly guilty.

Jan sat in a bright room, his left hand holding onto his right hip and his right hand holding onto his left hip. His shoulders were hunched over and he shivered. He didn't know whether the room was cold or whether he was shivering from elongated fear. Maybe it was both.

He wasn't sure how long he'd been in the room. It hadn't been hours, but it hadn't just been minutes either and there wasn't a clock. He had a scented cup of hot water in front of him – probably a type of tea, but not like the cups of tea he was used to at home – and he was completely, utterly, alone.

In the car, the policeman had sat in the back with Jan and once again Jan had found himself in somebody else's car not understanding somebody else's language. It sounded like the man might be called Oskyldig. He kept saying 'Oskyldig' and pointing one hand to his chest, but Jan didn't want to make assumptions. He'd made that mistake before with Hylad. Instead, Jan stayed silent.

When they got to the station there was another man at

the desk. He'd said a few foreign words to Jan's arresters and they'd said a few foreign words back. Then the man at the desk had turned to Jan.

'Eng-a-lish?' he'd asked with a bouncy accent and a smile. Jan nodded. 'OK,' the man said, 'you can wait in here.' That was when he'd led Jan into the bright room.

Since then, the policelady who'd spent a portion of her morning sitting on Jan's back had brought Jan the cup of what was potentially tea and now he waited for…well, he waited.

The room was pleasant enough, if a little sterile. There was a plant in one of the corners facing Jan. Presumably it had been put there to give the room a less intimidating vibe, but Jan had just been arrested in an unfamiliar country with no passport; at that moment he would have found a kitten licking the icing off a cupcake intimidating.

The door opened and the man from the desk came into the room. He was tall and lean, and now he had a pair of small circular glasses sitting at the top of his nose. He started talking before he'd even sat down.

'You have been arrested for theft,' he said. 'I don't know if you are guilty. I wasn't there, yah. But I speak Eng-a-lish and you speak Eng-a-lish, so now I think we can talk to work out if you are guilty.' Despite the implications of what the man was saying Jan was happy to hear him. He sounded jolly and it was nice to hear his own language again. 'Yah?' asked the man.

'Yes sir,' Jan said, through his still-shaking teeth, 'and I talk Old Fishton too.' The man started to say something and then stopped, gave Jan a quizzical look, and then continued.

'I am Liam,' he said, 'and you?'

'Jan,' said Jan.

'First, I will ask you a straight question,' Liam said, adding a 'h' sound before the t in straight. 'Are you guilty?'

'What?' asked Jan. This was going to be easy. He paused and put one hand on the table in front of him. 'No,' he said, flatly and clearly.

'OK, good,' Liam said. 'Please now prove it.'

'How?'

Liam shrugged before they both endured a long silence.

'OK, so you can't prove you are not guilty,' Liam said slowly. 'That's a shame. This isn't going to be as easy as I'd hoped. So, why are you in Shweden?'

'Norway.' Jan replied.

'No, Shweden.'

'I'm in Sweden?'

'You think you're in Norway?'

'I'm not?'

Liam sighed heavily.

'*Annan jävla självlysande,*' he mumbled to himself, which, roughly translated to English, means 'another poxy vest'.

11

AN OTTER

~~Norway~~ Sweden, 1970.

'Just one of Norway's many islands, you said, you were so sure, Nigel, you said you were sure.' Michael put his head in his hands and felt sick. 'It was Norway, not one of Norway's many islands. Norway. For Christ's sake, Hylad.' Hylad didn't like Michael calling him Hylad any more. He liked it when they'd all been together on the boat, but not now, not without Jan. It didn't feel right.

'You don't know that,' stammered Hylad. 'That could have been an island, and we could have landed in Norway, just at the wrong port.' Michael laughed a sarcastic one-syllabled laugh. 'We'll find him, of course we will. I'm not going to leave him. I was the one who wanted to show him Norway in the first place and you said no.'

'I thought you wanted a holiday with me, Hylad. Not with me and a kid I don't know, and I didn't say no. Why do you think we're on this boat? Tell me where you think we are exactly, because this doesn't look like England to me.'

'Well we're not in Norway, are we?' Hylad replied, not knowing quite how right he was. 'Only Jan's in Norway,' he said, not knowing quite how right he wasn't. 'I guess now at least you get your holiday with just me.'

'You know that's not what I meant,' Michael said sulkily, and then they both stopped talking.

This was the first time they'd stopped arguing since losing Jan. They'd already tried to moor the boat at the next town along the coast, but they'd been met with a similar resistance as before. Now they were on their way to the second town.

'What's the plan, then, if they let us off the boat, that is?' Michael said, his tone as deflated as his expression and posture.

Hylad thought. 'We'll go to the police station.'

'We can't just report a missing child,' Michael said, before putting on a mock voice without enough effort to quite pull it off. 'Oh, sorry, we appear to have left a kid in your country and then floated off without him. Give us a bell if you find him.'

'No. Think about it, Jan was arrested, and where do you go when you get arrested?'

Michael was leaning his head over the right side of the boat watching the coast drift by when he noticed two splashes in the water next to a sandy cove. An otter hopped out of the water and onto one of the rocks next to the sand. A smaller otter tried to do the same but didn't quite make it and fell back into the water. The bigger otter flopped back into the water after the little otter and gave the little otter a nudge up to the rock with her nose, before following.

'I'm moving us in,' called Hylad from the helm, 'fingers crossed!'

'Fingers crossed,' Michael called back.

He couldn't tell whether it was his sour mood along with the three days spent at sea playing tricks on him or not, but the bigger otter seemed to be looking sad. Michael wasn't sure if otters could feel sad. The bigger otter nuzzled her pup with her nose, dipped her head up and down twice and then slid off the rock into the water.

Michael watched the little otter look around the rock by himself. He didn't follow his mother. Instead, he nosed the edges of the rock as if trying to break it. Then he rolled upside down head-first in the middle of the rock until he was back on his tiny otter hands. Finally, he stood and waited for his mother to come back.

Michael scanned the sea between the boat and the cove for any sign of the bigger otter. He didn't even see a splash. When the little otter realised he was alone he yelped a high-pitched yelp – to Michael, to the sea, to nobody.

The boat was getting closer to land, and the rock by the cove was going to be out of Michael's line of vision in minutes. Just then the little otter dived off the rock. Michael watched the empty rock and thought about Jan. He hoped they could find him, and he hoped he was OK.

Seconds before the rock moved out of his sight Michael saw the little otter jump back onto the rock with something in his mouth. The little otter dropped his catch on the rock, batted it about a bit with those tiny otter hands, and then ate his first personally-caught fish.

It hadn't been hard to moor the boat at the town next to the next town along from where they'd lost Jan. In fact, it had been easy. No one questioned them, no one held them onto the boat like before and no one shouted or blew any whistles at them. No one was there. It wasn't until they walked up a grassy bank and along a sea wall that they found another person. This person, a slender lady with grey curly hair, sat outside the front of her blue-painted house and sipped a glass of juice.

'Where have you come from?' she asked in perfect, if heavily accented, English.

'England,' Michael responded in an out-of-breath and panicked hurry that slightly alarmed the lady. 'We need to be two towns that way.' He pointed. 'Please, how do we get there?'

'Give me two minutes and I will take you in my car. It is not far. But first, may I say, welcome to Sweden.'

'Norway,' Hylad said. Michael rolled his eyes and Hylad and the grey-haired lady had the same conversation that Jan and the policeman were having two towns down.

In the car Michael and Hylad told the lady what had happened.

Michael and Hylad's story was ridiculous and a little far-fetched but she believed them and decided that they were basically decent men that had been really quite stupid. She told them this and they agreed. She also decided from the looks that Hylad and Michael kept exchanging that they made a lovely couple. She told them this too, but they did not agree. Instead they said nothing, and Michael looked panicked once again.

The rest of the journey was stifled but not rude. When they reached the police station Hylad offered the lady some Norwegian Krone as a thank you. She declined, pointing out that she'd offered a lift out of kindness and not for personal gain.

'Oh,' she said, 'and as I've previously mentioned, I do not live in Norway.'

They thanked her and ran into the station talking over each other in their attempts to ask the man at the desk if he knew where Jan was.

The man at the desk did not speak English, but he did manage to ask Michael and Hylad to wait in reception for the English-speaking man to be available. He did this using mime and the only English word he knew – 'English'.

Once they'd sat down, Michael looked at Hylad. 'She knew,' he said, 'but how on earth?'

'I've got it,' Jan said to Liam. 'I know how to prove I'm not guilty!'

Liam was grateful. Guilty or not, Jan was clearly not a hardened criminal and Liam was beginning to feel he was wasting his time.

'You think I stole something from that girl,' Jan continued, 'but what? What could I have stolen? Look at me. I have no money, I don't have a girl's purse or anything on me. All I have is my clothes and they're dirty from being arrested.'

'That is true,' Liam said slowly, rubbing his chin. He looked at Jan's watch. It was green plastic and couldn't have been worth anything. The boy certainly seemed penniless.

'I don't even have a passport!' Jan shouted, elated.

'Well maybe not celebrate that, yah?'

'Fair enough, and I will deal with that later, I promise,' Jan said, meaning that he hoped that Hylad and Michael could deal with it later, 'but not having anything means I'm not guilty, right?'

Liam agreed. He led Jan out of the room and down a corridor that Jan hadn't seen before. 'We let the innocent criminals out this way to save them the embarrassment of leaving a police station.' Jan didn't consider himself an innocent criminal, nor did he think he'd know anyone outside, but he didn't protest. Instead he kept repeating his own sentence in his head – not having anything means I'm not guilty, not having anything means I'm not guilty, not having anything means I'm, not having anything means.

Not having anything means not having anything, but by the time he'd come to that worrying conclusion, he was standing outside the back of the police station by himself.

Hylad and Michael waited impatiently to ask someone in the police station if they knew where Jan was for about fifteen minutes. This was around the same amount of time it took for Jan to power-walk down from the police station to the docks to see if anyone knew where Hylad and Michael were.

They weren't the only people waiting in reception. There were another five people – a mother and daughter both sat silently with their hands on their laps, a lady taking the tiniest bites out of an apple core, and two men holding hands.

'Can we…?' Michael started quietly, 'Is it legal here to…?

I mean, it's not legal in Norway. I checked but…'

'I don't know,' Hylad answered nervously, before moving his hand over Michael's and rubbing his thumb over the back of it.

'I'm really worried about Jan,' Michael whispered.

'Me too,' Hylad said. 'I'm worried he'll be scared and I'm worried he'll be alone. I'm also worried that he won't be alone. What will he eat? Where will he sleep? I'm meant to be looking after him.'

They sat in silence for a few minutes, Hylad thinking about Jan, and Michael thinking about the otter he'd watched catch its first fish earlier.

'I think Jan will be OK,' he said. 'I think he'll find food and somewhere to sleep. He seems smart.' Hylad squeezed Michael's hand.

'It does seem like it might be OK, Michael. People have noticed us holding hands and no one has said anything. No one seems to mind,' and with that he leaned over and kissed Michael lightly on the cheek, and no one but the two of them thought anything of it.

12

HORSES

Sweden. 1970.

Jan found that there were quite a lot of English-speaking people down at the docks, but more importantly, quite a lot of boats that could be leaving for England. Here are just a few of the responses Jan received when he asked if he could hitch a ride back to England.

1.

'Give you a ride when you haven't got a passport? How do I know you're from England and not some Swedish homeless kid trying to hitch a lift?'

Jan had pointed out both his English lingual skills and his accent. 'How do I know you're not some English homeless kid then?'

'Well, I am, I guess,' Jan said, 'but I'm only an English homeless kid when I'm in Sweden.'

'I'm not having no homeless kid on my boat.'

Jan decided he didn't want to be on this man's boat either.

2.

'We're not going to England, we're going to Poland,' one of three middle-aged men told him. 'We're breaking through the Iron Curtain.'

Jan wondered what Poland would be like, and he seriously considered boarding the boat anyway.

'The Iron Curtain,' he pondered, 'sounds dark.'

The man nodded in agreement, and Jan nodded back. Neither quite knew what the other meant.

3.

'A gentleman wouldn't ask. A gentleman would wait to be offered.' Jan sat on the docks next to this boat for some time before it moved off out to sea without him.

4.

'We're not going to England, we're going to Norway.' Jan wished the couple a sincere good luck and told them that if they do manage to find the elusive Norway, they should watch a sunset.

5.

'We're honeymooning,' one man with curly dark hair and a moustache said. 'Do you know what honeymooning is?' Jan was about to say that he did, and that although he looked young he was in fact eighteen, but before he could start, the girl next to the man spoke.

'Oh Jerry, couldn't we help him? Imagine, helping a young stranger on our honeymoon – how romantic.'

Jan nearly spoke again, this time feeling more optimistic for the ride, but the curly-haired man responded quicker.

'It's not romantic,' he said sharply, 'it's foolish. We don't want him with us. Being alone – now that's romantic.'

'But Jerry, imagine the stories we'd h…'

'Shut up!' Jerry shouted, seemingly at the end of his tether. Then he softened his voice. 'I just want everything to be perfect for you, that's all.'

Jan walked away.

It was getting late by the time Jan gave up. He didn't want to sleep in the cold (and boy was it cold), nor did he want to have to try to make a bed in the dark. He decided to start looking for a place to set up camp before sunset. He remained penniless, so a hotel was not an option, and he knew he'd have to have his wits about him to get through the night. The problem was, Jan didn't really have any wits about him – ever. All his wits seemed to be about somewhere else. What Jan had was enthusiasm.

It was his lack of wits and abundance of enthusiasm that guided Jan in making an elaborate makeshift bed out of concrete, rubble, dust and twigs, only to find that not only was it not comfortable, but it didn't protect him from the wind in any way. He lay down on it and then he lay down on the floor next to it. They felt exactly the same.

Slowly, the docks began to fill with foreigners – foreign to Jan and foreign to Sweden. Jan didn't know many of the multitude of languages surrounding him, but before the night was over he would hear his first Arabic, French, German and Spanish words. People sat down, some next to each other, some alone, some holding hands and some in groups. Lots of people wore multi-coloured or luminous vests. It was sunset.

It wasn't illegal to be gay in England. Hylad and Michael could be together back home without breaking any laws; they just didn't dare to be. They were both big men who could handle themselves in a fight if necessary. They simply didn't want to make it necessary.

They had once gone on a day trip to a market town quite a way away from both Fishton and anyone they knew. They'd sat in a classic English pub, the kind they both liked, and they'd kissed. They'd only just met, and they thought they were out of view of the bar. It was barely a kiss, just a small peck of affection, but the barman hadn't taken kindly to it.

'Bloody poofs,' he'd said under his breath. It was a quiet pub. Hylad had heard, and looked at the barman as a reaction to the noise without registering what he'd actually said. 'I said, bloody poofs,' the barman repeated, only this time much louder. Hylad had looked down at his pint. On their way out of the pub, drinks only a quarter drunk, the barman had said, not shouted, but said with a distinctly casual disgust, 'Faggots.'

Hylad and Michael hadn't touched each other in public since. They didn't really mind. They sat and chatted over a drink sometimes after their respective work days were over and they saved their 'together' lives for behind doors.

In Sweden it was different. After they left the police station they power-walked the wide and beautifully paved streets looking for Jan. It was a panicked search and they both accidentally bumped into lots of people. After the fourth collision (this one by Michael) they began to assume that *förlåt* must mean sorry in Swedish. Hylad bumped into a young lady.

'*Förlåt*,' he said.

'*Förlåt*,' she said.

Michael bumped into a long blond-haired gentleman.

'*Förlåt*,' Michael said.

'*Förlåt*,' the blond man replied.

Hylad bumped into a beautifully moustachioed man.

'*Förlåt*,' Hylad said, and the moustachioed man just grumbled, but they do tend to do that.

They searched for three hours. They even passed the docks briefly but reasoned that Jan would a) be nervous to go there and b) try to explore the town. He was an inquisitive little thing. Eventually they stopped.

'What now?' Michael asked, exhausted and close to tears. Hylad wasn't used to seeing Michael like this; he was not an emotional man, and it broke Hylad's heart. He blamed himself for making Michael feel like this.

'We need to sleep, Michael. We need to sleep and we need to eat.'

'But, Jan…'

'I know,' Hylad said, holding Michael's arm with both of his hands. Hylad hated seeing Michael close to tears, but that was better than what came next: tears. Hylad looked around them. They were in a busy street, probably the main shopping street in town, but this time Hylad didn't care. He hugged Michael so tight that just for a second all their problems went away. Lots of people saw but no one cared, and neither Michael nor Hylad had to say *förlåt* to anyone.

Everyone made soft cooing noises at the sunset, and although Jan didn't understand most of the languages being spoken he could follow that there was a general appreciation of it. He sat surrounded by people but feeling ultimately alone, and watched it too. It was pretty, but he couldn't shake the feeling he was missing something that everyone else was seeing. Everyone was gathered to see what the docks looked like at sunset but to Jan they looked the same.

Although the sky was a light pink, the concrete floor remained grey, the boats continued to bob about in the same way they had done all afternoon and even the water stayed a similar greyish white as it failed to reflect the sky's hue. The main difference, Jan thought, was the fact that the docks were now busy with luminous tourists.

He looked to his right. Everyone was looking out to sea, all together and in a uniformed communal stare. He looked to his left. A further sea of tourists facing the same way. There was very little movement from anyone, and everyone, but Jan, was in awe.

Nevertheless, Jan felt proud to be in among this gaggle of tourists. To an outsider he would look like a true traveller – everything he'd wanted to be since his day trip away from Fishton and then back to Fishton.

He looked to his right again and accidentally made eye contact with a man in a baggy, tie-dyed t-shirt. The man smiled at him and nodded, as if they were both agreeing on something. Jan nodded back. He looked to his left again. This time the view wasn't as still. There was movement – a pale-skinned, dark-haired girl was crouching behind an embracing couple towards the back of the sitting crowd.

She lifted a flap on the couple's backpack, pulled out a purse on a drawstring, de-crouched, turned and walked away.

It's her, Jan thought, she's there, although it wasn't as if he'd been looking for her.

Jan stood up and moved to the back of the crowd but by the time he'd navigated a way through the compilation of crossed, kneeling and bent legs she had gone. Once again Jan sat and tried to enjoy the sunset. It was nearly over and very little had changed. The sea remained a greyish white and the sky was beginning to follow suit.

After another fifteen minutes people began to leave, while Jan remained. He was about to search for his makeshift uncomfortable bed when he felt a movement in his back pocket. Without looking he swung his arm round behind him and knocked it into another slender arm. He managed (with some awkwardness of elbow movement) to grab the other arm.

He turned to see the girl. Her eyes were dark, her skin was as pale as the sky had become and her cheeks smiled, even though her expression was full of shock and panic.

'Give me my passport,' Jan said forcefully. The girl yanked her arm but didn't free herself.

'Give me my passport,' Jan demanded again.

'I don't have the passport,' the girl said, at the same time as rummaging through her (or someone else's) bag with her loose arm.

'You stole my passport,' Jan said louder. 'Give me my passport.' The girl brought five passports out of the bag and gave them all to Jan. He let go of her, but she didn't run away. After finding his, Jan passed the other four passports to the girl, who had been rummaging further in the bag. She passed

Jan his wallet, said *förlåt*, and then ran.

'It's peaceful without Jan isn't it?' asked Jan's father.

Jan's mother stared at him. Since Jan had left four days ago she'd started biting her nails. She missed Jan and was already counting down the days until he was due home.

'I'm glad you feel peaceful,' she said sarcastically.

'I just mean,' Jan's father started, and then he stopped to think. He wanted to choose his words wisely. 'It's nice spending time with just you,' he said, and then he mentally congratulated himself.

Jan's mother continued biting her nails but did, if only momentarily, looked touched.

'This kind of trip can change someone,' Jan's father said. 'When I was younger I went to Devon.'

'I know,' Jan's mother replied.

'I'll never forget that trip. Aye, it changed my life.'

'I know,' Jan's mother interrupted again, annoyed.

'It was winter – a funny time to go to Devon I suppose, but it was beautiful nonetheless. Me and my mate, we stayed in a bunk house behind some stables.'

'I know this story,' Jan's mother repeated.

'That was fate, you see; I was meant to stay in those stables. I met the most beautiful lass there playing with the horses.' He paused. 'My point is, this could be the making of our Jan. He could come back a different person, someone more like...him. He might even meet someone.' This last sentence brought a smile to the face behind a now very short fingernail.

'He might find his bunkhouse lass,' Jan's father continued,

'if you know what I mean. His horse girl.' Jan's father winked at Jan's mother. 'It had such a nice setting that bunkhouse, a setting that changed my life.'

'Yes I know about the bunkhouse,' Jan's mother said. 'I was there!'

The crowds had gone, and the sun had set. There were a few streetlights on, spread at a distance from each other, giving the effect of several spotlights. Jan took centre-stage in one of them.

He sat on his painful homemade bed looking out to the relative darkness of the sea. His legs had gone numb. Occasionally he would move from his knees to his bum and occasionally he would move from his bum to his knees.

The sounds of the harbour had changed. There were no human noises any more, just the sound of some of the smaller boats bumping into each other. It sounded like Fishton in the quieter winter months, and once again Jan began to miss home.

A small spark of hope inside Jan spurred him to continually scan the horizon. Wasn't there a possibility that Hylad and Michael had planned to come back to the harbour to get him under cover of darkness?

He sat once more on his bum and stretched his legs out in front of him. He scratched the palm of one of his hands with his other hand and then used them to lean back on the hard bed. The ground under his right hand was much softer than that under his left hand, and it was warmer too. For a second, Jan smiled. Then the floor moved and his smile turned into a scream.

'You again?' the girl said hurriedly, as she tried to move backwards away from Jan. Jan held onto her hand tight and once again they found themselves violently holding hands.

'Me?' screamed Jan. 'Me?'

'Let me go!'

'Who are you?'

'Jan.' Jan loosened his grip and she pulled her arm free, but again she didn't run away. They both looked surprised.

'How do you know my name?' Jan asked.

'I don't,' replied the girl in a soft Swedish accent, 'but I could know if I wanted. I had your passport.' Jan sort of smiled at her and she half-smiled back. The wind blew her hair in almost every direction – behind her, to both sides of her, above her and across her face. It sounds awfully unattractive, but Jan found it mesmerising.

They both stood in silence for a few seconds, a metre apart but both fully in the spotlight of the street lamp.

'I can leave?' the girl asked eventually.

'Um. No,' Jan said. 'You said my name. You said Jan.' The girl looked at him quizzically.

'You are Jan too? How funny. My name is Jan,' said Ladyjan.

13

OTHER PEOPLE'S FACES

Sweden. 1970.

For most people the night that followed would be long. Sweden is not a warm country at night and Jan was not equipped for sleeping rough. His bed would surely testify he didn't really have the smarts to survive a prolonged stint on the streets. It was lucky, then, that at no point did Jan try to sleep that night. It was also lucky that this would be his last night on a cold Swedish street.

After a conversation that would have been uncomfortable to watch but pleasing to be a participant of, Manjan and Ladyjan had sat down together. It had taken them over fifteen minutes to work out that neither of them had run away from the other, not because of fear, but because they didn't want to. Each of them faced a night alone in the cold, and company, even that of a beautiful thief or a persistent victim, would be gladly accepted.

Ladyjan made a noise as if she was about to say something. Manjan looked at her, slightly flexing what muscle he had in his skinny arm in the hope that she might notice. 'What on earth are we sitting on?'

'I made this,' Manjan said proudly, hoping that she would be impressed.

'But what is it?'

'It's my bed,' Manjan beamed. 'I made it today.' Ladyjan thought about what Manjan had said and then disagreed with him. She told Manjan that it was not a bed and that they'd both be more comfortable if they sat next to it rather than on it. Manjan looked hurt and Ladyjan took pity on him and conceded. They both sat unnecessarily uncomfortably on the bed for the remainder of the night.

Manjan looked into the darkness of the horizon while Ladyjan looked at him.

'I've never seen you before today,' Ladyjan said. Manjan wanted to impress Ladyjan. After all, she was beautiful and the only person he knew in Sweden, so the next thing he said, although not strictly a lie, put a certain spin on actual events.

'I've been travelling for a while now,' he said, 'seeing parts of the world that, I guess, have inspired me. I visited this small island off the bottom of Norway actually. I really think you'd like it, it was quite something.' He paused. 'You should see Norway at sunrise, you really should.'

Ladyjan was impressed. They talked at length about Jan's travelling feats, how he'd stowed away on a boat in Fishton when he was younger and how only the other day he'd saved a cockroach from certain death. Again, Ladyjan was impressed.

'Wow,' she said, her subtle accent shining through in the word, 'I'm sorry. I would never have taken your things if I'd seen your, um, well, what you're calling a bed.'

'I don't mind that you took my passport,' Manjan said, 'but I don't know why you took it.'

Ladyjan didn't try to impress Manjan when she told him about her life. She just hoped that he wouldn't judge her and stop talking to her. She didn't want him to look down on her for being kicked out of her parents' house last year when she'd tried to defend her mother from her abusive father. She hoped that Manjan wouldn't disapprove of her subsequent decision to share a house with an alcoholic. That was when she'd started to steal, so she could pay the alcoholic the small amount that he charged for a bed. She held back a tear when she told Manjan that now she just stole for the sake of stealing. She lived here, outside.

They sat for a while.

'I still don't understand why you took my passport,' Manjan said quietly, not wanting to belittle anything Ladyjan had said.

'It's silly,' Ladyjan started to answer, 'I try to steal from tourists because they have money, and if I can get their passport too, I do.'

'But why?'

'So that one day I can give everything back.' She looked into Manjan's eyes, hoping that he might understand. 'But you didn't have any money,' she said quietly, the words almost lost in the wind, 'and I'd already taken your passport when I realised.'

Manjan didn't judge Ladyjan. He wanted to help her. 'Here,' he said, unbuckling his green plastic watch, 'take this, and you can take my passport back, too. You can sell the watch and use the money for what you like, but I want you to use the passport to one day find me again.' He held out the watch and the passport. 'You know, just to say hi.'

Ladyjan looked at the watch and laughed, and that made Manjan smile. Her laugh was pretty.

'I don't want to steal from you,' she said before adding, 'again.' Her eyes lit up as she told Manjan that what she really wanted was to travel, like him. She wanted to save a cockroach and visit unknown islands – so unknown, as Manjan had pointed out, that he didn't even know where they were or what they were called.

Some distance behind them a man whistled a tune. The sky remained a star-speckled black but Ladyjan knew it would soon be morning and she said so. The two didn't want to part and Manjan didn't want his first full day alone in Sweden.

'You can travel,' he said, again flexing his puny arm. 'Anyone can travel.'

Ladyjan looked sad. 'I have so many passports, but none of them are mine, with my face on it. Not anyone can travel. I can't travel.'

Manjan jolted his head around, first to his right, then to his left, and finally to the boats bobbing along the harbour front.

'Anyone can travel,' he said. 'How good are you at hiding?'

14

A PICKLED HERRING

Sweden. 1970.

Hylad and Michael had barely woken up from a night spent barely asleep. The harbour was wet and miserable, and the weather made them even more worried for Jan. Yesterday they'd searched the town, walked into every café and down every lane. They'd looked behind every Jan-sized object including bins, stairwells and one particularly large dog. Today they were back at the harbour.

They'd started early and found the harbour to be dark other than the occasional spotlight provided by the street lamps. A quick scan told them that there was no one there but one whistling man. They strolled up and down the harbour without much hope, let alone luck.

Now, in daylight and after a quick breakfast of

Surströmming, they were back. Neither Michael nor Hylad had known what *Surströmming* was when they'd ordered it, but it was the single option at the only seller they could find so early. It turned out to be pickled herring – an acquired taste and one that Michael had found trouble acquiring – he felt sick.

The harbour was much more bustling at this hour.

'Excuse me,' Hylad said to a couple who were clearly just waking up, 'have you seen a thin English boy around here? Eighteen, looks younger?'

'It could have been that boy yesterday,' the man said, looking at the girl to see if she agreed. 'He asked if we were going to England.'

'That'll be him,' Hylad said hopefully, as Michael put his hands on his knees and tried to calm his stomach.

'He was asking everyone with a boat,' the girl said, 'but we're going to Norway.'

'It's a slippery bugger, Norway,' Hylad said, before wishing them both good luck in finding it. Michael followed Hylad to the next boat, slow but optimistic. All they had to do was find the boat that Jan had managed to get a lift on.

'Have you seen an eighteen-year-old English boy around here? He looks a bit younger, might have asked if you're going to England?'

'That is not how two gentlemen addresses a gentleman,' said a man not too gentlemanly.

'Sorry,' said Hylad before pausing. 'Sir, have you seen anyone of that description?'

The rude gentleman told Hylad that he had seen Jan, but that he had not offered him a lift as he had only been planning a day trip on his boat, certainly not a voyage to England. Although the not-too-gentlemanly gentleman was speaking to Hylad, he looked disapprovingly at a now funny-coloured Michael throughout the entire conversation.

On the way to the next boat Hylad suggested that Michael go back to the hotel, but Michael refused. He wanted to find Jan, and that wouldn't happen in the hotel. The next boat had a man with an impressive moustache and curly dark hair sitting on a deckchair facing the harbour. He was sitting next to a beautiful, long-haired petite girl. He was either drinking a neat transparent spirit at an impressive rate or finding it hard to drink a very small amount of water slowly.

'Yeah, we saw him,' the curly-haired man said. 'Taught him a little something about romance, I reckon.' He slapped the thigh of his new wife and shook her leg.

'I wanted to help him didn't I, Jerry?' the girl said. 'We're leaving today, I thought we could take him with us.' Moustachioed Jerry gave her a sharp look. 'Jerry thought it'd be much more romantic if it was just the two of us. He's right. We're on our honeymoon.'

Hylad told them that Jan was lost and asked if either of them knew where he'd gone. The girl hit Jerry's arm with the back of her hand. 'I knew we should have taken him,' she said, 'I hope he's OK.'

'Will you shut up about that boy,' Jerry shouted, knocking the girl's hand away and spilling his drink, 'and just enjoy yourself.'

Then he let out a long line of swearwords that no one in the harbour wanted to hear but everyone in the harbour had to. The girl didn't cower; instead she stood taller than it looked like she should be able to.

'Shut up, Jerry,' she screamed. 'Just shut your stupid mouth up.'

Jerry looked shocked and he raised his hand.

'In front of all these people?' the girl asked.

Under his breath, Jerry mumbled, 'I swear to god, Connie, don't cause a scene.'

Then Connie let out a long line of swearwords. This time everyone in the harbour did want to hear; some even cheered. She was about to walk off the boat when Michael lunged forward, held on to Jerry's arm and threw-up down his shirt, leaving traces of pickled herring in his drink.

At the very moment that Michael's breakfast became Jerry's cocktail, Manjan and Ladyjan's boat left the harbour. Manjan and Ladyjan had heard the commotion but they couldn't see anything from the empty room they'd found to stow away in. Ladyjan was excited; this could be a new life for her. She held on tight to Manjan's hand. Full of nerves, Manjan looked at Ladyjan and the excitement in Ladyjan's eyes somehow made his nerves disappear. He was already lost in a foreign country. This boat would either take him home to England or to the same situation that he was already in, but in a different country. They both laughed quietly to each other, before they heard a woman's voice from upstairs on the boat.

'We're finally doing it,' she said, 'I can't believe we're actually going to India.'

PART THREE

15

A COW

Goa, India, 2016.

The sun had set, and the sea was resting. The light from the bar behind Shakey and Manjan was creating blurry them-shaped shadows on the sand at their feet. The COCK-tail bar down the beach was still thudding and now there were multi-coloured disco lights flooding the beach in front of it. Every now and again a green neon laser would shoot into the sky and a group of vests would cheer.

Shakey was torn. On the one hand, Manjan's story was interesting – Shakey wanted to know how Manjan and Ladyjan had parted. He wanted to know why they had parted. He wanted to know why Manjan cared so much for Ladyjan. So far in his story they'd only just met. What about Manjan's parents? Had Manjan gone home? Shakey wanted to know if Hylad and Michael were still together. He hoped they were. What had happened to them after Manjan had left for India? He cared. It might have had something to do with the small plastic buckets of vodka and Red Bull, but he really did care.

On the other hand – multi-coloured disco lights and green neon lasers shooting into the sky.

Manjan was completely lost in his own story. He liked telling it to people and he'd made the right decision to tell this vest, who, despite visible disco lights, was still listening. It may have been the red wine, but Manjan felt humbled by Shakey and offered to buy him another drink.

That was enough to make up Shakey's mind. He'd stay with Manjan, at least for now, and hear out his story. Lasers were great (there was no question about that) but it seemed unlikely that Shakey was going to get paid for handing out five silent disco flyers and then drinking with a stranger. He wasn't going to pass up a free drink.

While Manjan was at the bar, feeling stupid for ordering a small plastic bucket of vodka and Red Bull, Shakey looked up and down the beach. He wasn't sure what he was looking for exactly. Maybe a Swedish-looking thief? Perhaps she'd be wearing a mask.

'I get what you were saying about sunset,' Shakey said as Manjan placed the drinks on the table. 'I mean, we've just watched the sunset over Palolem but I didn't care. It wasn't that great.'

Manjan sighed. 'I think you've missed the point,' he said, but Shakey was pretty sure he hadn't. Manjan had been quite clear in his story – sunsets were stupid.

'Me and Jan, Ladyjan that is, we liked sunsets. But we also liked places when the sun wasn't setting.'

'Yeah I guess sunsets are pretty cool,' Shakey replied, and Manjan looked at him in disbelief.

'Look,' Manjan said, 'sunsets are nice, but Palolem is nice in the day too. It used to be nice at night as well but…' He gestured with his chin towards a thin green neon light in the sky, 'Well, things change.' He took a sip of his wine, tickling the rim of his wine glass with his moustache as he did.

'When I first met Ladyjan, she had other things to think about than the sun setting. Sunsets are for people who are already happy.' Manjan looked down the beach to where the cow was standing. 'Let's put it this way,' he said, 'that cow over there. That cow will have had a hard life. Do you think she cares about, or even sees, the sunset?'

Prisha, the cow, had been born in a field not too far from Palolem. Her childhood had been a happy one, living with her cow-mother in a relatively grassy field. She could see her bull-father two fields along, and although he didn't pay much attention to her, she loved him. Most days Prisha would eat the yellowing grass in her and her mother's field and when the sun got too hot, she'd lie down next to the fence parallel to her bull-father's fence.

Prisha couldn't remember ever having any physical contact with her father but she watched him from her field every day. She knew everything you could know about a bull just from observing his daily routine, his movements and his expressions. She felt certain that he was a good bull, and if they were able to share a field, he would be a good father.

On one particularly hot day, when Prisha was watching her father sleep, a thin old man attached a large sign around him with two thick black rubber harnesses. Prisha couldn't read, but if she could, she would have read the words 'FIT FOR SLAUGHTER' on her father.

The sign remained on the bull for a week. Prisha watched as the sign rubbed against her father's back and left sores on his underside. By the third day her father couldn't walk without discomfort and by the fourth he didn't try. When the thin man came back to the bull's field, Prisha's father was completely motionless.

Prisha didn't know that her family, and indeed all bulls and cows, had holy status where she lived. She also didn't know that her father had apparently lost his holy status when he became too old and quite ill. This was when the thin man had requested a 'fit for slaughter' certificate from the authorities. The old beast had become too expensive to keep alive.

Prisha knew the thin old man. He gave her and her mother water every few days – water which they needed. Nevertheless, the thin old man had killed her father. The next time he brought water to the field Prisha charged at him. She knocked the thin old man over and ran out of the gate in a panic. Her mother did not follow.

The next few years offered a lonely existence for Prisha. She'd stand by the roadside, eating what little grass could muster the energy to grow in the scorching heat, and she'd try to moo at the occasional motorbike. She normally managed nothing more than a dusty breath.

It was her own holy status that kept Prisha alive. People she'd never seen before would stop and empty their own water supplies for her. She ate all kinds of strange foods on her journey – jelabis, curried goat and lamb samosa. Despite this, grass was not easy to come by and life was hard. Never – not once – did Prisha notice the sunset.

It was seven years before Prisha found Palolem. When she first arrived in 2007 the beach had been surrounded by green fields with palm trees leaning out towards the sea. There were a few beach bars and maybe two dozen foreigners wandering the sands and waters. Although the people, trees and bars did not interest Prisha, the fields were her Mecca.

Every morning she would chew up some lovely fresh grass before being shooed away from the field by one of the farmers. She'd spend her afternoons eating unsatisfying dry sticks and driftwood on the beach.

Over the next few years more foreigners came to the beach. Not many stayed for more than a week, and almost none (bar one particular moustachioed man) stayed for longer than a month. A funny thing happened, though – as the population of foreigners increased, so did the number of beach bars and little shacks for sleeping. At the same time as beach bars and little shacks for sleeping increased, the number of farmers decreased, and as the number of farmers decreased the amount of time Prisha could spend eating their fields increased. It wasn't long before she was eating her fill every day without being shooed away.

After Prisha had spent a week comfortably filling her now quite skinny body with nutritious grass, she returned to the beach. This time she visited the beach out of habit rather than necessity. She wasn't hungry, and she felt no need to search for dry driftwood. Looking around her, she finally saw what the tourists were seeing – the beach was very pretty. The people she'd previously ignored were all smiling, and the bars were colourful. This was the first day that Prisha noticed the sunset, and it was glorious.

'How do you know that cow's had a hard life?' Shakey asked.

'Well I don't know for sure,' Manjan replied, 'but she's a cow on a beach and she looks pretty malnourished, although not as bad as the cows in Delhi.' Shakey had no idea what the cows in Delhi looked like, but India was India to him, so he assumed they were pretty much the same. 'My point is,' Manjan continued, 'that the cow is just trying to survive. She doesn't care about the sunset. Ladyjan was the same; she was too busy surviving.' Manjan had no idea how wrong he was about Prisha. Moustaches rarely do.

'She robbed people at sunset,' Shakey said.

'She survived,' Manjan said again, taking a sip of wine. 'On that boat Ladyjan told me that life wasn't romantic like it is in the films,' Manjan chuckled, 'and she hadn't even seen the Bollywood films then.' Shakey had never seen a Bollywood film either but laughed along anyway. 'Me, on the other hand, I was stowed away on a boat set for India with a beautiful girl. Life seemed like a film to me'.

There was a silence between them while Manjan thought to himself. It was true that Ladyjan's life had been hard, and it was a long time until she'd appreciated the beauty of a sunset, but he wondered why he himself had never cared for sunsets in his youth. They used to just pass him by, in the same way they seemed to now for Shakey.

The silence turned into a sort of grumbling sound from below Manjan's dark grey bristles.

'What about your parents?' Shakey asked, interrupting Manjan from what was now nothing more than a sleepy low growl.

'What about my parents?' Manjan snapped out of his trance.

'Well you sort of abandoned them, right,' Shakey asked, but with no question mark in his tone. 'Mine know I'm in India and I still call them every few days to let them know I'm OK. What about yours?' Manjan wasn't offended, but he was slightly surprised at being asked if his parents knew where he was, given his age.

'Oh, I see. I called them from Poland,' he said, waving his hand dismissively. 'I told them not to be cross with Hylad and Michael, that I was fine and that I'd come home soon. I didn't tell them about Ladyjan.'

'Poland?!' Shakey interrupted, spitting out a little vodka and Red Bull, catching it with his hand and then putting it back in his mouth. He'd assumed that Manjan and Ladyjan had travelled to India together, and that they'd both lived in this country since then. 'Is Ladyjan in Poland?' he asked.

Manjan said that she might well be. They'd travelled through several countries, including Poland, to get to India. Ladyjan could be in any one of them. They'd visited lots of countries after that journey too – Ladyjan could be in any one of those as well. Indeed, she could be in any of the countries that they hadn't visited. Then Manjan stood up. He looked to his right and then he looked to his left, just in case she was in this country, on this beach, right now.

Shakey got up too.

'If you do find Ladyjan,' he said.

'You mean when Ladyjan finds me,' Manjan corrected him. Shakey laughed but then instantly felt bad for doing so.

'Sorry, when Ladyjan finds you, can I give you some advice?' Manjan agreed that he could, but looked and felt uncomfortable about receiving advice from a vest.

'Don't compare her to a cow.'

Manjan thought for a second then agreed that he wouldn't.

16

WILD BOAR

Across Poland. 1971.

Manjan hung up the phone. He had just explained where he was, where he'd been and where he was going to his tearful mother. It had taken a long time to persuade her to pass the phone to his father and Manjan had no doubt that his father would now be having difficulty calming his mother down. Importantly, his father had understood and agreed not to be too hard on Hylad.

Back on the train, Manjan re-found Ladyjan, who was in a carriage with Saga and Valter. Neither Manjan nor Ladyjan had quite understood how far away India was. After only half a day of hiding on the boat, Saga and Valter had found them, greeted them and offered them food. It was a much better reception than expected.

Saga and Valter were a married couple who were both fearing their impending thirtieth birthdays. It had been Saga's dream to travel through Eastern Europe and to visit India, and Valter, being quite the romantic, made it his duty to help Saga live her dream. They had made the plan together. First, they would travel to Poland by water, and then on to Russia by train, then they'd fly to Nepal from Moscow, and finally they would cross over the Nepal/India border on foot. They didn't know how long it would take and they hadn't planned their way home.

Once the four of them had arrived in Poland, a member of Valter's extended family had taken the boat and they had gone through some very unsecure security. It was so unsecure in fact, that none of them were required even to give their names. Apparently, Valter was someone important.

The train clunked loudly, as it had done every time it had left one of the large mounds of grass masquerading as a station. Most of the journey had been through light green hills scattered with colourless wooden houses. There seemed to be a great deal of land per house, especially when compared to the rickety streets of Fishton. This was their second day travelling on a Polish train, and although they'd already seen three buildings that had been demolished and seemingly abandoned, overall the impression was of a pleasant country. They often spotted stalks flying over the horizon or shy wild boar running from the train and hiding.

The train itself was big but basic, with a single toilet and vending machine at the end of the seemingly endless trail of carriages.

'Prince Polo, anyone?' Manjan asked, after the train had been moving for about thirteen minutes.

'Please,' answered Ladyjan. Saga shook her head and

Valter waved a dismissive hand. All this travelling had made them tired. Manjan wearily started the long walk to the vending machine.

Much to Saga's disapproval, Manjan and Ladyjan had been practically living on Prince Polo chocolate bars since they'd boarded the train. Manjan felt he was experiencing Polish culture by doing so, and Ladyjan, well, she really liked chocolate.

'I can't believe we still don't know how you two met,' Ladyjan said with a cheeky smile. 'With an adventure like this, I bet it was romantic.'

Like Manjan, Ladyjan was full of questions and Valter, whose happiness was infectious, was eager to answer them. He held onto Saga's hands lovingly and looked at Ladyjan.

'It was fate,' he said in the same whimsical tone as a trained musical actor on a Broadway stage. Ladyjan's eyebrows raised in the middle while her lips made an 'aw' shape.

Valter told Ladyjan how he'd grown up as an only child in a wealthy family that owned a large estate. He'd received the best education that money could buy, wore the finest clothing and eaten a rich diet. He'd had acres of land to play on (albeit mainly by himself) and family staff who would fetch him what he wanted when he wanted. He told Ladyjan all of this in a sad voice, but then said: 'It was a great life. I was lucky. Saga on the other hand...'

And then he explained how Saga had grown up in a poor neighbourhood, how she was raised by her dad and how she'd worn the same five outfits for seven of her teenage years. Saga scowled at him when he said this last bit. Now she was dressed in a lovely bright red coat and she'd changed her outfit daily since they'd set off for India.

They'd met in their mid-twenties. Saga had been feeling

out of place in a posh restaurant that she'd grossly misjudged from the exterior. Valter had been feeling bored at yet another boozy lunch with the same investment professionals that he had known since university.

'It was a classic different-class romance,' Valter said proudly. He'd clearly said this line many times before. 'We spent the night talking,' he said, 'and it turns out that what Saga lacked in money, she made up for in dreams. Beautiful dreams of distant lands and new cultures.'

'And here we are,' Saga cut in. 'You see how it was fate?'

Ladyjan wasn't convinced that this was what fate was – convenience, maybe, but not fate. Valter and Saga both seemed happy though and Ladyjan was distinctly aware that they had found her and Manjan on their boat, helped them into Poland, paid for their train seats, helped Manjan call his parents and then taken them along on their adventure. They could have thrown her and Manjan in the sea. She smiled politely.

'Fate,' she said.

Manjan, eyes half-closed, with two Prince Polo bars in hand, walked straight past Ladyjan, Valter and Saga. Three more carriages down, without looking, he slumped into what he believed was his chair. The Polish lady next to him stared at him for a few seconds before he noticed.

'That's my brother's chair,' she said in Polish. 'Who are you? Get up.' Again, this was in Polish.

Manjan didn't understand her words but he understood her tone and panicked.

'I'm sorry,' he shouted in English. 'Where is Jan? Where

is Valter and Saga? I thought you were Jan.' Again, this was in English. As it happened, the Polish lady did look a little bit like Ladyjan. She was slightly older, mid twenties, and to Manjan at least, infinitely more terrifying, but her hair, eyes and complexion were, descriptively at least, of a similar ilk.

'Get up, get up,' the Polish lady shouted, still in her native tongue. Both voices were now raised but neither could understand the other. The lady picked up her bag and rummaged through it for her ticket. Maybe the boy next to her would understand that it was her name, Alaina, written next to her and her brother's allotted seat number. She took the ticket out, but then continued to rummage. Then she rummaged some more. Her passport had gone.

'Look, I'm sorry, you can't sit there,' she said eventually, 'there's bound to be another chair somewhere, but you can't sit there.' Of course, Manjan still couldn't understand what the lady was saying, but he could see that she was flustered.

There didn't seem to be any way of resolving this. Either the lady needed to use English, or he needed to attempt to use Polish. He thought for a second before saying the only Polish word he knew.

'Prince Polo,' he shouted, 'Prince Polo!' There was silence across the carriage. Between them they'd caused quite a scene. The lady looked at the two Prince Polo bars in Manjan's hand and then back up to his face. Manjan looked at the bars too and then back to the lady. 'Prince Polo,' he said much quieter than before. The lady nodded once slowly, calming down.

'Prince Polo,' she agreed.

It was admittedly limited, but they'd found a level on which they could communicate. Not sure what else to say, Manjan turned his statement into a question.

'Prince Polo?' he asked. The lady contemplated this,

before nodding again.

'Prince Polo,' she confirmed, with her hand out. Manjan gave her both bars, quickly stood up and stumbled back down the carriage.

'Where have you been?' Ladyjan asked as Manjan threw his body down on the chair next to her. 'Where's my...'

'I lost you,' Manjan interrupted.

Ladyjan wanted to tell Manjan about how Valter and Saga had met. She wanted to laugh about it with him, but Valter and Saga were sitting opposite so she would have to wait.

'You've been gone for ages,' she said instead.

'Jan even went to look for you,' Saga interrupted, nodding at Ladyjan, 'but she couldn't find you.' Ladyjan blushed, and fleetingly looked at her passport-shaped pocket.

Manjan told Ladyjan how, after he'd bought the chocolate bars, he'd met a Polish lady in a different carriage. He told her how he'd sat with the Polish lady and communicated with her on a different level. He said it was on a level which he'd never communicated with anyone before. This was strictly true. An old Polish man with a moustache a couple of rows back tutted and shook his head.

'Wow,' Ladyjan said, impressed.

Sensing that he was turning red, Manjan looked out of the window. A group of young wild boar picked up their heads on hearing the train, and ran through a clearing towards a group of trees.

'I'm glad you found us,' Ladyjan said eventually.

'I was bound to find you,' Manjan blushed, still looking out of the window, 'we're on a train.'

'But it's a big train,' Ladyjan replied sarcastically, 'and you found us. It must be fate.' She giggled, although no one but she got the joke. Saga's eyebrows raised in the middle while her lips made an 'aw' shape.

Manjan could still see one of the wild boars between the trees but it wasn't running. The boar obviously thought it was better hidden than it was.

Ladyjan wondered how to tell Manjan, Valter and Saga that, just occasionally, and mainly at country borders, she would like to be called Alaina. She placed her hand on Manjan's forearm.

'Jan,' she said. After a moment Manjan turned to face her. 'Where's my Prince Polo?'

17

A FRIEND

Goa, India. 2016.

'Valter?' Shakey exclaimed. 'Saga?' he exclaimed again.

Manjan looked at him, annoyed. Did he want to hear the story or not?

'You're just giving me a list of people you made friends with years ago!'

Manjan agreed that he had made friends with Valter and Saga years ago, but that didn't mean that he wasn't still friends with them. Shakey looked to his right and then he looked to his left. 'I'm sure they'll be here any minute,' he muttered sarcastically.

Here is a list of just some of Shakey's friends:

1. Shakey's mum and dad

Shakey wouldn't admit this to his other friends on this list, but his mum and dad were probably his best friends. His dad was fun, his mum was loving and between them they'd always 'had his back'. He was very aware that he wouldn't be in India without them (they paid), and if he had never come to India he would never have known the real him (the sand). And besides, he'd known them the longest – probably longer than he'd known anyone. Actually, there is one friend in this list who Shakey might mention his closeness with his parents to, but more on that later.

2. Mad Norman

Mad Norman was one of Shakey's closest friends from back home. His real name was Norman and no one really knew where the 'Mad' had come from. When Shakey had first met Mad Norman, Mad Norman had said, 'Hi, I'm Mad Norman,' to which Shakey had replied 'Norman doesn't sound that mad.'

Mad Norman got this response a lot when he introduced himself to people and it made him more than a little annoyed. In fact, it made him mad. This, according to Mad Norman was where the 'Mad' had come from – his displeasure at people not thinking Norman was a mad-enough name. Shakey wasn't sure whether the name had created Mad Norman or Mad Norman had created the name. Mad Norman wasn't sure either. It was all a bit chicken-and-egg.

3. The girl vest

Shakey had made friends with a few female vests since coming to India, but there was one in particular worth mentioning. They'd met on a fishing trip. As Shakey remembered it, they'd chatted before he'd thrown his rod overboard in a fit of passion and kissed her. She was beautiful, and she was clearly impressed, both by Shakey's bicep and his travelling skills. They'd spent the remainder of the fishing trip laughing and kissing. When they left the fishing boat, though, Shakey was told in no uncertain terms that he had to pay for the rod he'd lost. He was told that he was a 'stupid tourist' and he could 'kissy kissy somewhere else'. The girl vest had watched all of this and Shakey had secretly left the group shortly after when she wasn't looking. He hasn't seen her since and he doesn't know her name.

Remember I said that there is one friend on this list that Shakey might mention his closeness with his parents to? The girl vest is that one friend, but only if he thought it might impress her.

4. Zen

Shakey met Zen during his first day on the beach. Shakey thought Zen was the coolest person he had ever met. Her hair was tied up in short, messy dreadlocks and she knew how to do fire poi. She talked at length about fascists, why capitalism is bad and why Topshop is good. Zen and Shakey had hung out a few times on Palolem and Shakey felt sure that they'd remain friends back in England.

Zen's actual name was Sarah but Shakey didn't know that. Her dreadlocks would be shaved off before she started her business technology course next year but Shakey didn't know that either. Although Zen thought capitalism was bad, Sarah could see the benefits – especially with the job opportunities she hoped her course would provide. Zen would not exist in England and Sarah and Shakey would not be friends there, but Shakey didn't know that.

5. Manjan

Manjan was not like Shakey's other friends for many reasons. For starters, he was a moustache. A very moustache-y moustache at that . Not only was he set in his ways, grumpy and judgemental but he did actually have a huge, wine-doused moustache. He was forty-six years older than Shakey, and although Shakey had repeatedly told other people who were his age that he believed that people of all ages, genders and races could be friends, he'd never actually made friends with a sixty-four-year-old before. Manjan didn't claim to be 'mad' or 'mental' like Norman did, and he certainly wasn't cooler than Shakey in the same way that Zen was. He had insulted Shakey's intelligence repeatedly and he clearly looked down on Shakey, but he'd also bought him a drink, listened to Shakey's nonsensical 'found myself' speech and was now laying bare his whole life. Maybe he'd even come to the Silent Disco. Maybe. Shakey would almost certainly not feature on a list of Manjan's friends but Manjan fitted quite nicely on the list of just some of Shakey's.

'I guess, one day, when you tell other people about Ladyjan, I'll be in the story too,' Shakey said happily.

Manjan pushed the now chilled sand forward with his feet. He chuckled, but not in a mean way, and let out a sigh.

'Oh gosh, no,' he said.

18

A PAWN

Moscow, Russia. 1972.

Manjan placed his rook diagonally from Saga's king.

'Checkmate,' he said confidently.

'I don't think it is,' Saga laughed. Valter gave Manjan a sympathetic smile. They'd agreed that they should learn something Indian before actually getting to India and Saga had suggested chess. Valter already played so he'd been teaching Manjan, Ladyjan and Saga since Rostov-on-Don, their first stop after Poland. They were now in Moscow and Manjan still wasn't grasping it. Saga moved her knight.

'You've lost your queen,' she smiled, tapping her fingers together mockingly.

'No I haven't,' Manjan replied, a little too certain of himself as he moved a pawn in the way of her knight, 'my pawn's in your way.'

'But knights can jump.' Saga looked at Valter to check she

was right and Valter nodded. She picked up Manjan's queen and circled it in the air before placing it next to her gathering of Manjan's pieces. 'You've lost your queen,' she said again.

They'd been waiting in Moscow for several weeks now, waiting for Valter's very unofficial-sounding contact to contact them and provide them with some very official-looking papers. In another seven days they would be boarding a plane to Kathmandu before driving down to the Nepal-India border. The last leg of Poland had been pleasant enough, although they'd only seen the eastern half of the country through the train window while they'd travelled for two days straight.

The more Manjan had relaxed around Ladyjan during the journey, the more she had found him to be funny, charming and endearingly stupid. She liked his inquisitiveness of people and enjoyed watching him as he'd listen at length to Valter and Saga's stories. For hours he'd ask questions about them and about Sweden. He'd got into full discussions with other passengers about their lives and the places they'd been. He had even asked the Polish train conductor about Sweden in a stupid (endearingly stupid, in fact) error. When the Polish train conductor said that he'd never visited Sweden, Manjan had suggested that he should talk to Valter and Saga, who could tell him all about it, which they did, with Manjan listening intently all over again.

What Ladyjan liked most, though, was the way that Manjan listened to her. He seemed infinitely interested in her. What were her parents like? Where had she been in Sweden? What was her favourite food, colour, music? Where would she like to visit? Manjan asked her everything that could be asked with an eager attentiveness that flattered Ladyjan.

But it also scared her.

Ladyjan was used to hiding from attention. She was a thief, after all, and thieves succeed best when they are hidden. Luckily, people don't usually want to see a thief anyway, which makes hiding and thieving that much easier.

'Move your pawn,' Ladyjan said to Saga, before receiving an approving nod from Valter. Saga moved one of her two remaining pawns.

'Checkmate?' she asked.

'Checkmate,' Valter confirmed.

'Yes, checkmate!' Ladyjan cheered, looking directly at Manjan.

Manjan didn't realise it when it was happening, but he had become everything he had dreamt of in Fishton. He was moving from country to country with two, new, older and more sophisticated friends plus a beautiful girl by his side (although he could only really refer to her as a friend, too). He'd tasted new food (Prince Polo bars) and learnt new things (how not to play chess). In short, Manjan was a traveller.

The group had made a fair few stops since Rostov-on-Don. Rostov-on-Don itself was simultaneously the dustiest and neatest place Manjan had ever visited. It was in Rostov-on-Don where Manjan finally understood what his mother had meant when she'd ranted about the difference between tidying his room and cleaning it.

They'd taken a bus to Voronezh from Rostov-on-Don, passing green Russian countryside and driving along dangerous track roads. It felt like (and in fact was) thousands of miles away from Manjan's little Fishton life. The city of Voronezh itself was wide and open. The few buildings looked old and worn, the streets were crooked, and the majority of the cars coughed as they drove. Valter hired one of the coughing cars in Voronezh and together they set off to Moscow, stopping at several villages for repairs on the way.

'Hello,' Valter had said, at the last village they visited, 'our car has a flat tyre.' He and Ladyjan had left the car to seek help from a group of people eating next to a water well. The group, who were mostly middle-aged men, looked blankly at them.

'Have you got a pfff pfff?' Manjan shouted from the back of the car, recognising the familiar blank expressions of a language barrier. He mimicked the action of pumping up a tyre when he said 'pfff pfff', by holding an imaginary pump in his left hand and pretending to pump it with his right hand.

'That didn't look like a pump,' Ladyjan joked, looking back to the car.

'Yes, have you got a pfff pfff?' Valter repeated, copying Manjan's actions. Most of the villagers flinched at each 'pfff' and one shouted something angrily in Russian.

'Pfff pfff,' Valter said again, raising the intonation of the last 'pfff' to imply a question mark. Again, the villagers flinched.

The tallest man in the group ran towards a building behind him while the shouter shouted something in Russian again. Seconds later the tall man reappeared, yelling 'pfff pfff', striding forward with a powerful and threatening advance.

'Run!' Valter shouted to Ladyjan, 'he's got a gun,' but when Valter turned around to run himself he could see that Ladyjan wouldn't have heard him. She was already at the car swinging open the back door. Saga turned the ignition and the car coughed and cut out. Jumping up and down in a panic she turned it again. Again, the car coughed but nothing else. They were trapped. Valter jumped into the passenger seat as Saga repeatedly turned the ignition again and again, screaming words that she wouldn't normally say.

The car coughed, then it choked, and then it coughed again. The tallest villager hit the bonnet and held up the gun. The car coughed, then it growled, then the engine turned over and then it purred (the sort of purr that a cat with a serious illness might make, but a purr nonetheless).

As they drove away, they heard a small explosion behind them, and then silence. No one said anything. Saga held on tight to the steering wheel, biting her lip, and Valter held on tight to his door and Saga's leg. In the back seats Manjan and Ladyjan found themselves holding on tight to each other.

After eight whole minutes the silence was broken.

'What was the explosion?' Valter asked. Saga looked at him.

'You didn't recognise it?' she said. 'We've popped another tyre.'

By the time they'd reached Moscow the car had two flat tyres, no windscreen wipers and only one working door. At the car drop-off point they all piled out of the one working door and in front of one of the men who worked at the garage. He did not look happy.

'What do I owe you?' Valter asked, expecting to be extorted but aware that he was the only one of the four with enough money to pay for the damages. The unhappy man shrugged his shoulders.

'Cars,' he said, 'what are you going to do?'

'Let me know how much,' Valter offered again, reaching for his wallet in a way that Ladyjan found very unattractive and Saga found very attractive.

'You paid when you pick car up?' the unhappy man asked

in a gruff Russian accent.

'We did, but...' Valter started.

'Then you get me coffee and,' he paused as if he were thinking about something, 'and then we are even. Come. I know a place.'

Valter ordered five black coffees although there wasn't much of a choice. The shop consisted of a counter, a Soviet Union flag, a shelf and a single pot of coffee. There was a pay phone next to the toilet and a Russian sign that Valter assumed to mean 'do not use this toilet'.

'I'm going to call my parents,' Manjan said, feeling a little guilty. Valter was still paying the extortionate international charges. 'I said I'd call when we got to Moscow.'

Manjan's phone calls with his parents had calmed down. His father had stopped his mother from 'getting on a plane herself and bringing him home by his ear' and instead they had loaned Manjan a little money for food, and to thank Valter and Saga for their help. That, and for not killing their son when they'd found him stowed away on their boat.

At the end of every phone call with his parents Manjan asked his father the same question.

'Have you seen Hylad?'

At the end of every phone call with his parents Manjan's father gave a similar answer.

'He's not come back to Fishton yet son, I'm sorry,' or, 'Jan, do you not think I'd have told you?' or, one time, 'quite possibly, but I'll be damned if I've seen him!' Every time his father gave an answer which essentially equated to 'no', Manjan's heart sank.

Back at the table the unhappy man looked a lot happier thanks to the effect of coffee.

'Hylad's still not there,' Manjan said, as he took a seat

on a metal stool between Ladyjan and Valter. Valter put his arm around Manjan affectionately and explained to the now happier man who Hylad was, why Jan called him Hylad and where Hylad still wasn't.

'He enjoy Sweden,' said the unhappy-then-happy man, 'and he will go back to your Fish-town when he is done. Just you wait.' The man looked down at his coffee and became less happy again. 'The people you love and the people you lose,' he said before trailing off into a short, muttered monologue aimed at no one and in Russian. Eventually he lifted his head. 'They always come back,' he said.

When Manjan, Ladyjan, Valter and Saga had met the unhappy, then happy, then unhappy man, he had already gone through several relationships. Some were friendships, and some were romantic. It was these relationships which made him truly believe what he had said about people coming back.

He had old friends he had fought with and who he regularly bumped into on the street, he had ex-lovers he saw out and about with their new lovers and he had family members who hadn't turned up to his wedding but often turned up at his garage, unwelcome. He even saw his estranged wife most Thursday nights before Soviet curfew, when he was outside her new house after a few too many drinks. But she would have to deal with that, because, frankly, the people you love and the people you lose, they always come back.

It seemed to the unhappy, happy, unhappy man that relationships were like a coiled spring trailing behind him wherever he went. No matter how far away the two people at each end of the coil were, they would always spring back to the middle and meet again.

It is worth pointing out here that the unhappy, happy,

unhappy man had never set foot outside of Moscow. No one he knew had. In fact, the unhappy, happy, unhappy man had spent the majority of his life so far in one particular district in Moscow. The same district that he was in now and the same district that all of his previous lovers, friends and family members lived in. His metaphorical coil never stretched too far.

Later, when Valter, Saga, Ladyjan and Manjan left the coffee shop, Valter secretly placed 3,500 rubles in the unhappy, happy, unhappy man's coat pocket, and when they had gone the unhappy, happy, unhappy man found it. Although he hadn't managed to say thank you he felt certain that he would meet Valter again when their coil contracted, and this made him happy again.

'I talked to Saga earlier,' Valter said, as he moved one of his pawns forward two spaces. Manjan was yet to make his first move. 'This money your parents are offering us to say thanks. We don't need it. We've got everything we need for the trip. We've got more in fact. We're grateful, but we think you should keep the money.'

Manjan looked a little hurt and reached for his rook.

'You can't move a rook on your first go,' Valter stopped him. Manjan moved one of his pawns two spaces forward, exposing his queen. Valter moved his pawn again, taking the pawn that Manjan had just let go of. 'Your go,' he nodded at Manjan.

'But you pay for everything,' Manjan said, 'so I don't really need any money either.' He moved another pawn. Valter laughed and advanced his knight before Manjan moved his queen forward, excitedly taking Valter's pawn. 'Yes!' Manjan celebrated.

While Valter weighed up how cruel his next move should be, Manjan thought. He could give some money to Ladyjan. She'd stolen his money back in Sweden anyway and then she'd given it back, so in a way it would be like giving back the money that he had taken from her. It just so happens that the money he had taken from her was money she had made by stealing from him in the first place. But that was her job.

Valter decided to be kind.

'Do you want to change your last move?' he asked, snapping Manjan away from his thoughts, which were beginning to confuse him anyway.

'What? No. I just took your pawn,' Manjan protested.

'If you're sure,' Valter said.

'I'm sure!'

Valter moved his knight again. 'You've lost your queen,' he said.

19

A GOAT

Moscow, Russia. 1972.

Ladyjan refused Manjan's money. If she wanted it, she told him, she would just take it. She'd done it once before and she could do it again. She was, in her own words, an expert in her profession.

'Challenge accepted,' Manjan said. He placed the money in his back-pocket and looked away. He was going to tell Ladyjan to steal from him again but as he turned he was instantly distracted by St Basil's Cathedral, which stood like a grand multi-coloured flame in front of him.

'Why do you think it looks like that?' Manjan asked quietly to himself. Ladyjan smiled at what she understood to be his awe, spontaneity and inquisitive nature. It hadn't crossed her mind that what Manjan actually possessed was a lack of an attention span. She told him that she didn't know why it looked as it did but suggested that maybe the answer was in the question.

'What do you mean?'

'Perhaps they built it to inspire,' Ladyjan continued, 'so that people like you and me would look at it and say, why do you think it looks like that?' She mimicked Manjan as she said this last bit.

'It looks like it should be built on a cloud,' Manjan said as Ladyjan took his parents' money out of his back-pocket.

'You should write,' she joked, as she waved the money in front of his face. Manjan looked at her and smiled. 'I'm not keeping it,' Ladyjan told him sternly, 'I'm proving a point.'

Michael watched Nigel from the window. He was pulling the ropes on his boat to test how tight they were, and he was grunting a lot. Michael watched Nigel lift the hatch on the floor and he watched him look through the safety equipment underneath. It was obvious why Nigel was spending so much time on his boat and it annoyed Michael that Nigel hadn't told him. He'd clearly given up. Nigel was going back to England.

With another grunt, the door slammed open and Nigel walked into the rented flat. Michael was sitting at the table drinking a bottle of beer. In front of him sat another bottle of beer, which he'd taken from the fridge after he'd seen Nigel leave the boat.

'Beer,' Michael said, rather than offered, tilting the top of his bottle towards the bottle on the table. Nigel picked up the bottle but didn't take a drink. 'Hylad,' Michael said sadly.

'Hylad?' Nigel said. 'I haven't been called Hylad in a while.'

'But you will be,' Michael replied quietly, 'when you're back in England.' There was a long pause and Nigel took a swig from his bottle. 'What are you going to say to them, Nigel? You can't go back.' Nigel grunted again.

After Jan had accidentally started his journey to India with Ladyjan, Nigel and Michael had spent two days searching for him, catching two full sunrises and two full sunsets. On the third day, with blisters on his feet, Nigel had called Jan's parents. He didn't think that he was telling a lie when he'd told them that he'd lost their son but that he wouldn't come back to England without him. He'd promised. Jan's mother was understandably in pieces and Jan's father was more than a little angry.

Before the call had ended, Jan's father had spoken slowly and softly but with a real emphasis on each and every word. Words that Nigel heard in his sleep every night.

'Bring...Jan...home.'

Since the phone call, both Nigel and Michael had spent every day looking for Jan. They'd put *'förlorat'* notices in several Swedish newspapers and they'd visited all of the surrounding towns. Eventually, realising that the task might take longer than they'd hoped, they'd rented a flat, and Michael had taken up odd jobs on people's boats for a bit of extra cash.

Three days ago, Nigel knew that he had lied to Jan's father. He took another long swig from his bottle.

'You don't have to come,' he said. Other than the continuous worry that they both had for Jan, Nigel and Michael found they actually quite liked the life they'd accidentally acquired in Sweden. Their flat was small, and money was short, but they had a lovely view of the harbour and they were spending more time together than they'd ever managed in England.

'If you're giving up,' Michael said, 'write to them. Jan's father won't want to see you. Neither will his mother.' Nigel agreed before there was a long contemplative pause.

'I'm not giving up,' Nigel said, before heavily breathing out of his nostrils, 'but I am going back. We should speak face to face. I owe them that.' He put his head in his hands.

Michael sighed.

'Of course I'm coming,' he said. 'If you can miss Norway, you're never going to find England.'

The carton had a picture of a cartoon goat grinning on it so there was every chance that it was milk. They couldn't tell, though, because neither Manjan nor Ladyjan could read Russian. It wasn't just the words and the spelling that were different; they didn't recognise most of the letters either. So far, in Russia, they'd bought a savoury cake when they were trying to buy bread, a sweet garlic sponge when they were trying to buy a fruit cake and a hard, miscellaneous white substance that tasted like dust when all they wanted was cheese. It didn't really matter if the carton didn't contain milk, though; they would laugh at their mistake together. It didn't take much to make Manjan and Ladyjan laugh together.

They had eventually agreed that they would share Manjan's parents' money. If they both wanted something, Manjan's parents would pay for it and they would share it. They shared food, toiletries and travel costs. It was surprisingly intimate. They both ate what the other would eat and drank what the other would drink, they learned about each other's routines and, thanks to Ladyjan's choice of toiletries, Manjan had never smelt better. Now they would share what was potentially a carton of milk, but potentially not. The lady at the counter frowned when they asked for two straws.

They were meeting Valter and Saga in Gorky Park. They'd been to the park several times since they'd come to Moscow, but they'd taken a different route each time, on Manjan's request. He was adamant that they were still travelling, even though they'd been in Moscow now for weeks.

On the way out of the shop Manjan saw a bright-blue payphone hanging, partially covered on the wall.

'I'd best ring my...' Manjan started, but he didn't bother to finish his sentence because there was only ever one place he rang. Ladyjan nodded with a smile. She knew the reason he was ringing his parents so often and so did Valter and Saga.

Hylad.

He picked up the phone and Ladyjan showed him her crossed fingers. 'You go on,' he said, pointing in the direction of the park with a head nod, 'the others will already be there.'

'Aye,' the receiver whispered in that Northern, Fishton accent that Jan would miss if it wasn't for the regularity of his phone calls home. As had become tradition, Jan greeted his father and asked how his mother was. Jan's father told Jan that they were both doing well but that they missed him, and Jan replied that he missed them too.

'Jan, I've got something to tell you lad,' his father said. 'Guess who knocked the other day.' Jan exhaled sharply and quickly before holding his breath in anticipation so that his chest felt collapsed. There was a silence on the line. 'Jan, lad?'

'Tell me,' Jan said exhaling even further.

Now, I know and you know who it was that had knocked

on Jan's father's door. But put yourself in Jan's position for a moment. Picture having not seen one of your closest friends for nearly two years – someone who taught you a whole language and to whom you had taught a whole different language in return, someone who had taken you abroad for no other reason than knowing that you wanted to go abroad, and someone you know is looking for you, un-contactable and in the wrong country. Jan knew the guilt that Hylad would have felt since they'd separated at the docks in Sweden, and Jan had felt that guilt in return.

Now imagine hearing that the person, who you hadn't seen for nearly two years, had come home and found out that you were OK. Imagine the guilt lifting, the relief setting in and the sheer happiness that Jan must have felt at that very moment.

He shouted.

'Weaaaaaaaaaaaaaaaaaa!'

It wasn't a word as such, he was too full of emotion to form an actual word, but what it lacked in sense it made up for in volume.

In the park, Valter and Ladyjan were sitting on a bench with Saga spread out on the grass in front of them. They were leaving for Nepal in two days and were taking it in turns to say what they were most looking forward to. It was refreshing for all three of them to talk in their native tongue when Manjan wasn't there.

Valter was looking forward to Kathmandu. He said that he thought the city might give them their first taste of what India would be like. He was also keen to spend some time in Nepal's countryside and jungle area. Ladyjan confessed that she didn't actually know anything about Nepal, but that she'd enjoyed Poland, and had absolutely loved Russia. She told Valter and Saga that she was just keen to learn more about another country.

Saga started to say that she'd heard about a large and beautiful lake in Nepal that she'd like to visit but that now she really just wanted to get to India. Ladyjan interrupted.

'That is Jan?' she said, returning to English, and pointed at a small Manjan-shaped figure running full pelt at them from the park entrance. Saga sat up and they all watched as Manjan's gangly legs sped his flailing body towards them as fast as they could. He started shouting something before he was in their earshot.

'He'll be there,' was the first thing Ladyjan heard him say about half a minute later, 'when I go home. He'll be there.'

'Hylad?' Valter asked.

'When I go home,' Manjan continued, out of breath but nearly reaching the group, 'he'll be there.'

Ladyjan stood up excitedly, and as Manjan reached the three of them, without thought, he and Ladyjan kissed.

Valter and Saga fell silent. Saga held her hands together tightly. Valter nodded and raised his eyebrows. They'd both been waiting for something to happen between these two for some time – as, I'll wager, have you.

Manjan held Ladyjan's shoulders and their lips parted. They looked at each other for a few seconds. Manjan was still out of breath but beaming and Ladyjan looked surprised and wide-eyed. Was it Manjan, or did her eyes have a hint of sadness to them?

'When did you say you are going home?' she asked.

At the airport Manjan considered ringing his parents. There was a bright-blue, partially covered payphone hanging on the wall between a fake plant and an advert for yoghurt. Manjan had rung his parents nearly every time he'd seen a payphone but today he didn't feel any need to.

He could ring them and tell them that he was about to fly for the first time. He could tell them how nervous he was and how he hadn't slept all night. He could let them know that, despite all this, he was still safe and well. But he didn't. Hylad was home.

Manjan looked closer at the yoghurt advert. A big cartoon goat was jumping from a carton of milk grinning manically. Manjan recognised the goat and realised that he hadn't drank his half of the shared milk. Was it milk?

'Saga, where did Jan go?' Manjan asked. There was a yoghurt and milk-based joke to be shared.

'She went to the toilet,' Saga replied, looking at the big clock on the wall, 'just after they started boarding. She said she'd meet us on the plane.'

Manjan looked at the payphone again. Hylad was home and well. He should ring anyway, he knew he should, but he didn't.

'Shall we get on the plane?' he said.

Manjan did not understand the air host when he explained to the passengers in Russian that they would shortly be taking off. He did not understand the air host when he said the same thing in Nepali. Manjan didn't understand any of the safety procedures that the air host ran through. He just kept looking at the door waiting for Ladyjan. He did understand why the air host was shutting the door though, and he started to panic.

The air host did not hear Manjan's first attempt to call him due to the buzz of the other passengers. He didn't hear Manjan's second attempt to call him because the pilot had started the engine. By the time the air host had heard Manjan he was next to him and the plane had started moving.

'Stop,' Manjan ordered, manically pointing at the empty seat next to him.

Calmly, and in perfect English, the air host told him that the plane couldn't just stop. Then he started saying something about the terms of the very official-looking but ultimately illegitimate ticket. Manjan had stopped listening.

'Let me off,' he shouted, but the air host told him it was not safe. 'Let me off,' he shouted again, but the air host told him that he wouldn't. 'Let me OFF!' he screamed while the air host looked at his ticket. 'JAN!' Manjan cried, losing all control.

Seeing the name on the ticket, the air host felt sorry for Manjan who, mentally, was clearly not all there. 'Look, look, let me show you something,' he said, holding onto Manjan's shoulder and ushering him to the window over the empty chair where Ladyjan should have been sitting. Outside the window, Manjan could see Moscow. Not just a bit of Moscow, not just St Basil's Cathedral and not just Gorky Park, but all of Moscow, and it was tiny.

What Manjan couldn't see was Ladyjan standing outside the airport. He couldn't see her drop her barely lit cigarette and immediately take another one out of the packet, and he couldn't see her slump her back against the wall.

Ladyjan loved Manjan but she couldn't be his Saga. She couldn't live off his parent's money and pretend that they were meant to be together; it wasn't right.

Manjan sat back down in a hot sweat. Saga put her hand on his leg, shook it and gave him a sympathetic look. From 15,000 feet, Manjan couldn't see Ladyjan's cheek slowly dampen and he couldn't see her eyes turn a bright and painful red. From the ground, Ladyjan couldn't see his do the same.

20

A BUMBLE BEE

Goa, India. 2016.

'You see?' Manjan asked.

'Yes,' Shakey responded, but it was clear that he didn't. He was grinning an insanely large grin and staring at Manjan with that hint of crazy that never seemed to leave the enormous vacuum behind his eyes. Manjan noticed how Shakey's hair seemed to sort of glow now that the sky had grown dark, probably due to some neon left over from a previous night's vest party.

'I had lost my queen,' Manjan said, and Shakey let go of his intense stare with an elaborate head nod.

'Right,' he said, 'I get it. Yeah. So that was the last time you saw your lady-you then?'

'My lady-me, Ladyjan, Jan,' Manjan corrected himself.

Shakey was certainly good at making nicknames. 'No, of course not. I don't wait on a beach for just anyone. That is the first time I lost her, the first time that I realised how much I needed her.'

Manjan noticed that Shakey had started drawing a pattern in the sand with his foot but he decided to continue anyway. 'I spent some time in Kathmandu with Valter and Saga. I hated every second. Ugly city, polluted, crowded...' He paused and thought. He normally liked crowded cities. Looking again at Shakey's pattern in the sand, he mumbled, 'It's amazing how lonely a crowded city can feel.'

Manjan continued to watch Shakey etch out several parallel lines while he told him about the rest of his time in Nepal. He had nothing good to say about it, despite Nepal being one of the most beautiful countries he had ever visited.

After Kathmandu, the three of them had travelled to Pokhara together. Saga and Valter had left Manjan in Pokhara, deciding to go onto India quicker than originally planned. They'd asked Manjan to go with them, but he hadn't gone, and, honestly, he barely noticed them leave. He barely noticed anything in Nepal. It was agreed that they would all meet in a month in Varanasi, India.

Pokhara is a quaint town next to a huge crystal-clear lake. There are majestic sun-peaked mountains reflecting on the water and small pink flowers growing along the banks. Every evening in Pokhara Manjan would sit on a grassy mound by himself next to the lake, watch the sunset and think of Ladyjan.

'That sounds good,' Shakey said, monotonal and absentmindedly staring at the sand. 'I bet you found yourself there?'

'No,' Manjan answered. 'I hated every second of it. I hated

how the mountains reminded me of how big the world was, I hated how the flowers would die and wilt in the water and I hated myself every time I saw myself reflected in the lake. I hated it.'

Not sure what to say, Shakey dug deep into the sand to create another circle above his stripy sand pattern. 'It's amazing how loneliness can turn paradise into hell,' Manjan said bitterly.

Manjan had met Elaine on his normally solitary mound in Pokhara. She'd sat next to him and introduced herself but Manjan had remained quiet. He didn't want company.

In another story, it would be mentioned how stunningly attractive Elaine was. You would read about her long dark hair and the brightness of her eyes. Many details would be given about her soft smile and smooth olive skin. But Manjan didn't see any of this and so, in his story, you won't hear about these things.

You will hear about how Elaine wouldn't leave Manjan alone for three days and how she mistook his silence for a sensitive soul and deep spirit. You will also hear how she drove him to the Chitwan Jungle on their fourth day together. During the two-hour drive to the Jungle, Elaine realised that Manjan did not have a deep spirit. What he had was something nearing depression. Manjan and Elaine did not spend time together in the Chitwan Jungle.

The jungle, Manjan told Shakey, was too hot, too damp, too muddy and too inhabited. At least that's how it had seemed to him in 1973. 'It's amazing how lonely an inhabited jungle can feel' he mumbled.

Shakey had stopped drawing his pattern in the sand with his foot. Manjan looked at it, took a little sip of his wine, and coughed.

'A bumble bee,' he said, and Shakey beamed at him having clearly not listened to Manjan's admittedly very moustache-y thoughts on Nepal.

'A bumble bee,' Shakey repeated back at him, still smiling a smile so big it seemed to disappear around each cheek. 'What do you think?' Manjan wasn't offended by Shakey's brief lack of attention. In fact, he was humbled that Shakey was still sitting next to him.

'It's a good bumble bee,' he answered, and Shakey looked down at his art without releasing his grin, 'but there is only one. Bumble bees work together.' Without hesitation Shakey dug his big toe deep into the sand next to the first bumble bee and started to create more parallel lines. Further down the beach, Prisha the cow let out a low, satisfied moo and Manjan continued.

'That's when I first came to India,' he said, 'not with Jan, Ladyjan that is, but by myself, to keep a date with Valter and Saga.'

Manjan's first glimpse of India was at the Nepali-Indian land border. In all his time in Sweden, Poland, Russia and Nepal he had never seen anything like the Nepali-Indian boarder. Nepal had a population of 12 million and India had a population of 554 million. From what Manjan could see as he stood in Nepal's last few metres of calm, unpopulated land, all 554 million Indians must have decided to enjoy a day out at the border.

What struck Manjan most was the sheer contrast. Behind him were three Nepali men and six travellers. In front of him, just past the gate, stood a human wall. A mass of moving, weaving, shouting people all connected at the arms and shoulders. Everyone seemed to possess the ability not to fall into Nepal. Not one person on the Indian side stepped over the border into the country in which Manjan stood. Completely in awe of what he saw, Manjan thought of Ladyjan and how he would have loved to share this experience with her.

For the first time, taking advantage of his empty spot in Nepal and the sheer volume of people in front of him, Manjan looked to his right, just on the off-chance that she would be there. Then he looked to his left. It was unlikely, but he may as well check. She wasn't there. He looked to his right again. A short round woman was looking back at him inquisitively. Then he looked to his left again.

He saw no sign of her.

There were now six bumble bees, all different sizes, circling the original bumble bee. Shakey was looking down at them. Something wasn't right.

'You know what,' he said, 'I don't think you're right. I don't think bumble bees do work together. All the bumble bees I've ever seen are flying about on their own, sniffing flowers.'

'Ah,' Manjan responded, slightly miffed that Shakey had nothing to say about the wall of people he'd just been talking about. He sniffed hard and the bristles on his moustache moved up and then down again. 'That's when they're working. When they're at the hive they're together. They're meant to be together.'

Shakey looked at his picture and quietly repeated that it didn't look quite right and that he thought there were too many bees. He couldn't find the original.

'Isn't that the truth?' Manjan exhaled. Then he slapped both his legs with his hands and said 'Toilet.'

In Manjan's absence, Shakey looked down the beach to his cheering peers. He saw the neon lights circle the stars and watched a puppy walk away from the vests, away from Prisha and towards the rocks at the end of the beach. For the first time since he'd come to India, Shakey wondered what was on the other side of the rocks at the end of the beach.

'Where were we?' Manjan asked, sitting back down next to Shakey. The presence of red wine and the absence of vodka and Red Bull in Manjan's hand didn't go unnoticed.

'Wall of people; India,' Shakey replied.

'Oh yes,' Manjan continued. 'It's amazing how lonely being one in 554 million people can feel.'

21

A DEAD BULL

Varanasi, India. 1975.

Manjan spat. The paan hit the floor with an echo and the man in the shower next to him made a disapproving noise. The shower was terrible – the water was brown, the floor was concrete and there was a drop toilet directly below the flow of water.

'I'm done anyway,' Manjan mumbled, grumpily grabbing his towel and sliding his hard-soled feet into an old pair of flip-flops.

'Good. Go. The shower's not for spitting. Don't spit,' returned the echoing voice. Manjan scowled loudly. He could hear that the voice in the next shower was chewing paan too and he would have to spit it out sometime. Whether or not he did it in the shower, Manjan doubted very much that it would be in a bin.

When he had first arrived in Varanasi two years ago, Manjan, Saga and Valter had lived three days together as tourists. They had visited temples, they had rowed up the river Ganges together and Saga and Valter had treated Manjan to his first thali (something they themselves had first tried in Gorakhpur). For a short time, Manjan had enjoyed travelling again.

But for Saga and Valter, India was end game. It was where they'd set off to get to and it was everything Saga had hoped it would be. In Varanasi Saga started to receive an increased amount of male attention. If she was being honest with herself, she sort of enjoyed it, but Valter had noticed it too and he didn't seem so keen. After three days, once again, Valter and Saga left Manjan by himself, and once again, Manjan stopped travelling and became resident.

On his way out of the shower and back to his small brick cell of a room, Manjan nodded a hello to Kalem, who was coming in from his morning shift. Kalem lived with his wife in 'Sunshine Hostel' where Manjan lived, and it was Kalem who had found Manjan a job shortly after Valter and Saga's departure.

Kalem's English was incredibly good and he liked to show it off. He never really stopped showing it off in fact.

'Good fish today, are you going back up to your room, yes? How was your shower? You have to stop using the shower, Jan, I've told you; wash at work, wash in the great Mother Ganges.' He held his hands in the air. 'The great Mother Ganges.' He put them down again and shrugged his shoulders. 'You know, wash at work. The shower here is no good for you and it is no good for me, my friend. You will never see me in this shower.' He looked at the man sitting behind the counter. 'This is not an insult to you, sir, you run a fine establishment, you do and you know I love to live here.' Then he looked back to Manjan sadly. 'You cannot go back upstairs now, Jan. You can't just sleep all day and then sleep all night.'

'I'll see you tonight for a drink,' Manjan said.

'Yes I know, every night, a drink, and every day? A bed and nothing else, and then every night after a drink also, a bed. Work in the morning. Shower in this hole.' He waved his arm at the shower before looking back to the man behind the counter. 'No insult sir, no insult.' Back to Manjan. 'Come with me today. We will go somewhere in this beautiful city and appreciate what we have.'

Manjan thanked Kalem for the offer (an offer which he received and thanked him for every day) but told him 'no' and continued up to his room.

Manjan heard the same chant and ringing of bells that he heard every morning as he walked down to the river for work. He knew that a group of mourners were about to push past him on their route to the ghats, a dead body on their shoulders, and hope for a loved one's eternal afterlife in their hearts. It was in many ways life-affirming, but in many other ways it was a constant inconvenience to Manjan. He stood to the side and watched the small parade light the darkened streets as it passed by.

Varanasi was considered a holy city, but in these early hours of the morning all Manjan could see was the dirt on the walls, the faeces on the street, and death. So much death. Down at the concrete bank he picked up as many rusty metal cages as he could carry and threw them into the rickety wooden boat that Kalem had previously assigned to him. Then, when he had paddled out to the middle of the dark river he dropped the cages into the water. Before sunrise he would be back at the hostel and Kalem would take over, collecting the cages and packing their catch into boxes to be sent to nearby towns. Holy fish from a holy river.

Once Kalem had finished his work, he would bathe in the river with his wife, several local people who they were friends with and hundreds of individuals and families at the end of a pilgrimage.

Kalem had explained the religious benefits of washing oneself in the Ganges to Manjan several times before, and he'd expressed his desire to be cremated into her one day. He firmly believed that if Manjan would just walk into the river, he might be released from the terrible slump he seemed to be in. Maybe a small splash of the mother Ganges, and his woes, his longing for the girl who had left him on an aeroplane and his partially self-inflicted loneliness would all just wash away.

After he had bathed and brushed his teeth, Kalem walked his wife to her work and went back to the hostel alone, ready to try once again to persuade Manjan not to spend all day in bed. He pushed the door open into the hostel reception and instantly noticed the quiet. He was used to the sound of running shower water and complaining voices. There was a distinct lack of activity, too – where were the towelled men sitting waiting on the hostel's constantly damp sofa? Where were the small pile of flip-flops outside the shower rooms? Where was Manjan?

Kalem walked over to the man sitting behind the counter.

'Sir,' he said, 'where is everyone? No one is showering.' He pointed to the empty shower/drop toilet rooms. 'Alas, no one could actually shower in these showers, which is, of course, meant as not an offence to you, but they couldn't, and now I look and see for the first time that no one is showering in these showers.'

'Broken,' the man sitting behind the counter said, without looking at Kalem.

'Yes, yes they are broken,' Kalem continued, 'I know that. Every day I am telling you they are broken. Any shower above a toilet is broken, I agree, I do, but where are the people that feel happy bathing in them?'

'They're broken,' the man said, a little more sternly, this time looking up at Kalem. 'Water isn't coming out of them.'

'No. Again, sir, I agree. What comes out of these showers is not water. It is brown and smelly. The people who shower here come out worse than they went in. They should be cleaning in the Mother Ganges. You know, I've seen you down by her side with your children, who, I notice, do not stay here. The river is brown from the sins it is cleaning away, but these showers', he grimaced, 'these showers are brown from, I have to assume, excrement?'

'The people aren't here,' the man sitting behind the counter growled through gritted teeth, 'because the showers do not work.'

Kalem smiled. If these showers were broken then Manjan couldn't have cleaned today. He ran up the stairs to Manjan's room and pushed open the heavy red door. He wouldn't normally do this – he would normally knock – but when he saw an opportunity to help a friend he got carried away.

Inside, Manjan was face down in his pants on his bed. Some clothes were strewn among the paan stains on the floor and there was an inefficient fan, whirring noisily but not actually spinning, on the ceiling. Kalem made a show of waving his hand in front of his nose and pulling a face.

'You need to wash, Jan,' he said. 'You should use the shower downstairs, please.' Manjan knew that Kalem would have seen the broken showers and he knew why Kalem was in his room.

'They're broken,' he said.

'Oh no, they're broken?' Kalem repeated. Manjan turned over to see a huge smile spread across Kalem's face. 'They could be broken for a long time, Jan. My friend, you will start to smell even worse.' There was a couple of seconds' silence.

'I'm not going to the river,' Jan said, as he put more paan into his mouth.

Sunshine Hostel did not live up to its name. It was down an alley and overlooked by four taller buildings. In a very literal way, Sunshine Hostel lacked sunshine. But in a metaphorical way too, Sunshine Hostel truly was down an alley and overlooked by four taller buildings. Even the word 'hostel' wasn't really appropriate, as all the residents were permanent. Occasionally a traveller would come for one night, complain and then leave in the morning, but for the most part it was the same people every day.

The facilities were shared. There were showers, a kitchen and a telephone. As a general rule, no one touched the walls to save their hands from the grease and no one used the kitchen because none of the appliances worked. Some people showered because they needed the toilet anyway and it was possible to do both at the same time, and most people didn't use the phone because it was sticky.

Manjan didn't use the phone either but not because it

was sticky. Manjan didn't use the phone because he didn't want to. He didn't know how to get hold of Ladyjan and he couldn't think of anything positive to tell his parents.

Sometimes Kalem used the phone, but only to persuade Manjan to ring home. He would pick up the phone and thrust it at Manjan but Manjan never took it. Kalem's hands were often sticky.

Knee-deep in the murky brown river, Manjan looked back to the bank, where he saw that Kalem had already stopped watching him and had started chatting to young boy. Kalem was looking proud.

'Work hard,' Manjan heard him lecture, 'and you can have it all. You live here?' The boy nodded. 'You live in the best city in the world, my friend. You live with the divine and in the divine, and that will help you. God and Varanasi are on your side.'

Manjan looked back at the river that he was standing in. He was used to seeing it in darkness. Now, with the sun up, he was joined by crowds of people picking up water in cupped hands and splashing it onto their faces. Some were lying on their backs in the water while children were throwing water at each other and laughing. Behind him Manjan could hear Kalem go on.

'Look at me young friend, I have worked hard in this city and I have a happy and fulfilling job. I pick up freshly caught fish off my best friend' – he pointed at Manjan in the muddy river and Manjan waved back – 'and I package them. I am the best at packaging here and so I am chosen to do it. God has been kind and he will be to you, too.' Kalem looked at

Manjan and shouted. 'Get in all the way so that all your body is wet.' Manjan laughed. 'And have you brushed your teeth?'

Kalem really was a good person and Manjan did not deserve his friendship. Facing the river and away from the shore, Manjan bent his knees and felt the cool of the river high up his legs. Two years ago it would have bothered him that a few meters down the river they were burning dead bodies into the water but now he didn't mind. He put his hands in the water and watched them instantly disappear under the surface. Shutting his eyes he lifted his hands up to splash his face and breathed out. Kalem clapped and cheered as the boy ran off.

Manjan's toothbrush was worn and barely had any bristles left, but knowing it would make Kalem happy now he was finally washing in the river, he dipped the remaining bristles in the river, opened his mouth and brushed frantically. It tasted awful.

When Manjan opened his eyes he saw a dead bull floating past him on the other side of the river. He spat and gagged a little, while the man next to him made a disapproving noise before continuing to wash with his wife and three children. Nearby, a large moustachioed man started to brush his teeth. Manjan stared at the dead bull – why was no one fazed by it?

Back at the bank Kalem had started talking to an elderly lady about his love for the city and his wife. Sitting at the water's edge, a young couple were washing each other's arms and a huge middle-aged bearded man helped his mother slowly enter the river. Even the dead bull was joined by a stork, who was standing on the bull's head. For the first time in a long time, Manjan acknowledged how he was feeling, and he found that how he was feeling was alone.

That evening Kalem stood outside the heavy red door of Manjan's room as he did every night, waiting for Manjan to come out so they could get a drink. He hoped that Manjan would be a changed man after he had cleansed himself in the holy river. He hoped that he would be greeted by a happier Manjan.

The heavy red door didn't open. Kalem knocked again and waited for a further half a minute before trying to push the door open. It was locked. He lifted himself up to the bars on the small square window at the top of the door. Pulling his face up so his nose was just above the lower edge of the window, he peered inside. There were no clothes strewn across the floor, the fan had been mended and Kalem thought he could smell air freshener wafting through the bars. Manjan wasn't there.

Panicked, he ran downstairs. The man sitting behind the counter was listening to a man complain about the amount of paan spit on the floor in the showers.

'They are broken,' said the man sitting behind the counter, and he shrugged. 'What does the paan matter?' The complaining man got louder and the man sitting behind the counter shrugged again. He shrugged a lot.

'What is happening in room 254?' Kalem shouted above the complaining man. 'Where is Jan, the man in 254? Has he gone?'

The man sitting behind the counter had completely forgotten the note that Manjan had left him to pass to Kalem. The note that said a long and heartfelt thank you. The man behind the counter shrugged.

The phone rang. Manjan's father stood up from his armchair and walked over to the hall. It would probably be the florist.

'Aye,' he said, deflated, dropping his intonation at the end of the word. There was a couple of seconds' silence before a stranger's voice started talking, completely void of emotion.

'I have a Jan on the line from Varanasi. Will you accept the charge for this call?'

'Aye,' Manjan's father said, with much more enthusiasm, and then he said 'yes', just to clarify. There was a click and another brief silence before anyone spoke.

'Hello,' Manjan said.

'Jan?' Manjan's father asked without inferring a question. There was a further pause, but some pauses can be understood. 'Jan! How are you, lad?'

Manjan's father asked questions solidly for a few minutes without leaving any space for answers. Where was Jan? Where had he been? Who was he with? How was he keeping? Manjan smiled. It had been a long time since he had heard his father's northern English accent and he had missed it.

Once his father had settled down, Manjan began to answer the many questions. He didn't lie, but he did pick which truth he wanted to tell. He told his father how he had been staying in a place called the Sunshine Hostel and mentioned what a beautiful name the hostel had. He talked about Kalem and Kalem's wife and how thanks to them he now had a job. Manjan spoke about Varanasi the way he had heard Kalem talk about Varanasi. He told his father how the deceased were burnt into the river to escape the reincarnation cycle and to enter the afterlife and how the living bathed in the river to cleanse themselves of their sins.

'I bathed in the river myself an hour ago,' he exclaimed proudly.

'Your accent has gone lad,' Jan's father said. He hadn't heard his son's voice in a long time and he was actively taking in every syllable. 'You sound like you're from many different places. Not Fishton at all.' Manjan asked his father what country he sounded like he was from. 'I don't know lad. I can hear – I think I can hear, anyway – Swedish. Aye, there's Swedish in there.'

Manjan paused in his tracks. He was unsure what to say. His father didn't know about Ladyjan and his comment had taken him aback. But some pauses can be understood, so Manjan's father changed the subject.

'Tell me about your friend Kalem.' Grateful for the diversion, Manjan told his father about how he and Kalem worked as a team to catch and sell food to the surrounding villages. He said he respected Kalem and that he was proud to work with him.

'I drop the cages early – it's still dark. Then Kalem collects them and packages them,' he said.

'Sounds technical,' Manjan's father agreed.

'Kalem seems to think his role is very technical,' Manjan continued, 'but he's very good at it.'

His father interrupted. 'A specialist?' he asked.

'I suppose so,' Manjan replied, unaware of the trap he was being led into.

'Oh Jan,' his father said in a mocking tone. Manjan had not missed this mocking tone and he prepared for a joke about an odd number of socks. 'Kalem,' his father continued, 'is a box-packaging specialist and technician.'

Manjan quietly listened to his father laughing before

asking to speak with his mother.

'Oh.' Manjan's father stopped laughing abruptly. 'Jan.' For just a few seconds, time and everything in it stood still. 'Your mother i…' Manjan's father paused, but some pauses can be understood.

PART FOUR

22

A CAT

Fishton. England. 1975.

Jan's father stood in the arrivals waiting room holding a cold battered fish with some soggy chips in a wet newspaper. He'd been standing there for an hour. He'd seen people his age returning from trips with floppy sun hats on their heads, he'd enviously watched reunited couples and he smiled in anticipation at other parents picking up their teenagers.

Jan wasn't a teenager any more – he was twenty-three – but the last time his father had seen him he had been. This last week, Jan's father had found himself wondering what Jan would look like when he saw him at the airport, and would he still be the chatty and inquisitive explorer he had always been, or would he be a sensible young adult? A lot can happen to a person in five years. Of course, he was certain that he would recognise his own son.

There hadn't been any delay. Jan's father had arrived at the airport an hour early because he didn't want Jan to get home and for no one to be waiting for him. At least, he knew that Jan's mother wouldn't have wanted Jan to get home and for no one to be waiting for him. Jan's mother would have told him to go early, so that's what he did. That was pretty much why Jan's father did anything now. That's why he was holding a cold battered fish with some soggy chips in a wet newspaper. Jan's mother would have told him to buy Jan a welcome-home gift. So he had.

'Jan,' he called as his son walked through the gate with no bag in his hands or shoes on his feet. Jan's father felt his eyes well up and he felt embarrassed. He shuffled uncomfortably on his feet and called his son's name again, on an inhaled breath, in an attempt to hide the tears.

Jan ran to his father and hugged him. They both cried, partly through joy and partly through grief; neither knew which.

'You've grown a beard,' Jan said into his father's greying curly hair, without letting go. Although Jan's father was aware of the harsh stubble all around the lower half of his face, he had not grown it intentionally, so he muttered an awkward 'aye'. Jan could feel the grease from the cold fish and chips dripping down the back of his head.

A few moments later, with drying eyes, Jan said, 'I'm sorry.' He heard his father breathe in loudly through his nose and then out through his mouth.

'You don't need to be, lad,' he said, 'but you stink.' Jan laughed as they released their embrace but his father's face was straight. 'No lad, you stink. You need a shower.' He looked Jan up and down. His feet were yellowing and cracked, his legs were dusty and his clothes were filthy. Jan's father couldn't see the picture on Jan's t-shirt either, because it had worn off from over-use or because of the mud it was caked in. Perhaps both. Jan's face was creased beyond his twenty-three years and his hair was long and greasy (although the fish and chips could be partly blamed for this). More than anything, Jan was thin.

'Got you some tea, lad,' his father said, and passed Jan a cold battered fish and some soggy chips in a wet newspaper. Jan accepted them gratefully and held them by his side.

Jan and his father had a good relationship but they didn't normally hug. Neither said anything for a while as they stood facing each other in arrivals. Jan wasn't sure if he could handle mentioning his mother yet and he didn't know whether his father could handle it either. Jan's father didn't mention Jan's mother because Jan's mother wouldn't have wanted him to. Not yet. He gestured towards Jan's bare feet.

'Lost all five socks I see.'

'I think I left three on the side.'

It would take Jan and his father three hours and twenty minutes to get home. The first ten minutes were spent hailing a taxi, the next five were spent searching for Jan's father's wallet and the following five were spent despairing over other items he'd lost while waiting for Jan's plane to land.

'My poxy passport,' he said, emphasising nothing in particular with his hands in front of his chest. 'Why take my poxy passport? So the culprit must look like me. Poxy...' He stumbled through some other words that didn't conjoin to make a sentence before adding, 'and my torch.'

The next hour was spent talking fruitlessly with airport security, looking for someone who looked like Jan's father, and then looking for a phone to call a friend of Jan's father who would come to pick them up. So they sat on the curb outside the airport for another hour, and then the following one would be spent in the back and passenger seat of Jan's father's friend's car, on their way home to 31 Western Crescent, Fishton.

While they waited for their lift to arrive, Jan's father placed two of the plastic bags he always carried around with him on the pavement as protection for their bottoms against the wet. As they sat, they talked, grateful for the cold battered fish and soggy chips in wet newspaper.

'How's Hylad?' Jan asked, after again relaying the countries he'd visited to his father.

'Moved away,' Jan's father said. 'Said he liked Sweden. Found a lady friend out there, I reckon.'

Jan nodded slowly with his bottom lip out further than his top. There was a short silence before he ventured into his next topic of conversation, a topic that neither of them had managed up to this point.

'Dad,' he said, 'how are you doing?' His tone gave the question more context than the words, and his father understood the meaning.

'Aye,' he replied, and then looked up. It had started to rain, but they were sheltered. 'Y'know.' Jan did know and he told his father as much. Quietly he spoke again.

'Why do you carry plastic bags?' he asked, 'and why a torch?' His father didn't know.

'Your mother always made me carry things,' he said, as the rain picked up, 'for emergencies.' Jan looked at the bag he was sitting on and shivered. Northern England was colder than Northern India.

A small white paw patted at the top edge of the coffin. Then a black furry leg reached up, swiped at something that wasn't there, and disappeared. A stifled titter could be heard in the congregation through the multitude of tears, but it wasn't obvious who the offending noise came from.

A black tail with a white tip raised itself above the coffin and then zipped straight back down again in one smooth sharp movement. Jan's aunt kept struggling to talk through sniffing and holding back her tears as a large cat leapt onto the coffin lid.

The cat was mostly black except for one white paw, the tip of her tail and half a stripe around her front leg and chest. She stuck her tail in the air, stretched her front paws out in front of her and yawned.

There was another titter in the congregation, and a now cleaner and healthier Manjan frowned. His father looked at him and gave a half-smile. One of those sad smiles that people give at funerals that seem to say, 'I'm so sorry' and 'it'll be OK' at the same time. Jan's father's smile said 'I'm so sorry' and 'it's not the cat's fault' at the same time.

'Cats do what they want,' he whispered, as the cat lifted one of its hind legs up and licked its own private parts on top of Jan's mother. 'Your mother wouldn't mind. She was the same.'

The cat jumped down from the coffin, proudly walked up to Jan's father and rubbed her head on his leg. Jan stroked the cat's ear and picked her up. Looking directly at the cat and with the cat looking directly at him, he focused – focusing on the cat helped him to hold his emotions back.

'You're the same, too,' Jan's father quietly said. 'You do what you want, just like your mother.'

Jan's father knew that his wife would have loved to have seen Jan before she died. Since they had lost contact with Jan he had spent sleepless nights comforting Jan's mother that Jan would be well. He was probably exploring in a different country the way he used to explore Fishton, he told her. After weeks had turned into months Jan's mother had started to believe him, or maybe she hadn't, but they had started talking about the adventures Jan might be having rather than the empty space ever-present at the table.

When Jan's mother had fallen sick, she and her husband had spoken more firmly about how Jan was well and how he would be enjoying his life. They made up stories together about where he would be and what he would be doing. One day he would be riding a horse in the Middle East and the next he'd be climbing a Nepalese mountain. Jan's mother had once suggested that he might have learnt chess.

'Our lad would be crap at chess,' Jan's father had said, and they had laughed. The week before she died, in her eternally worried but loving voice, Jan's mother had told Jan's father that she was grateful that Jan had got to explore the world and that she knew he was OK.

'He's out there enjoying himself,' she had said, 'just as he should be.' A week later Jan's father stopped creating stories about what Jan might be doing. He had no one to share them with.

Jan's face was stern. He continued to focus on the cat (although she had stopped looking at him) but his wet cheeks deceived the stare.

'Jan,' his father whispered. Jan continued to look at the

cat but his father knew he could hear, 'I've got some money from the chip shop. If you promise to ring me every week, I'll pay for you to go back to India. For your mother.' It hadn't sounded like Jan had been having the experiences his mother had dreamed of. Jan's father put his hand on Jan's forearm. 'You can come back any time you're unhappy, but try to enjoy it.'

She had never expected to bump into Manjan nor had she expected to bump into any of his friends or family, but Ladyjan had the travelling bug, and from everything that Manjan had said, Fishton sounded wonderful.

It was OK.

Fishton didn't quite have the excitement she'd experienced in Russia. The food was similar to Swedish food (everyone ate fish) and she didn't laugh even half as much as she had done in Poland. There was one thing in particular missing from Ladyjan's recent trip to Fishton, and that was Manjan.

She was certain that people in Fishton would be as interesting as Manjan had said they were but she hadn't spoken to many of them. She'd stolen from them instead. She'd liked the idea of continuing to travel but she was beginning to give up. If she could take enough money from enough people she could fly back to Sweden and live how she used to. Life had been exciting for a little while, but she had been right when she'd told Manjan that life wasn't like it was in the movies.

'Check-in for the A1056 flight to Delhi will open in 30 minutes.' Ladyjan looked up from her latest spot in the airport. She'd found it relatively easy to hitchhike the forty miles from Fishton to the nearest international, and the people in the airport had more to steal than those in Fishton.

It's surprising how little people notice each other in an airport. Ladyjan had been living on different chairs in different rooms for three weeks and no one had batted an eyelid. Absentmindedly, she pulled some foam from the chair she was currently sitting on and watched the screen. She'd paid attention every time the announcer had mentioned Delhi. It had only happened three times in three weeks but it always made her smile. Delhi was in India. India was where Manjan was. Somehow, the planes connected them.

She reached into her deceivingly deep pockets. Rummaging past several passports and a great deal of cash, which she kept in a stranger's leather wallet, she felt for the passport with two bent corners. She often felt for this passport; there was something comforting and familiar about the man in the picture's face.

She didn't know what.

'Do you live here or something?' a large man in a security uniform boomed. Ladyjan looked up at him, surprised.

'I'm waiting for my flight,' she stuttered, preparing to run. The security guard laughed and frowned at the same time.

'Look,' he said with a fake smile plastered over his wide, stubbled face, 'you've been waiting a long time.' He paused for effect. 'You're not waiting for a flight. You want to know what I think?'

Ladyjan ran.

She ran past two large unattended suitcases and a small unattended suitcase, she ran past a queue of people waiting to check-in to fly to Delhi and as she clocked the doors, she ran past Manjan and his father. She only noticed the doors.

'Something's kicking off, lad,' Manjan's father smiled

at him but Manjan hadn't noticed. He was folding a page back in his new *High-Tide Travel Guide to India*. He was determined to enjoy India this time, Ladyjan or no Ladyjan, for his mother. No. He was determined to enjoy himself for his father.

Ladyjan ran out of the airport doors as Manjan looked up at his father. 'I'll ring,' he said, 'I promise.'

Outside, Ladyjan was certain she'd got away from Mr wide-stubble-face. She rested her hands on her knees and breathed deeply. In and then out. In and then out. In and then...

'Don't run,' came the man's gruff voice as he put a heavy hand on Ladyjan's shoulder and hardened his grip. She couldn't have run if she'd tried. 'Why,' the man heaved out a lengthy wheeze and then coughed, 'why have you been in the airport for so long? You need money?' It was a nice question but it was asked in a terrifying way. Ladyjan doubted very much that he was about to offer her money. She didn't reply. 'Somewhere to live? Look, I can help you.' Still, Ladyjan didn't reply. In her experience, people in uniforms rarely wanted to help her.

The man coughed again, a loud, phlegmy cough and then lowered his voice to a whisper.

'I'm going to pretend to take you to the security office, but I have a job for you. It'll make you money and take you...' he wobbled his head, thinking of the right word, '...places.'

His grip implied that this wasn't an offer.

'You ever worked in a fish factory before?' he whispered, before looking up and shouting, 'OK lass, you're coming with me,' and jolting her back into the airport.

23

AN INDIAN SEAGULL

Delhi, India. 1977.

Manjan hung up the phone. He had stuck to his word and rung his father every week for the past two years from different parts of India. One week, when he had joined a group of travellers on a desert excursion far away from a phone line, he had even asked Kalem to call on his behalf. His father had been confused, but grateful. One way or another, Manjan had been in contact every seven days, religiously.

In a week, he would be going home. He wasn't sure what he would do when he got there but he fancied work as a box-packaging specialist and technician. He had experience, and after seeing Kalem's pride at his job he thought it might be quite rewarding.

Manjan was ready to stop travelling again. After landing

in Delhi he had travelled back east to Varanasi and met with an excited Kalem who had feared the worst for Manjan when he had left. Kalem was certain that Manjan's return was another of god's miracles. He was also sure without doubt that Manjan's shaven face and clean feet were two more of them.

From Varanasi, Manjan had travelled north to the mountains, where he had lived with an old married couple for a while. The couple liked the way Manjan made weekly phone calls to his father and they appreciated his help growing tea leaves on the plantation. They also enjoyed watching as Manjan completed his twice-daily ritual of standing at the highest point of the plantation and looking right, then looking left, then right and then left again. They didn't know why he did this, but it was oddly endearing.

In the west of India, Manjan had enjoyed all the 'pur' towns and cities, before one last stop in Varanasi to say goodbye to Kalem (who assured Manjan that it was not goodbye – people had a tendency to do that). Now he found himself back in Delhi hanging up the phone for the last time and wiping his sweating face with the bottom of a luminous t-shirt.

On his way back to the hotel Manjan browsed the market. He needed to get a present, something that would show how much he appreciated his father's insistence on sending him back to India. The market made it hard. It seemed unlikely that he would manage to get spices through customs at the airport and most of the home furnishings on offer were too big to travel with. A lot of the ornaments depicted obscure sexual positions and his father never wore a suit, let alone a tie.

'Hey, man, what you after – a lamp?' shouted a man with a trolley full of lamps. Manjan instinctively waved his hand, no. 'Expensive lamps man, but a good price,' the man went on undeterred, as Manjan received an accidental elbow to the chest from the dense crowd in front of him. Maybe looking at lamps would be better than continuing to fight through the rabble.

'What kind of lamp you want man?' the seller asked, forcefully handing Manjan a red glass lamp with a picture of a bird that looked like a seagull on it.

'We have lamps that look like these in a shop where I'm from,' Manjan said. 'What type of bird is that? Ours have seagulls on them.'

'Seagulls? No. My man, these are Indian birds. Very unique. You want green?' He thrust a green lamp into Manjan's free hand.

'How much?' Manjan asked, waving the red lamp. His father might quite like an Indian version of a classic Fishton lamp.

After a short haggle, Manjan agreed to purchase the lamp at less than a tenth of what people paid for one of the seagull lamps in Fishton.

'Very good price,' the man nodded.

'Very good price,' Manjan agreed, but the man already looked distracted, peering over Manjan's shoulder into the crowd.

Manjan followed his stare and froze. Not to the right of him and not to the left of him, but standing right behind him, waiting to talk to the man selling lamps, was a dark-eyed, pale-skinned girl with bits of hair stuck to her face from the heat.

'Um, hello?' she said in a soft Swedish accent.

'Hello, yes, how are you?' replied the man who had just sold Manjan a lamp.

'You've not bought that lamp, have you?' asked Ladyjan, with an emphasis on the word 'bought', but Manjan couldn't reply. He couldn't say anything, in fact.

'Yes, you too,' the lamp-seller continued, 'same place tonight, I can meet you at eight.'

Ladyjan giggled. 'You did buy that lamp didn't you?' A man from the crowd bumped into her and she held onto Manjan's wrist to stop herself from falling. She didn't let go. 'You do know where else you can get those lamps?'

'You got the...' the lamp-seller started. Ladyjan raised her dark brown eyes to meet his. Her smile disappeared as an idea swept across her face.

'Jan,' she said, looking back to him, 'you trust me?' Manjan still hadn't said a word but his face said that he did. 'Eight,' she said to the man, 'at eight,' and the man frowned hard at her.

When Manjan had finally regained the ability to speak, he stuttered.

'It wasn't a carton of milk,' he said, 'it was yoghurt.' Ladyjan held onto his arm tight and they both ran together through the crowd.

In shock and wanting to say something less stupid than his only sentence to Ladyjan so far, Manjan kept trying to pull her to a halt. Ladyjan would not stop. There was something of a panic in her run, and that, along with the density of the crowd, meant they crashed into strangers regularly.

'Where are we going?' Manjan asked loudly over the noise of the market.

'Goa,' Ladyjan replied. Manjan panted. He wasn't as fit as Ladyjan and they'd been running for over ten minutes.

'I can't run to Goa,' he said. 'It's too far.' At this remark, Ladyjan stopped running and instead fell into a side alley laughing. Manjan followed, half-laughing at his own comment and half-panting. He was aware that he was not looking his best, but Ladyjan wouldn't have agreed with him. To her, he looked like the best thing she'd seen since the day she hadn't left Russia.

She rested her sweaty forehead on his chest and felt every heavy rise and fall as he re-caught his breath. She lifted her head to face him.

'Why...' Manjan started and then took another deep breath, 'are we running?' He smiled. 'You don't have to buy a lamp.' Ladyjan laughed and took the red lamp out of Manjan's hand.

'You bought a lamp,' she said. 'You came all the way to India and bought this lamp.' She raised the lamp to his face. 'It has a seagull on it.'

'It's an Indian bird.'

Ladyjan pulled at a string in her pocket and a leather pouch came out. It didn't really look like something she would normally keep on her.

'He wanted me to give him this,' she said with a fading smile. 'Now he expects me to give it to him at eight. At eight, I will be in Goa and I hope, maybe...' She didn't say it but Manjan understood this was an invitation. He didn't reply.

'You can get this lamp in Fishton,' Ladyjan said quietly, and Manjan's eyes narrowed. What had Ladyjan been doing in Fishton? Equally quietly, almost inaudible over the market noise, he told her that he was going to Fishton in a week and Ladyjan replied mysteriously that she can't go back. 'Not now,' she said, at the same time as gesturing to the leather pouch with her eyes. 'Poxy fish factory,' she muttered in her soft Swedish voice, and Manjan felt such a strong surge of love that he kissed her.

For the rest of the day they talked, and laughed, and kissed. Neither of them noticed the person on a bicycle who knocked a man right into Ladyjan's back. They didn't feel the jolt of the impact or hear the lamp smash below them. They didn't notice the man apologise in a different language or the person on a bicycle shouting at all three of them in good, if a little abusive, English. They didn't notice the market quieten and they didn't notice a stray dog lie down next to them, fall asleep, wake up and leave. At eight fifteen, they didn't even think about the lamp-seller as he paced his room on the other side of town cursing Ladyjan with each step. They just talked, and laughed, and kissed. They didn't even notice the sun setting (which is of course the best time to experience a Delhi market).

'Goa?' Manjan smiled.

24

A DONKEY

Fishton to Delhi. 1975-1977.

'We want you to be our regional sales manager,' the man
paused to think of how to phrase it, 'for a rather far-off
region.' He was much smaller than the wide-faced security
guard from the airport, but he had the same menacing and
imposing demeanour. The fish factory, back in Fishton,
where Ladyjan had now spent the night, was equally
imposing – a large warehouse full of industrial machinery
and buttons she was scared to touch. The floor (her bed) was
made of cement and she hadn't been offered a pillow. The
airport security guard had watched her sleep, which meant of
course that she hadn't slept at all.

Before the workers had come in the morning after, the
security guard had moved Ladyjan into an office and left,

locking the door behind him. Ladyjan waited there for three hours.

She watched through the large office window as the workers arrived and tried to get their attention, but they all seemed to actively ignore her. They had definitely seen her. One lady caught eye contact with Ladyjan and looked at her sadly while putting on her white cap and overalls, before quickly looking away again and starting to work.

'Of course you'll report back to Fishton,' the smaller man said, now pacing the office. Ladyjan looked right towards the window but without moving her head. The workers were still there. The man followed her eyes. 'You're not in danger,' he said. 'They don't respond to you because the window is soundproof. They just can't hear you.' Then he picked up his chair and slammed it hard on the ground. 'Work!' he shouted. Ladyjan looked out the window, this time turning her whole head to see the workers pick up the pace. Those at conveyor belts moved their hands quicker and those walking across the room broke into a jog. Soundproof indeed.

Ladyjan wasn't one to show fear, but at that moment she felt it.

'India,' the man said quietly. The workers were already beginning to slow down to a normal pace again. I need you to pick some things up for me from a city in India. I notice that you carry many passports. None with your face on though, no?' He picked up one of the many passports sprawled across his desk and pretended to study it. It was the passport that Ladyjan had used to get from Poland to Russia and then from Russia to England. 'You're not…Alaina,' he stated, not asked. She shook her head. 'Who would notice if you disappeared?' Ladyjan didn't say anything but swallowed a lump in her dry throat. 'Oh no,' the man said, 'I didn't mean it like that,' and then he laughed. 'I just meant if you were to go on holiday for a while.' He waved his hand dismissively and then drew his eyelids close together and said, 'although', implying something non-specific but specifically not very nice.

Ladyjan was yet to say anything to the man. He didn't know what she sounded like and he didn't really know anything about her. All he did know was what he had been told by his wide-faced security friend. He knew that she'd lived in an airport for three weeks stealing from strangers and he knew that she wasn't English. From that, he'd deduced that no one important would look for her and that she probably needed money.

'We've been working on something quite lucrative at the Fish Factory, and we want you to be a part of it. Let me let you in on a little secret,' he said, and then he let her in on his little secret.

His little secret:

'You see, our last regional sales manager, poor sod, she fell very ill. Terribly ill. She was working out in the field and she was seen, um, applying for a different job, shall we say. That's the thing with this job, by the way, you're always seen. There's always someone who knows you nearby. When our last regional sales manager was seen doing the job correctly, she was rewarded. When she was seen doing the job... incorrectly, unfortunately she fell very ill. Terribly ill. So now there's a position which has opened up. I think you would be perfect. Here's how it works.

'I will give you an inordinate amount of money and you will take it to the airport. The security guard – you've already met him – he can give you a lift, it's not close you see, but you know that. He'll also let you into departures and you can skip security if you'd like. I'd recommend it with this kind of cash. He'll be able to see you when you're in departures. He's a lovely man, but a violent sod and an erratic driver, so be careful what you do.

'You'll board the plane to Delhi. Now, I've got a mate who flies to Delhi every so often and he'll be on the same plane – big fella, you want to watch out for that one. Anyway, he probably won't introduce himself so you won't know who he is. When you land – and when you do land, be careful of Harry who hangs out in the airport – you need to take the money to a bloke who sells lamps. I'll give you an address. It is a lot of money for some lamps I know, but they're very good lamps. This bloke who sells them, he's a close friend of mine. It was him who, unfortunately, witnessed our last regional sales manager get very, very ill.

'I want those lamps on every third lorry travelling down to Surat port. You can join the lamps on one of the lorries. I know the lorry drivers – great guys – but you should be careful of them – fiercely loyal. At Surat, you'll see a man fishing in the port. He will be the only man fishing in the port. He never catches anything. He will get you on a boat and that boat will land in Fishton. When you're back, we'll chat and I'll make sure you get paid. Any questions?'

Ladyjan couldn't help but notice that the man's little secret wasn't actually very little at all, but she wasn't sure what questions she could ask that wouldn't make her ill. Terribly ill.

'Drugs?' she breathed with a slight cough.

'Nice lamps,' the man responded.

'If I do it. After that, I can go?' The man rubbed his chin as if in thought before responding that, no, she could not. After she had come back, she could fly to Delhi again, with more money.

'It's a lifestyle,' he said, emphasising the word 'life'.

There was one perk to Ladyjan's new 'job' and that was that she would visit India. Manjan might be in India. But for this small perk there were many disadvantages. She was presumably being watched all the time, although she couldn't always tell if this was true or not, and she seemed to constantly be in possession of illegitimate money that she couldn't spend. She had a wage of her own, but it was very low and she was often in the company of terrifying people. Travelling in the back of a lorry across India was uncomfortable and drawn out and although she never inspected the lamps through fear, she was fairly certain she was travelling with narcotics, internationally.

By the end of her first year working she began to realise that the one perk that she thought she had with the job didn't feel like a perk at all. She'd made three round trips and hadn't seen Manjan. India was big, and she wasn't even sure he was in India.

On her third trip back to Fishton, Ladyjan had been forcibly told to stay on the boat behind a crate of lamps. She had listened as two voices spoke old Fishton to each other and rummaged around the ice crates filled with fish.

'They never check the lamps,' a worker at the docks winked at her when the voices had gone, but Ladyjan didn't care. She'd stopped caring about anything.

By the sixth time Ladyjan visited India she'd resigned herself to being a mule. A donkey with no true home and no true friends. A donkey who barely spoke to anyone in Fishton other than people she worked for and hated, and a donkey who spoke to even fewer people in India. Once, in Fishton, she'd considered talking to a lonely-looking man who was sitting in a café drinking tea by himself. He looked like the man she'd stolen a passport from in the airport a few years ago and he had a friendly face. As Ladyjan had stood up to move to his table a large, balding man had sat next to him, apologised for being late and said he was only in Fishton for a few days. So she continued to walk past the table and out of the café. The large balding man had smiled at her as she passed.

Ladyjan walked off the plane in Delhi for the sixth time, looking respectable and holding an inordinate amount of cash in her clothes but feeling like a donkey. In a few months, after she'd purchased and transported the lamps, she would be treated with hay. A small amount of money to keep her alive. That evening she slept in the same hostel she always did when she was Delhi. It had been specifically picked by the man at the fish factory because it had everything she needed – a mattress, his friend, who could watch her (mental little so-and-so, apparently) and no official check-in procedure.

In the morning, she ate a cereal breakfast at the same café she always ate a cereal breakfast in Delhi, picked by the same donkey owner who picked everything this donkey did. Then she took her inordinate amount of cash to the same market to pass to the same lamp-seller before meeting him later in the same place to pick up the same number of mysteriously illegal lamps.

She stood behind a tourist like she always did. The tourist was purchasing a lamp and she secretly cursed him under her breath. He had no idea how little this sale meant to the lamp-seller or how much the lamp-seller would get from his next international customer.

The man in front of her turned around.

'Um, hello?' she said in a soft Swedish accent.

One of Shakey's eyes was facing slightly upwards and his other was facing directly at Manjan. His eyelids were moving like they couldn't stay open or shut and his mouth hung slightly further open than normal. He was clearly quite drunk, but he was listening very intently.

'She sounds awesome,' he slurred, 'like a film.'

'No, she was forced to run drugs,' Manjan protested. 'She was very unhappy. But then we met again, and that was down to fate. The same fate which has bought me to Palolem and the same fate which will lead Ladyjan back to Palolem, back to me.'

Shakey looked at Manjan, impressed. He thought Manjan looked quite on-edge. Maybe it could be the wine, but he wanted to relax him. Shakey took hold of Manjan's hand and wiggled it up and down like you do to a baby. Manjan looked at their hands moving together.

'What are you doing?' he asked, but felt surprisingly relaxed at the gentle movement.

'I'm Shakey,' answered Shakey. Manjan still wasn't really sure why Shakey was called Shakey. He went on.

'The fish factory sent Ladyjan to Delhi over and over again, and I was in Delhi. Fate wanted us to find one another. If she hadn't found me that day in the market, I'd have travelled back to Fishton and we would have met there. We were magnets, swinging around each other until eventually our gravitational pull brought us to the same spot, in the same market, at the same lamp stall.'

Shakey's eyes continued to concentrate. They were concentrating hard, but they were also both looking in different directions and they both looked confused.

'Would you like another drink?' Manjan asked, and stood up to go to the bar while shakey nodded for a prolonged amount of time.

At the bar, he ordered a small glass of red wine and a small bucket of Red Bull. He did not ask for vodka.

'Fate will bring Ladyjan back to Palolem,' Shakey said, again a little slurred. 'But why back here? Why not Russia or Poland or Sweden or Fishton? Why Goa?'

25

AN ALIVE BULL

Delhi to Palolem. 1977.

You wouldn't expect to see a 25-year-old man imitating a bull. But that's exactly what Ladyjan, and a bull, could see.

Manjan and the bull started eye-to-eye, staring at each other. The bull snorted. Manjan snorted. The bull stepped backwards. Manjan stepped backwards. The bull picked up litter from the dusty street with its mouth. Manjan frowned, thought about it, and then picked up litter from the dusty street with his mouth.

'No, no,' shouted a man who was walking on the other side of the street, 'is bull.' He made horn signs with his fingers and imitated charging, but Manjan didn't care. Ladyjan was in fits of giggles and that was what mattered to him. Besides, he was winning.

'You're crazy,' Ladyjan shouted through laughter. The man the other side of the street agreed, waving his finger round his ear with a very serious expression on his face. 'Yes, crazy,' he shouted before leaving in disbelief at other people's stupidity.

The bull snorted again and looked at Manjan, who again copied and looked back. Ladyjan tried to stop laughing to tell Manjan to stop, but her laughter was uncontrollable, and she couldn't. Manjan saw her struggle though, and emphasised hunching his back like the bull to make her laugh more. He couldn't help it, Ladyjan's laughter was like fuel. The bull stomped his back legs hard on the floor, kicking up dust and Manjan jumped hard on the floor too. Ladyjan stopped laughing.

'Run!' she shouted and Manjan turned to look at her. Ladyjan started running forward to...what? Tackle the bull? She didn't know what her plan was and she didn't need to because before she reached the pair, the bull had bucked forwards and hit Manjan in his side, knocking him against a wall. The bull bucked again but Manjan was slumped at the bottom of the wall and out of the way. He groaned.

Ladyjan kept running, but with more focused purpose – to help Manjan, who, frustratingly, was the other side of the bucking bull. She ran straight into the bull's backside, stumbled and rolled onto the floor next to Manjan.

'Wow,' Manjan grunted.

'You thought that was intentional?' Ladyjan asked, dazed, but once again laughing. Manjan let out a breathy laugh as the bull calmed himself, re-picked up the litter he had previously dropped, chewed it and swallowed it.

'I still would have won,' Manjan muttered.

Ladyjan and Manjan had taken their time getting to Palolem. They'd left Delhi the night they'd bumped into each other in the market, they'd waited until it was dark and then boarded a small, colourful bus. Delhi's streets were full of small, colourful buses and, on Manjan's suggestion, they'd picked the bus that looked the most like all the other buses. Ladyjan laughed at this but Manjan didn't know why.

On the bus, Ladyjan sat underneath Manjan's bag with a scarf around her face. Provided no one saw her board the bus, there was no chance anyone would see her on it. They got off the bus three hours later in a city called Rewari.

'Could they find you here?' Manjan had asked at 4 am, knowing that neither of them knew where they were.

'I don't know,' Ladyjan answered. 'On the lorries I travel from Delhi to Surat, and it takes a whole day and night. Where I go in between is...it would be a guess. There were no windows.' She had apologetic eyes but Manjan refused to let her feel bad.

'Good,' he said. 'Shall we get another bus then?' He smiled an insanely wide smile and Ladyjan laughed.

Thirty-nine hours of the next three days were spent on buses, twenty were spent walking and studying maps to see where they were, four were spent eating and nine were spent sleeping. When they knew they were a safe distance from anywhere Ladyjan had been before, they slept for fifteen hours under a statue in a park.

'So where are we?' Ladyjan asked, waking up. Manjan rubbed his eyes.

'Safety,' he said calmly, and they kissed. That night, they

talked, drank wine, laughed and, um, well…did something rather more intimate, but I won't go into that here.

It was in Bombay that Manjan told his father about Ladyjan. He'd rung and apologised for not coming home when he had planned to, and his father had been understanding.

'You have to stop apologising,' he'd told Manjan, shouting so his son would hear him over the traffic.

'I've met a girl,' Manjan shouted back, 'she's called Jan too.' Manjan's father couldn't hear his son, so he told him that he was very well and thanked him for asking. 'No, I've met a girl.' Again, his father told him to stop apologising. Manjan looked at Ladyjan. 'He can't hear me,' he said and Ladyjan took the phone from him.

'Hello,' she said. It was Ladyjan's feminine voice that helped Manjan's father understand what his son had been trying to tell him and his eyes filled with tears. He welled up and thought about how happy his wife would have been.

'Oh Jan, lad,' he said, instantly forgetting it wasn't his son on the other end, 'that's why you stayed in India.' The doorbell rang. 'I've got to get the door. Stay there, I'll be right back. I'm so happy for you lad.'

'I can't hear him,' Ladyjan said, 'but I think he knows what you're trying to tell him.' She passed the phone back to Manjan who held it up to his ear to find that his father had gone, so he hung up.

'Can I help you?' Manjan's father said to the wide-faced man at the door. The man looked at a passport in his hand and then at Manjan's father. He nodded to himself and walked straight into Manjan's father, pushing him back into his own house and away from the view of the street. The wide-faced man looked behind him and then shut the door.

Bombay was home to Manjan and Ladyjan for a few weeks. Ladyjan didn't want to keep moving. She was finally free from her captors and frankly sick of transport. They used some of her newly acquired inordinate amount of money for lavish accommodation and good food and Manjan treated the city how he had treated Fishton when he was younger. He met people and asked them questions about themselves, their lives and the places they had been, although now he was a little older he was more tactful about it. The truth was, he was just trying to impress Ladyjan. That's all he was ever trying to do and, to that end, it was in Bombay that he started repeatedly imitating different animals to make her laugh. Ladyjan always took over to see if she could keep it up for longer but in her eyes, Manjan had changed her life. She didn't need impressing.

Everything about Bombay was fascinating to Manjan; the huge white monuments that scattered the city, the wealth that dominated the skyline and the poverty that spread under its bridges. Together, they'd watched a Bollywood movie being filmed from on top of a grassy hill just outside the city and they'd walked along a littered beach lined with fully clothed sunbathers. The beach was depressing, but because they were together, it didn't matter what they were seeing or doing; everything seemed right.

'We should visit Nepal,' Manjan had suggested, while enjoying a walk along the beach and stepping over a crumpled can that had at some point been on fire. He'd hated Nepal, but with Ladyjan he'd probably quite like Pokhara's huge crystal-clear lake and majestic sun-peaked mountains. He might not mind the jungle's heat and the wildlife that lived there and, in Kathmandu, he and Ladyjan would probably embrace the bustle and live in the moment. Actually, now he thought about it, Nepal sounded quite fun.

Ladyjan finally felt safe and thought it seemed quite unlikely that she'd end up back in the rear end of a truck hauling fish and lamps across the country again, so she nodded.

'Nepal sounds good,' she said, 'maybe after Goa?'

'Goa sounds good too,' Manjan had replied. 'Everywhere sounds good.'

Manjan and Ladyjan spent their first night together on Palolem, Goa, the way they'd spent their first night together in Sweden – outside and talking. They talked about how Ladyjan had, once a week, stared at an airport screen wistful of coming to India. They talked about how Manjan had only seen the bad in the places he'd gone after Russia. They spoke about the day Ladyjan had missed their plane, why she had done it and what might have been if she hadn't. They even spoke about Manjan's mum's funeral and how his father had lost his passport. Manjan made a joke about Ladyjan stealing his father's passport but Ladyjan didn't laugh. Instead, she looked through the passports she had left in her bag.

'I don't have them all any more,' she said sadly. 'They took most of them. Maybe I did steal it.' Manjan just laughed and told her it didn't matter. Then they spoke about his father and how on the phone earlier he hadn't seemed himself. He had been more...shifty.

In the dark hours of the morning, Ladyjan told Manjan that life really wasn't like it was in films. In films, people go out of their way to make things happen; someone offers a romantic gesture or solves a crime. In reality fate offers the gesture and solves the crime. It was fate that Ladyjan had stolen from Manjan that day at the harbour in Sweden and it was his life experience that had taught him that stowing away on a boat was a 'good idea'. Ladyjan could have missed Manjan at the market a few months ago (just a minute would have made the difference) or she could have been sent to a different country to collect illegal lamps. Fate had bought them together then, too, and if it hadn't have done this time, it would have done soon enough. Ladyjan held Manjan tight and he held her back...

...For a really long time.

As the sun started to rise, Manjan and Ladyjan paddled in the same water that nearly forty years later Shakey would drop a fishing rod into, and they watched as the beach started to fill with Indian tourists.

During their single week on Palolem they visited a spice farm, learnt to ride motorcycles and tried yoga for the first time. One day they climbed over the rocks at the end of the beach and found another beach with rocks at both ends. Over those rocks they'd found yet another beach which they walked down for about an hour, and then, at the other end of this beach, they'd found more rocks. It was a magical week.

Nepal would have been magical too, had they have gone.

The late afternoon sun was cooling down and Ladyjan and Manjan had just enjoyed a fruit salad from a health restaurant that had recently opened on Palolem. Manjan sat on the sand and rested on his elbows. Ladyjan joined him.

'Should we go to Nepal?' she asked, 'or should we just live in our little beach bubble?'

'I don't think the bubble is the beach,' Manjan said. 'Nepal would be a bubble too.' Ladyjan rested her head on Manjan's bare stomach. She was feeling tired and hot.

'I've got a bad feeling,' she said. Then she stopped talking. A few birds communicated in their bird way ('Cacaa?' one bird asked and another agreed, 'cacaa!') and a crab rolled some sand into a ball (bubbler crabs do that). Manjan stroked Ladyjan's hair and made a noise that prompted her to go on.

'Not a bad feeling,' she continued, before pausing again, 'but, it depends on what you think.' Manjan made the same noise but he wasn't in any rush. Ladyjan could say whatever it was that she wanted to say whenever it was that she wanted to say it. He looked out to the sea and enjoyed its gentle lapping along the soft golden coast while the words 'I'm pregnant' washed through him.

The phone rang in Manjan's father's house and Manjan daydreamed about his mother answering. Would she have been happy if he'd been able to tell her his news? She did like babies, but she wouldn't have liked the fact that neither she nor Manjan's father had met Ladyjan. He imagined her ordering him to get the next flight home and to bring Ladyjan with him. She was never rational under pressure. Despite this, Manjan would have given anything to speak to his mother now. The phone rang again.

Manjan hadn't reacted badly. After a long but not uncomfortable silence, he'd told Ladyjan that their bubble would just get bigger and that now it would never pop.

Ladyjan had already decided that she would keep the baby regardless of Manjan's reaction but was nevertheless relieved with his response. They'd slept early that night after buying a melon from a teenage girl who sold them along the beach.

The phone rang again. Manjan thought it odd that his father hadn't answered already. He normally answered on the second ring and it was still early in England. It was unlikely that he'd have gone out yet. Again it rang, and Manjan had the most unsettling thought. His father might be with a woman. He shook his head and threw this thought away. His dad was dedicated to his mother.

Just as Manjan was about to hang up the phone there was a noise on the other end.

'Hello,' said his father, who normally said 'Aye'.

Manjan paused and listened to his father's heavy breathing before asking him how he was. There was another breathy pause before his father uncomfortably answered that he was well.

'Are you sure?' Manjan started, 'You sound...'

'I, I need to you to come home,' his father interrupted. Behind his father's breath Manjan thought he could hear whispering.

'You need to come home, and bring your girlfriend with you,' his father said. The whisper sounded like it was happy with Manjan's father.

'Um...' Manjan replied, unsure of what to say and increasingly aware of his distance from home.

'I haven't met her yet,' his father said quickly before more heavy breathing. 'I need to meet her'.

Manjan didn't reply for a while and listened closely to the line, pressing the receiver hard against his ear. There was someone else there and whoever it was wasn't a new woman.

In the pause in conversation Manjan could hear his father's need to tell him something that he couldn't. Desperation dominated the shared silence and Manjan could hear fear in his father's breath.

There was a large crash in the background and the whisper turned into an inaudible shout. Before the line went dead Manjan heard his father's panicked voice shout 'Don't come!' and then there was silence.

26

A FISH OUT OF WATER

Fishton. 1977.

There is only one road into Fishton. There are two ways in total, if you include by boat, but Ladyjan knew that the lamp-smuggling fish factory had a heavy presence down at the docks. Driving was their only option. She also knew that there was at least one dangerous man patrolling the nearest airport, so when Manjan and Ladyjan returned to England they landed at Victoridon airport, 300 miles south of Fishton.

They visited a charity shop (a classic and authentic Victoridon charity shop, or so they were told by the owner) to search for a disguise for Ladyjan. Something she could wear on the journey north. She was too feminine for fake facial hair and it was too cold in the UK to shave her own hair, so in the end they decided on a large woollen hat that could be pulled down over her forehead, and some large sunglasses. They bought an extra-large jumper in the men's section which would hide both her feminine shape and ever-expanding pregnant belly. She would have to concentrate hard not to keep touching the bump. She liked touching her bump.

'How do I look?' Ladyjan asked, after changing into her new outfit in the bathroom of a small car rental on the outskirts of Victoridon. Manjan made a jokey purring sound and smiled but neither of them laughed.

They'd discussed what they would do when they got to Fishton all day on Palolem, all night on the bus back to Bombay and for the majority of the flight to Victoridon (they slept for the rest), but there hadn't really been any outcome. All they knew was that Manjan's father had shouted down the phone instructing Manjan not to come home and that he seemed to have someone with him. Someone Manjan's father sounded scared of.

Fishton was a dangerous place for Ladyjan so before they'd boarded the plane Manjan had told her not to come, but Ladyjan had insisted. She'd spent a lot of her life alone and, on reflection, she hadn't liked it. Besides, she'd already left Manjan at one airport and as it had been the worst decision of her life, she certainly wasn't going to do it again. Neither Ladyjan nor Manjan knew what they would find back at Manjan's childhood home, but as Ladyjan kept nervously pointing out, it was unlikely to have anything to do with the fish factory. They didn't know who Manjan or his father was.

Ladyjan wore her hat, sunglasses and jumper for the entire drive from Victoridon but her disguise didn't stop her from holding her breath and shrinking into herself every time they passed a lorry or van. She offered to drive, but Manjan said no. He thought she was too shaken up, but kept quiet when he was so lost in his own nervous thoughts that he went the wrong way, adding an hour to their journey. He also decided not to tell her when a bus nearly scared him into the barrier at the side of the road.

By the time they got to the town down the road from Fishton it was dark. Had they looked upon entering the town they would have seen the most beautiful clear winter sea, but that's the thing with fear – you always end up missing something wonderful. Manjan drove down the quaint and cobbled streets to Hylad's old house. There was a light on upstairs and a figure was in the window but it wasn't Hylad. It was a small lady's figure, probably mid-twenties, bouncing a baby on her shoulder. Manjan's heart sank, even though his father had told him that Hylad didn't live there any more. Seeing Hylad really would have helped rationalise what they were doing.

The baby in the window cried and the lady's figure bounced more vigorously. Manjan looked at Ladyjan with love in his eyes. Then he looked at her hidden bump.

'We should sleep in the car,' he said a little sadly. Ladyjan didn't reply straight away. She held her tummy with her right hand and nervously stroked her little finger with her thumb on her left.

Eventually she said, 'It's dark,' without looking at Manjan. 'We should go to your father's house tonight.'

Lots of people in Alistair's line of work lived for assignments like this one, but not Alistair. He worked for the money only. When he'd knocked on the door he'd expected to see a junkie, not a lonely old man. But work was work and he'd pushed his way through.

It hadn't taken Alistair long to tie the old man to a chair in the living room, and thankfully he hadn't had to use much force. The man had submitted, probably realising he wouldn't stand much of a chance against a man of Alistair's stature.

Alistair had been trained to torture people to get any information he needed, but it soon became clear that the old man didn't have the information he needed to give. For starters, he thought Jan was a boy.

'This is your passport, yes?' Alistair had demanded, and the old man had spluttered a yes (it was pretty obvious; his face was in the picture). 'You know Jan?' Alistair had continued with a stern, wide face.

'Why?' Manjan's father answered, but a look from Alistair prompted him to continue, 'Yes, I know Jan. He's my son. He's in India, miles away, so you might as well leave.'

The old man was clearly mad. He thought Jan was an English boy, not a Swedish girl, and he was convinced he was related to her. But he was definitely the man on the passport (the first person on Alistair's list of passports to intimidate) and he knew that Jan was in India. And, as it turned out, Jan rang the old man regularly. Alistair locked the doors and set up camp.

For the next few days Alistair and the old man survived on the out-of-date cans of baked beans and lentils that the old man hadn't cleared from the cupboards when his wife had died. Alistair sat opposite the old man every day and every night. They chatted and, as it turned out, got along rather well, given the circumstances, but the old man remained tied to the chair and next to the phone so he could answer when it rang and instruct Jan to return.

'Hello,' the old man had said, while breathing heavily the first time he'd answered, only to be asked about his car insurance.

'Hello,' the old man had said, while breathing heavily the second time he'd answered, and then had a very short conversation with one of his fellow fisherman. He wouldn't be down at the docks for quite some time he told them.

'Hello,' the old man had said, while breathing heavily the third time he'd answered. 'I'm well,' he said after a long pause. 'I, I need you to come home.'

Manjan barely recognised his old house when they pulled up opposite with the car lights off. The upstairs curtains were open, the lawn was overgrown and the light outside the front door hadn't been turned on. Manjan couldn't be sure whether these small oddities were something he should worry about or just the result of his father living alone. He hadn't seen his father for a while – maybe he was now the type of man to forget to close curtains, mow lawns and turn outside lights on.

'I'm just going to knock,' Manjan whispered, and Ladyjan nodded with an unnatural speed. Even through her fear, she noticed how nice it was to see where Manjan had spent his childhood. It was nothing special, a terraced house with a tiny weed-covered path leading up to a dark door. Two windows upstairs, one window downstairs. Once loved.

'Don't forget I'm here,' she muttered, and Manjan kissed her.

Outside, the air was cold, and Manjan wrapped his arms around his torso. The gate creaked the way it always had when it opened and Manjan looked down at the familiar cracks in the path. Did the downstairs curtain move? Maybe his father would be in.

He knocked. No one answered but Manjan thought he heard a snuffling noise inside. He knocked again and waited, rubbing his arms to keep himself warm. After a minute or so he opened the letterbox. It was dark inside and there were newspapers strewn across the floor. If it wasn't for the snoring the house would seem abandoned, but there was snoring.

Manjan held onto the small roof that protruded out above the front door in the same way he had when he was a child, lifted himself up onto it and wedged his fingers into the crack between the window and the frame. With a little wriggle of his ice-white hands it opened, and he managed to squeeze himself into his old bedroom. It smelt of whisky.

The landing outside was also covered in newspapers, baked-bean cans and mouldy-smelling towels. Towels Manjan recognised as the subject of many of his mother's mad washing weekends. She'd wash everything on those weekends, dirty or not. Manjan stepped over a large sweatshirt that he did not recognise and moved downstairs as quietly as he could, towards the snoring.

At the bottom of the stairs, Manjan froze as a set of pale, slender fingers pushed through the letterbox.

'Jan,' a whisper came into the hall. Manjan breathed a stifled sigh of relief and quietly walked to the door past the room which contained the loud sleeper.

'Shh,' he shh'd in a more hushed voice than people normally shh. His fingers slowly opened the door to see a clearly pregnant girl wearing a hat, sunglasses and a very baggy men's jumper. She mouthed the words 'I couldn't leave you' but made no sound. They looked at each other without moving for a few seconds before Ladyjan turned her head towards the snoring room. 'Your father?' she mouthed and Manjan shrugged, but his eyes said that he suspected not.

Together they carefully trod to the doorway and peered round. There, spread out across Manjan's old living-room floor, with one arm across his chest and the other resting by his side, was the wide-faced man from the airport. He was dressed in a large military jacket and jeans and the room stank of smoke and booze. Ladyjan put her hand to her mouth, her eyes shifted to sadness and tears began to silently roll down her cheeks. She pushed her back against the wall, so she couldn't see into the living room any more.

Manjan didn't recognise the wide-faced man, but it wasn't his father.

Alistair awoke with a banging head, as he had for the past few days. He knew how his day would pan out. He would make himself a strong black coffee, read the newspaper (not the newspaper he would normally read but some tabloid tosh the old man had delivered every day). Then, he'd watch daytime television until 3 pm, when he would eat whatever was left at the back of the cupboards. He'd spend his evening continuing to empty the old man's drinks cabinet. Waiting really was easy.

He went to rub his eyes with his left hand. His hand moved but his arm wouldn't budge. He pulled harder and felt a pain in his forearm and bicep. He turned his head and saw he had been tied to various things in the room – curtain rails, chairs, the doorknob. One of the ropes even left the room, out the window and presumably onto a tree.

Alistair roared angrily and thrust his body upwards in an attempt to break free but he remained stuck to the spot. Focusing his eyes through the pain in his head he saw a girl sitting on the chair where Manjan's father had been tied. It was Jan. He spat in her direction, but it landed on his own chest. Ladyjan laughed and called him something she'd never called anyone before. She sneered when she said it.

'Where's my father?' A man's voice came from a different direction. Alistair frowned and looked around him. Someone he had never met was sitting on the sofa next to him.

'Who are you?' he asked.

'Where's my father?'

Alistair looked confused. 'You are Jan too?' he concluded. No one said anything for a long time. At last Alistair shouted angrily, 'You are Jan too?'

Both Manjan and Ladyjan jumped, and Manjan shouted back, 'Where is my father?'

'Screw your father,' Alistair screamed again, thrusting his body like a fish out of water. Without words he continued to yell and writhe. All the furniture and décor to which Alistair was attached began to shake and Manjan and Ladyjan felt as if they were in the centre of an earthquake. Alistair broke his right leg free, smashing a nest of glass tables as he did. He kicked the floor repeatedly, moving his other leg violently to the side, over and over again.

Ladyjan jumped out of her seat in a panicked frenzy and attempted to hold Alistair's free leg still.

He kicked her arm.

He kicked her chest.

He kicked her stomach, hard.

Manjan leapt across the top half of Alistair's body and held him down, while Ladyjan managed to restrain the rogue leg.

Alistair spat again, this time right into Manjan's face. Their eyes were only inches away from one another.

'Your father is at sea,' Alistair smirked. Manjan looked confused. His father was a fisherman. Alistair raised his eyebrows and quietly laughed, so close to Manjan that he could feel the breath on his cheeks.

Manjan had never been a violent person. It wasn't how he'd been raised. But now it appeared the people who had raised him were no longer around to see his demise, so he lifted his arm behind his head, tucked his thumb underneath his fingers and made a fist that would have hurt himself as much as it would have hurt Alistair, had it landed.

But it didn't land.

The veins in Alistair's thick neck raised and his face went purple as he lunged forwards, managing to head-butt Manjan in his chin at the same time as pulling the rope that was wrapped around his shoulders. The oak drinks cabinet at the other end of the rope fell and hit Manjan in the back of the head, and Alistair in the front of the head. For both of them, the world went black.

They hadn't found much on Alistair's sleeping body before they'd tied him up – a wallet, a clock on a pendant, some cigarettes – but there was one thing that Ladyjan had deemed worth keeping. Manjan's father's passport.

She'd seen it in the breast pocket of Alistair's jacket while Manjan had been looking for weapons in his wallet (there weren't any), and not wanting Manjan to see the passport, she'd tucked it into her jeans.

She let go of the unconscious Alistair's now still leg and

shook Manjan, but he didn't wake. She pushed the drinks cabinet off the two men, grazing Manjan's back against the lock and accidentally cutting Alistair's face with a broken liquor bottle as she did.

She tightened the rope back around Alistair's foot and tied it to the chair where she had been sitting, and lifted both of Manjan's feet in the air. She'd lifted Manjan once before, when they'd been trying to reach some bananas from a tree in Goa, but it was much harder without his cooperation and this time neither were laughing. She dragged his body through the door, into the hall and out of the house. Outside, she lifted him from under the armpits down the path and finally into the back of the car. She could hear him lightly breathing and she smiled.

She went to sit in the driver's seat but paused with one foot inside the car. Then, she took her one foot back outside the car and walked confidently back into the house. She didn't look at Alistair as she walked straight past the living room and up the stairs, stepping over a large sweatshirt which, for all she knew, could always have been there. She stepped into the first door she could see and into what used to be Manjan's father's bedroom. She opened the top drawer next to the bed, pushed aside some old handwritten letters from someone who referred to themselves as 'stable girl' and found a passport. The picture on the back page was of an attractive lady a bit younger than Manjan's father.

She reached into her jeans, pulled out Manjan's father's passport, placed it in the drawer, and wept as she held the pain in her stomach with both hands.

27

A FISH IN THE WATER

Not so far from Fishton. 1977.

'You're scum,' Alistair had hissed, holding Manjan's father's head back by his hair so his neck was facing the sea. 'What are you?' Manjan's father gasped.

'Jan,' he stuttered, 'my son.'

'What are you?' Alistair said louder, and Manjan's father quietly agreed that he was scum.

'That's right, you're scum.' Alistair pushed his hand forward, forcing Manjan's father's face back into the water.

The night air was cold, and Alistair's face had gone white. He could barely feel his hands and his thick scarf was unravelling from his neck. He'd tighten it, but he needed his hands on Manjan's father, one of the many downsides of his job. Alistair didn't enjoy dunking Manjan's father. The man seemed nice, and Alistair knew that he was only protecting his son. But there was a chain of command and, just as so many people feared Alistair, Alistair feared the chain.

He pulled Manjan's father's head back again. There was a loud splash which was shortly interrupted by choking.

'What are you going to do when Jan rings again?' Alistair spat into Manjan's father's ear. There was no reply. 'What are you going to do?' Manjan's father finally managed to take a proper breath. 'Say it.'

'Bring him home,' came a weak and whispered voice.

'Say it!' Alistair shouted.

'Bring him home,' Manjan's father said, trying to sound more convincing. They both knew he was lying.

Alistair pushed the old man's head back underwater and shuffled on his knees. Each dunk had bought a strange calm to their surroundings. The sea was rough, but the light from Alistair's car was casting a beautifully sharp ray through it, and the grass behind them could be heard in the wind. Alistair knew they were alone; no one would be anywhere near this spot. He relaxed and took in the moment. When they were back at the house, he would apologise to the old man and make him a cup of tea. He just needed to get the message to him, that if he did not comply in the finding of his son and his son's girlfriend, it was curtains for the three of them.

Alistair thought about his future. He wasn't sure he wanted to stay in this line of business forever. He quite liked being a security guard at the airport, but he couldn't help but feel that his other line of work, the line of intimidating and killing, might be hindering his prospects somewhat. But he didn't know how to stop. The two Jans were quite good at escaping, and he felt he'd had a certain rapport with the female one a few times in the airport. Maybe he could use the old man to find them, and then leave with them.

He thought about this for a very, very long time.

The lake was colder than the night air and Manjan's father wasn't wearing a scarf. He was wearing his pyjamas and they were soaking through. He felt hot. Heat comes with panic.

Under the water, he wondered if he would live. He thought about Jan and he thought about Jan's mother. His stable girl and their renegade colt.

Then he thought about Ladyjan, whom he'd never met. Maybe she was Jan's stable girl.

A school of fish went past Manjan's father's face, but he didn't notice them in the dark, and they didn't notice him. They had their own lives to deal with and each other to think about.

Manjan's father had always done what he could do for an easy life. Such chaos always seemed to happen around him.

His thoughts focused solely on Jan as his consciousness faded. He wanted to tell him how proud he was of him and how, even in his absence, Jan had made life worth living.

Manjan's father passed out, feeling nothing but the gratitude and the love he'd felt all through his life.

'That's enough,' Alistair said calmly, pulling Manjan's father's head back out of the water. 'I'm going to let go of you, and then I'm taking you home. Then, we wait.'

Alistair released his grip and the old man's face fell back into the water, lifeless.

28

NO LIFE

Sweden. 1978.

Ladyjan drove to the airport from Manjan's old house. She knew they hadn't killed Alistair because he'd been breathing when she'd dragged Manjan off him, but they needed to leave England if they were to be safe. By the time Manjan had regained consciousness, she'd already purchased two flights to Sweden.

Ladyjan found them a small flat on the South Coast to live in. It was small, dark and damp but it was enough to keep them warm through the winter. They didn't have much money left and what they did have they spent on rent and food. After a week, Ladyjan found part-time employment at a very low rate, serving tea down at the harbour, and she used the income to buy second-hand baby clothes and a small bed.

She spent the other part of her time carefully constructing a letter to a group of people she had seen but never actually met. It needed to be striking, apologetic and anonymous, ready to be pinned up in the sheltered statue house outside the city hall. Maybe Manjan would pin it up for her.

Manjan did not find employment, nor did he look. He spent his days sitting next to the only window in their small flat, looking at the spot where, eight years ago, Ladyjan had shouted '*hjälp! Hjälp!*' to the little and large policemen before they arrested Manjan. He missed his father and he missed his mother. Ladyjan was all he had now but he was too depressed to be grateful for her presence. He couldn't see past his grief to appreciate her efforts down at the docks to provide them both with shelter, and he didn't much care for her gentle persuasion for him to look for work. He knew that the baby would change their lives and he was looking forward to the distraction, but until then, he would sit.

To the people listed below,

I am sorry that I took your passports.

I will leave them under the furthest west tree in St. Djurgården on 31st March.

I also took your money. Please know that it has helped me in my life and that I am grateful.

These are the passports I have managed to hold on to.

If I took you passport and you do not find yourself on this list, I am sorry.

Yours apologetically,

x

In early January 1978, Ladyjan started bleeding. Six months into her pregnancy she still hadn't felt anything kick and she hadn't gotten any bigger. For his part, Manjan felt responsible for leading Ladyjan into his father's house and Ladyjan felt stupid for following him and even stupider for trying to restrain the man with the wide face. More than anything, and overwhelmingly, they both felt unhappy.

CHAPTER 29

THE PEOPLE LISTED BELOW

St. Djurgården. 31st March 1978.

Under the furthest west tree in St. Djurgården sat a stranger's leather wallet. It hadn't been there the day before and no one had seen who had placed it there at midnight. Well, a small quail who occupied the tree had, as it stirred from slumber, but it wasn't going to tell anyone.

At six-thirty that morning, a lady walking her dog paid no attention to the wallet. In fact, she paid no attention to anything around her. She didn't notice the now wide-awake quail and she didn't notice the sun beginning to rise. She didn't notice her dog having a good sniff of the wallet before chewing the strap right through and then jumping up at a squirrel in the tree, and she didn't notice that she was being watched.

At quarter past seven a man in a suit walked briskly into St. Djurgården through the west gate and straight up to the tree. He looked up the trunk and then back down the trunk quickly, stopping at the chewed leather wallet. He lifted it by the strap, opened it up and rummaged through the passports, paying no attention to the pictures of strangers in the other passports. When he found his, he gave himself a small smile, dusted his already-clean black shoe with his hand and hurried out of St. Djurgården the same way he had entered.

For the next five hours the wallet remained watched but untouched. It was a cold Friday and St. Djurgården was reasonably quiet. Until lunchtime, that is. Around 12.30, a man in a novelty bowtie strolled towards the tree from the north gate eating a sandwich. He stopped at the tree, having seen the wallet, but continued to eat his sandwich. He was in no rush to look for his passport and why should he be? It had already expired.

At 12.37, a lady with large purple glasses and a blond perm entered St. Djurgården from the south gate. She was in no rush either. She'd never used her passport before and she didn't expect to, but she had no one to meet on her lunch break and fancied the walk.

'Passport?' the novelty tie-wearing man asked. The lady in the purple glasses smiled a tight-lipped smile and nodded. 'Same,' the man said. The lady picked up the wallet in her thumb and forefinger, being careful not to touch the chewed-up strap too much. 'I bet you can't guess which one's mine,' the man challenged, with a mouth full of sandwich. The lady quietly laughed a one-syllable laugh but didn't reply or attempt to guess which passport belonged to the man. 'Seriously,' the man encouraged, 'go on, see if you can find me.'

'Um…' the lady replied, fingering through the pictures in the different sleeves, part looking for herself and part looking for the man. 'This one?' The man looked at the passport in the lady's hand. The man in the picture was a little younger than he was now, but then what picture of him wasn't? The hair was fuller and the jawline stronger. Put simply, the man in the picture was a better-looking version of himself.

'That's not me,' the man said, and the lady looked up at him as if maybe he was wrong. 'But thank you, I'll take it as a compliment.' The lady took her purple glasses off to look at the passport closer. It did look like the man.

'You're better-looking than the man in this passport,' she said, looking away.

The man shifted on his feet awkwardly and his cheeks turned red. Neither of them said anything while the lady continued to rummage through the wallet. Finally, she looked her younger self in the face and placed her hands on the floor to lift herself up. The man offered her a hand and she took it.

'It's expired.' She offered him his passport and he looked at the picture.

'That's me,' he said.

'You've travelled.'

'Not much.'

'More than me.'

'Well…' he started, before taking her passport from her other hand and looking through the blank pages, 'yes. More than you.' He gave her passport back. 'Where would you like to go?' The lady saw from the open page in his passport that the man had been to Poland.

'Poland,' she answered.

The man flinched, but then smiled. 'The north coast is beautiful,' he said.

From the other side of the park, behind the public toilets, Ladyjan and Manjan watched the man offer the blond, permed, purpled glasses-wearing lady some of his sandwich. They watched the lady decline the offer but point to the coffee kiosk across the park. The lady and the man queued together, bought two coffees and sat down.

Over the next hour six different people visited the wallet under the tree. Five left with passports and one looked through the wallet and, not finding any money, walked away again. The lady and man noticed each new visitor from their table and quietly laughed together at the hopeful one who left empty-handed.

Ladyjan thought about the night she and Manjan had first spent together down at the port before stowing away on Valter and Saga's boat. They'd had so much to talk about that night. All through Poland and Russia they'd joked and laughed. They'd made each other feel good. In India they'd helped each other – she'd helped Manjan during a hard time grieving and he'd helped her escape her life in a terrifying illegal lamp ring. They were closer than ever in India.

But now...now they barely talked at all. Ladyjan spent a lot of her time now, at work, feeling deeply unhappy, or at home in their little flat arguing with Manjan. Manjan spent his time arguing with Ladyjan, or not doing anything. She started to cry silently.

Manjan did the same but neither of them noticed one another.

The lady and the man stood up either side of the table and left through the same gate. After their respective work days, they went to their respective flats before meeting again that night in a restaurant. After a meal, they returned to their respective flats to pack. The next morning, they met at the docks, and boarded a ship for Poland.

CHAPTER 30

A SMALL QUAIL WHO OCCUPIED THE TREE

Sweden. 1978.

The small quail who occupied the tree had enjoyed five peaceful weeks. Other quails in the park had chosen to nest in bushes low down, which gave her and her eggs some privacy in the high branches.

She hadn't found it easy building her nest. The weaving was a doddle, but she could only fly short distances, so every time she found a good twig for insulation she'd have to make several short flights back to the nest, and that made the whole process very slow. In the cold early morning light she looked at her eggs lovingly, and sang a merry tune. In only a few weeks they would hatch.

The five boxes that surrounded the only door made the already small flat even smaller by a third, but to Manjan it felt bigger. To him, the boxes were a reminder of an absence that greatly upset him. Ladyjan, who was currently at work down at the port, would return to the flat in an hour. She would pick up the boxes one by one and put them in her friend's car. Then she would leave.

Manjan looked at the door, each box was labelled in black marker, as if Ladyjan owned enough to require a filing system.

CLOTHES
HOUSEHOLD
KEEP
OTHER PEOPLE'S THINGS
JAN

Ladyjan's life packed into five boxes. The box marked 'KEEP' implied that she didn't feel the need to keep the contents of the other boxes but Manjan knew that wouldn't be true. She would at least keep other people's things – that was, until she had returned them to other people. With the exception of 'OTHER PEOPLE'S THINGS', none of the boxes were full. Manjan had checked through 'CLOTHES' and 'HOUSEHOLD' to make sure Ladyjan hadn't forgotten anything and that she would be OK, although he knew that she would be. He did not look through the box labelled 'OTHER PEOPLE'S THINGS'. Instead, he opened it, rummaged through a pile of his own things that he had ready to pack in the corner of the room, pulled out a phot of the two of them and placed it inside the box.

Manjan did not look in the box labelled 'JAN' either. In his naivety, he thought this box would be private to Ladyjan. It was only later, when he was packing his own boxes, that Manjan saw some of his things were missing.

The quail watched St. Djurgården from her branch. Her eggs had started moving last night and she felt an overwhelming need to protect them now more than ever. It was 6.30 and the sun was beginning to rise. The park was nearly empty, with the exception of an absentminded lady walking her dog and two other people whom the quail had watched hide behind the public toilets on the other side of the park. Thankfully, the lady walking her dog paid no attention to the quail or to the eggs high up in the tree. She didn't notice her dog having a good sniff of a wallet that had been left below the quail's tree and she didn't notice her dog chewing the wallet's strap straight through.

The quail looked towards the public toilets. The wallet had been left there in the night by the people hiding behind them and she wondered if they minded the lady's dog destroying it but there was no movement from the pair.

Neither the lady nor the quail noticed the dog drop the wallet and jump up at the first branch in the furthest-west tree in St. Djurgården. They didn't notice the squirrel running up the tree away from the dog and the lady didn't see the squirrel knock into a small nest of eggs in a panic.

The quail saw. The quail watched as her nest wobbled to one side of the branch she was sitting on. She bobbed her head forward to hold on to the straw to protect her eggs, but the nest fell. The quail watched the nest hit the ground. She watched as her eggs broke and she watched as the dog ate them.

Ladyjan's friend looked forward awkwardly. She'd known Ladyjan when she was a little girl but she did not know the man Ladyjan was with. She didn't want to interrupt but she also wanted to start the long night-drive back to Sollefteå, a small riverside town further north.

Manjan's skin was pale from the cold air and his eyes shone with motionless tears.

'Where will you be?' he asked. This wasn't the first time he'd asked.

'It doesn't matter,' Ladyjan replied. Her tears weren't as motionless as Manjan's and bright thin streams were running down her cheeks. She stood tall on her toes and kissed Manjan softly. For a moment everything was still. The sound of the icy air returned to their ears as they parted lips and Ladyjan said the last thing Manjan would hear her say.

'We'll meet when fate next decides.'

The small quail who used to occupy the tree now occupied an old, unused car engine. There were two quails to the right of her and one on the left. There was also a nest but it didn't belong to her and she tended to ignore it.

The day after the small quail had lost her eggs, she'd flown out of St. Djurgården (over the north gate), across several roads and over many small buildings until she didn't know where she was any more. Then, tired and emotional, she'd stopped to take stock of her surroundings. Since leaving the park she had only seen suburbia, people and man-made machines. This suited her fine – she never wanted to see a tree, a squirrel or a dog again.

A large yellow dustbin truck drove slowly down the road, stopping at every few doors to allow the men working behind it to catch up. The noise was deafening and the quail basked in it. It seemed the more sound that entered her ears, the less thinking could happen inside her head. For three streets she hopped alongside the truck, concentrating only on the whirring of the engine and the hissing sound the mechanical arm made every time it lifted a bin. At the end of the last street, the men behind the truck hopped into the cabin and it drove away down a highway.

For quite some time the quail couldn't hear anything. She saw two people talking and one person looking in their bin, annoyed, but she did not hear any of them. After a while there was a ringing sound that she had never heard before, and finally, after the ringing sound had gone, she heard the sound of a small quail.

She was startled. Looking around, she saw the end of a wing as it disappeared into a large garage. She had already flown further than she had ever flown before that day but she picked up her feet and darted at the garage.

Inside it was dark and noisy. She saw the quail hop onto the bonnet of a car and under a raised hood. Hoping to find some form of safety she followed, pushing her little plump body between two pipes and into a clearing where the engine should be. The three quails already occupying the engine space didn't acknowledge her and the noise from the garage filled her ears as her thoughts once again escaped her head.

The small quail who occupied the old, unused car engine, did so for the next year and thought she was happy. From the engine and the street outside she did not see any trees or any squirrels. She did not see any dogs either. The noise allowed her to not think about her eggs, and the darkness felt a million miles away (although it was in fact less than one) from the natural light of St. Djurgården. But every evening, when the noise stopped, and the ringing sound had died, there was something in the back of the small quail's thoughts that just wouldn't go away. The old, unused car engine miles away from her old home felt good. Not thinking felt good. But the small thought that occupied her mind knew that it wasn't right.

Manjan made no effort in packing his own boxes. There was nothing he cared about keeping and he didn't know where he would be taking them. He had a flight booked back to England but he didn't know why. He didn't know anyone there any more and the boxes wouldn't be able to fit on a plane. But the flat needed to be cleared in two days so Manjan put everything haphazardly into boxes. He didn't label the boxes but he could have labelled them all 'Jan' because everything he owned made him think of her.

Late that night Manjan drank and chewed some old paan he'd found in one of his old travelling bags. It didn't taste good but he didn't care. After spitting it onto the living room floor and putting more into his mouth, he passed out.

The next morning he woke up alone. He rubbed his eyes, got dressed, walked past the newly packed boxes and out of the door.

Down at the Port, Manjan saw that three of the large vessels had people on them preparing to set out to sea, and he waited. When no one was looking he stepped onto the middle vessel, hid in a storage room and waited to find out where he was going.

'When fate next decides,' he said to himself, as he felt the ground beneath him move with the waves. Once again, an unknown ship sent Manjan into the world, this time completely alone and with nowhere to return.

PART FIVE

PART FIVE

CHAPTER 31

A MOSQUITO

Goa, India. 2016.

The night was quiet again, if not peaceful. The thudding had stopped but it had been replaced by a new sound.

Tapping.

The sound was frantic and was presumably intended to be rhythmic, but it didn't quite hit the mark. If it was broken down into bars, each bar would last a different length of time and include a different amount of taps. Shakey's head nodding certainly implied there was supposed to be one, but there was no pattern.

'Quiet now, isn't it?' Manjan observed through gritted teeth. Shakey continued to beat out not-a-rhythm on his thighs with his hands and smiled an insanely wide smile in agreement, completely oblivious to the pretext in Manjan's tone.

The exclusion of alcohol from Shakey's last drink had meant that his bucket had been filled with caffeinated stimulant. Without the depressant to level it out, Shakey was, in his own words, buzzing off his tits.

'It's probably the vodka,' he said, staccato, turning his head towards Manjan, and then back away from Manjan in the same short sentence.

Manjan agreed that it was probably the vodka out loud, but he was well aware that a bucket of Red Bull may not have been his best decision of the night.

'Where do you think,' Manjan started, before waiting for Shakey to jolt his head back towards him, 'the music – if you can call that music – has gone?' Shakey continued to bob his head in time to the music that wasn't there and tap his thighs to create a noise that no one in their right mind could call music. 'Every night the music stops at eleven. I can last longer than eleven.'

Shakey laughed, not unlike the Count from Sesame Street, but a little more gormless. He reached down to the sand on his left where he'd left his flyers.

'Would you say it's silent?' he asked, his insanely wide smile getting insanely wider.

'Well no, I wouldn't say...' Manjan started, but Shakey hadn't finished.

'Silent disco tonight, old-timer?' he asked, handing Manjan a flyer.

It is a curious thing when a vest turns into a moustache overnight. Most moustaches will have spent a couple of months as a vest

in a previous existence but there is normally a transition period of around forty years before they become a moustache. The vest would usually meet another vest on a beach in the 'spiritual home' (initially attracted to the neon) and then re-meet up after their flights in their 'actual home'. Here, they realise that the less vest-y version of the vest they met is actually quite nice. It's more than a little convenient that vests almost always mate with a vest from the same 'actual home' as them.

They normally rent a flat, become something useful like doctors, builders or teachers, buy a house and have children. When their children are older they re-visit the spiritual home only to see that it's been taken over by new vests. They mumble to themselves. I don't think I need to tell you what they mumble...

At this point you can be sure that the former vest has become a moustache.

The morning that Manjan stepped onto that ship down at the Swedish port and hid in the storage room was the morning that he truly became a moustache. He didn't know how long he was in the storage room because it didn't have any windows, but it was clearly rarely used as it didn't seem to store anything. On the deck above him he could hear what sounded like hundreds of people stomping on the wooden floor, laughing and presumably dancing.

In the dark, Manjan sat, holding onto his knees with his hands, arms folded. He planned to wait until the rocking had stopped and the noise had died down before he would disembark quietly to see where he was. His mood was in stark contrast to the jubilee above him. He didn't care where he ended up, but wherever it was, he knew it wouldn't be far enough away from his own life. A mosquito landed on his top lip and he hit himself in the face.

'Poxy...' he started, but then stopped and held onto his knees

again. A glass was smashed on the wood above his head, much to the party goers' delight. Manjan's moody face remained the same. By himself, the wait felt long, and was made longer by the fact that he didn't know where he was waiting to go or how long it would take to get there. After an hour or so, another glass was smashed and again there was a cheer. But then the cheer turned into two muffled men's voices seemingly having an argument with each other. The other voices hushed as a high-pitched buzzing sound landed once again on Manjan's top lip. Again, Manjan hit himself in the face, saving himself from being bitten.

He mumbled so far under his breath that no one would know that he was saying 'poxy' again. He looked around the room for his blood-sucking companion but couldn't see it.

Rolling onto his side and behind a large box, Manjan shut his eyes. It was cold and there was nothing in the storage room he could use to cover himself, so he began to shiver. Every now and again he could hear the high-pitched buzz coming from different places in the room. Looking for one mosquito would be pointless, there were clearly a family of them.

'I could've killed him,' a man shouted at another man, bursting into the room and holding his nose with a handful of blood. That's all I'll tell you about what this particular man said during his time in the storage room, as the language he used was indecent and it made it almost impossible to follow his train of thought, but let's just say he probably couldn't have killed the man who'd bloodied his nose.

Frozen to the spot, Manjan listened, hoping to get an idea of where they were going, but to no avail. While the man who said he could but definitely didn't kill another man washed his face, Manjan silently watched a tiny mosquito buzz around his face and then land gently on his top lip.

When the only red that remained on the man's face was from anger rather than blood, he waved his hand dismissively and stated that 'he wasn't worth it anyway' before opening the door to leave. Seconds before the door closed and Manjan would be free to hit himself in the face, the mosquito dug the forty-seven sharp edges of its mouth deep into his upper lip.

'Poxy mosquito,' he shouted, thankfully now out of earshot of the angry man.

Now, I don't know whether there was something in that mosquito's bite that stimulated hair growth, or whether the bite was simply the last straw for Manjan, but within a few hours he had grown wispy fluff either side of his lips. The next day the stubble under his nose was stronger than that on his chin, and by the end of the week he was sporting a full and flowing moustache.

Manjan scoffed, because he was by now a fully-fledged moustache and it was in his nature to do so, but he was lying when he told Shakey that he had no interest whatsoever in going to the silent disco. His story had clearly made Shakey a little sad and he was finding it difficult to watch the juxtaposition of Shakey's energetic thigh tapping and sad eyes (that retained their hint of crazy even in this state).

'You say you want me to travel beyond this beach,' Shakey started, in the complete belief that he was about to blow Manjan's mind with his wisdom, 'so I say to you, *you* should travel beyond this beach'. He emphasised the words 'this' and 'beach' to imply that they meant much more than they actually did.

'Come with me, man, broaden your mind, see something

you've never seen before.' Shakey did want Manjan to come with him, but it wasn't so that Manjan could broaden his mind by way of a silent disco. He wasn't sure if the girl from the boat would be there, and if she was, he wanted her to see him talking to an older gentleman. That would surely prove to her that Shakey is a worldly traveller, and then she'll want to kiss him. It's basic logic.

'Will it be silent?' Manjan asked, and Shakey nodded.

'Will you stop tapping your thigh?' Manjan asked, and Shakey looked down at his legs, surprised to see that he was tapping his thigh, and nodded.

'Will you stop tapping your thigh now?' Manjan asked, and Shakey nodded. There was silence.

'Then I'll come to the silent disco.'

CHAPTER 32

AN OTTER

Where Manjan next shored. 1978.

The ship was still and most of the noise had died down. The party goers had disembarked (none of them in a straight line) and Manjan was about to find out where his new life would be – not that he cared particularly.

He could hear someone mopping the deck above him where the glasses had been smashed but he wasn't too worried about one person seeing him; he had become quite good at talking himself out of situations like this. Maybe the person mopping could tell him where they were. Again, not that he cared particularly.

The mopper did not tell Manjan where they were. Instead he cast a glance over at Manjan, assumed he was a drunk lost member of the previous party, waved and continued mopping.

Manjan looked out across the land. It was a lush green with patches of yellow where leaves had been raked into piles. The sea was restful (much to the displeasure of one otter trying to play in waves that weren't there) and there were no other ships in sight. If Manjan had given his surroundings any thought at all he would have concluded that his new home was peaceful and beautiful. But he didn't, so he didn't.

He stepped off the ship, walked up a grassy bank and along a sea wall, which was long enough to have no visible end. Eventually, he would come across somewhere to live.

'Where have you come from?' asked a frail old lady with thinning grey hair. Manjan had been walking aimlessly for some time (although he didn't know how long, and nor did he care). The lady was sitting outside the only house Manjan had seen since disembarking from the party ship. Manjan pointed back behind him.

'Sweden,' he replied.

The old lady nodded and sipped from a glass of juice through a straw. 'And where are you going?' she asked in perfect, if heavily accented English. Manjan recognised the accent and tried to put his finger on where he was.

'That depends,' he answered, walking up to the faded blue-painted house and leaning on the fence. 'It depends on where I am?' The lady nodded but didn't seem to notice the question mark implied in Manjan's intonation.

She looked quite ill and Manjan noticed that her skin went paler as she sucked on her straw, making that slurping sound that straws make when a drink is nearing its end.

'Can I have some tea?' she called faintly behind her, indicating that she wasn't alone.

A rattle came from the kitchen and then something

dropped on the floor.

'Aye, course you can, Ebba,' came a voice from inside the house. Manjan was still trying to put his finger on the accent when the voice from inside walked through the door with two cups of tea. There was a stunned silence until the voice (now outside) spoke again.

'Hi, lad,' Manjan repeated the same words back to Hylad.

Ebba had been born in Sweden in 1912 and had enjoyed a happy childhood. Her parents not only stayed married but also remained very much in love, and Ebba looked up to them for that very reason. She used to pretend to be her *mor* and one of her friends would play her *far*. They would look after Ebba's only doll and push it around in the pram that Ebba's *mor* used to push her around in.

When Ebba reached her teenage years, she started finding life a little harder. She'd finished attending an all-girls school where she'd met Olivia, a stunningly attractive girl who was shy but with whom Ebba had managed to start a secret romantic relationship.

Romantic relationships were not allowed at Ebba and Olivia's school, but a shortage of teachers made it relatively easy, and of course they never really considered that they were doing anything wrong. It was only after Ebba had finished school that her parents noticed her and Olivia spending so much of their free time together. That's when they started introducing Ebba to a long line of strange boys.

She became good friends with two of the boys but it wasn't enough for her parents. They were worried about her, although they wouldn't tell her why.

A year later Olivia's parents (who hadn't been as subtle as Ebba's) moved Olivia to Sollefteå, a small riverside town north from where she had grown up. It had taken Olivia two whole days on a train to get there – one day crying, one day dehydrated. She moved in with a distant relative whom she had never met, and found out in her first month in her new home that her parents considered her to be mentally ill (as did her relative).

Eventually, after several years of 'playing up', Ebba married one of her friends (if this story was about Ebba's husband, I would tell you about how he was madly in love with Ebba, but it isn't about him, so I won't). Once a year she would travel up to Stockholm 'with work' for a week and Olivia would travel down to Stockholm at the same time on holiday. For one week every year, Ebba and Olivia would re-discover that they were still very much in love, and that Olivia was not yet cured of her 'mental illness'.

When Ebba was thirty-two, the Government Offices of Sweden decriminalised same-sex relationships, Ebba told her husband about Oliva, and they separated. She bought a small house, painted it blue, and the next time she was in Stockholm, she invited Olivia to come and live with her (if this story was about Ebba's husband, I would tell you about the years he spent longing to be with Ebba after they separated, how he developed a drinking habit and how he sobered up after meeting and rescuing a stray dog, but it isn't about him, so I won't).

Shy Olivia turned down Ebba's offer to live with her, so Ebba lived alone in her small blue house, once a year visiting Stockholm. She would have been happy in the house if it wasn't for those weeks in Stockholm. In Stockholm Ebba knew what true happiness was.

In 1970 Ebba met two Englishmen who were searching for a lost boy. She gave them a lift to the police station and told them that they made a lovely couple, but she knew only too well the denial in their lack of response. Later that same week, the two men had stopped by to thank her and to tell her that they would be staying in Sweden a little longer as they liked how accepting everyone was – would she like to go for a meal with them?

Ebba told them that she would – if only Olivia would feel this comfortable in HER own skin as quickly.

Three years later the two men were still in Sweden, and they accepted Ebba's offer to visit Stockholm to meet the Olivia that they had heard so much about.

It was in a restaurant in Stockholm that Michael and Nigel had convinced Olivia to join the three of them on the journey back down south. Olivia knew by now that she wasn't mentally ill, but it took her seeing the English couple being so openly affectionate with each other in public without judgement to realise that she might be – dare she think it – normal.

So, in 1973, twenty-nine years after Ebba had bought it, Olivia came to visit the small blue house.

A year later, when they were both sixty-two, Ebba and Olivia started living together in the blue house, and for the first time they lived the life that they should always have been living.

One morning, two years later, Ebba woke up, happy to be waking up next her Olivia, but Olivia did not wake up happy to be next to her Ebba. In fact, she did not wake up at all.

Olivia's funeral was small (Ebba, Michael and Nigel attended), local (down the sea wall on the grassy bank) and terribly interrupted. Ebba had decided to give Olivia a private funeral to reflect the person she had been, but the day that they picked to send off the love of Ebba's life was the same day that the soon-to-be-monthly booze cruise would first shore up on the grassy bank to drop off a party of pissed-up tourists.

Shortly after, Michael and Nigel moved in with Ebba to keep her company, help her with the upkeep of the house and fend off the boozers if they got too close. It wasn't long after Olivia died that Ebba started to feel weak.

'*Förlåt*, let me understand this…this is the boy you were looking for?' Ebba asked for the third time, looking again at Manjan, the twenty-six-year-old man drinking tea in the chair next to her. 'And he has just walked into our garden?' She couldn't stop laughing.

'*Förlåt?*' Manjan repeated, and he put his head in his hands. 'I'm still in Sweden, aren't I?' It seemed every time he tried to run away from a country, he ended up back in the same country, usually with Hylad.

There was a lot of laughter that day and a great many tears. Michael came home in the early afternoon and completely broke down at the sight of Manjan. Eventually he managed to speak.

'We have to tell your father,' he said and Manjan's face fell. Hylad and Michael's faces followed suit and it went silent. Sometimes silences can be understood.

'Um…' Manjan started, after Ebba had looked at all of them with a smile before understanding the subtext.

For the first time Manjan told his story. He told them about Jan, how they'd travelled to Russia together with Saga and Valter, and how Jan had left him on a plane. He told them about India without Jan and then he told them about India with Jan. He told them about the lamp business and how this had effectively killed his father, his unborn child and his relationship with Jan.

Only one day after Ladyjan had left, Manjan told Hylad, Michael and Ebba how much he missed and loved her.

Ebba went to bed very early that night (as she had started doing every night) but before she did, she looked at her three companions and smiled. Nigel and Michael had been so kind to her, and by persuading Olivia to live with her, they had given her the best years of her life.

'Where is your Jan now?' she asked. Manjan told her that he didn't know and that she could be anywhere.

'Poland?' Ebba asked, and Manjan said that she might be in Poland, but that she also might be anywhere.

'Russia?' Ebba asked, and Manjan said that yes, she might be in Russia too. She could be anywhere.

'Nepal? India?'

'Maybe,' Manjan replied. 'She could be anywhere.'

'How did you look for your Jan when you lost him?' Ebba asked, turning her attention to Hylad and Michael.

'We tried everything,' Nigel said.

'We really did, lad,' Hylad said sincerely to Manjan. He tried to remember the specifics about the everything that they tried. 'We started by retracing our steps down at the harbour and...' Ebba interrupted.

'Retracing your steps, you say? There's a thought. I've never been to Poland, or Russia... Come to think about it, I've never been to Nepal or India, either. I could do with leaving this place behind.' Then Ebba shrugged her shoulders and wished them all a good night.

'What do you say lad?' asked Hylad. Manjan thought for less than a few seconds.

'I don't have any other plans for the rest of my life,' he replied.

CHAPTER 33

A COW

Goa, India. 2016; Poland and Russia. 1978 – 1980.

'And that's what we did,' Manjan said, as he took a sip from his red wine, which was now in a plastic cup, followed by a sip from his bottle of water. The wine really did taste like piss.

They were sitting at the bar of an outside silent disco. To Shakey's credit, the disco was quieter than most other discos, but it was far from silent. Most people had headphones on their heads (Manjan had discussed at length with a man at the door why he didn't wish to purchase headphones) but every time the silent DJ played something that the dancers particularly liked, which was about every three and a half minutes, the crowd would cheer. Manjan's thoughts and now fairly slurred story were constantly interrupted.

Shakey also took a sip from his plastic cup of wine. Manjan

thought it was nice that Shakey had ordered the same as him, if a little sad.

'You travelled to all those countries again?' Shakey said in disbelief.

'We did,' Manjan replied. 'Hylad, Michael, Ebba and myself. Ebba sold her house and we went everywhere, starting at the docks where Ladyjan had worked before she left.' There was a cheer from the crowd. 'She wasn't there though.'

Poland

'Prince Polo?' Manjan offered on their first day in, what was for three of them, a new country. Hylad, Michael and Ebba all accepted. 'The first bite's the best,' Manjan told them as he enthusiastically unwrapped the bar and hungrily took his first bite in seven years. The first bite wasn't as good as he remembered. Neither was the second. Had they changed?

Manjan ate a much more varied diet during his second visit to Poland – *pierogi*, *bigos*, borscht – but he made every attempt to rekindle his relationship with Prince Polo bars as they travelled. He ate at least one every day and every single one of them was fine. They were all just fine.

They hadn't planned on staying in Poland for very long. Manjan and Ladyjan had just passed through by train, so it stood to reason that this time should be no different.

'I agree that searching by train makes sense,' Hylad had agreed, when they'd been planning the journey, 'but if we're going to search a country for someone we should do it properly,' and so the three trains they caught zig-zagged from the East German border to the North coast, from the

North coast to the Czechoslovakian border and from the Czechoslovakian border to the Russian border.

The East German border was reasonably barren. Two sticks bearing the colours of each country's flags stood in some tall, dry grass. A group of officials was taking pictures of the sticks, but after checking each one (from afar), it turned out that none of them was Ladyjan. It was at this point that Manjan, Hylad, Michael and Ebba realised that only one of their party knew what Ladyjan looked like. Manjan briefed them; they were looking for a witty, strong, brave and beautiful Swedish girl who did not look stereotypically Swedish.

This really wasn't going to be easy.

The North coast of Poland was much more populated. There was a beautifully decorated wooden shack hosting a wedding on the beach. Manjan checked all the guests and found that, sadly, none of them was Ladyjan. He waited for the bride and groom to come out of the shack and, for the first time in his life, he hoped with all of his heart not to see Ladyjan. He heaved a huge sigh of relief when a lady in a wedding dress, large purple glasses and a glittering blond perm walked into the crowd. She looked at her groom, who was wearing a wedding-themed novelty bowtie and smiled a tight-lipped smile before saying something in Swedish. Manjan thought he recognised the couple, but neither one of them was Ladyjan.

The Czechoslovakian border was situated just a few miles from the nearest town, where the four of them ate (Ladyjan wasn't in the restaurant), drank (Ladyjan wasn't in the bar) and explored (guess where Ladyjan wasn't…)

Before they entered Russia, Manjan had his last Prince Polo bar. The manufacturer had not changed the way in which they made Prince Polo bars since Manjan had left Poland the first time, but he was sure something had changed.

'Poxy Prince Polo bars,' he said through his upper lip hair as the group entered Ukraine, 'they don't make them like they used to.' Of course, they did make them like they used to, and they still do.

At the Russian border, the group learned three things:

1. Ladyjan wasn't there.

2. Prince Polo didn't only supply Poland with chocolate. Once again Manjan tried the bar and longed for the taste he remembered, only to inform Hylad, Michael and Ebba that it was even worse in Ukraine than it had been in Poland. It wasn't, though. It was the same.

3. Russia was not an easy country to enter in 1980.

Russia

A line of dusty green military vehicles stood still, some in Russia and some in Poland. Every hour or so one vehicle would move from Poland to Russia and join the line on the other side of the border, but no one really went anywhere.

Manjan, Hylad, Michael and Ebba were on foot and walking alongside the vehicles. If it wasn't for Ebba's fragile image, gender and age, the four of them would have been shot before they saw the Soviet army soldier pointing his rifle at them. They stopped dead (but not actually dead, as could have been the case) and stared at the soldier who was lying alone in a small trench.

'Friend,' Hylad shouted.

The sound of a rifle cocking is a terrifying sound.

And the sight of a soldier quivering in a trench is a depressing sight.

'Friend?' the soldier shouted back as another military vehicle moved through the border. He didn't want to shoot anyone today, so instead he shouted 'Down. Get down.' The group did as they were told, and the shaking soldier ran at them, continuing to hold his rifle in front of him as he did.

'Who are you?' he shouted, and this time it was Manjan who spoke up through the mud in his face.

'We want to come into your country to look for someone.'

The soldier had heard this line lots of times from lots of travellers, lost family members and lovers, all wanting to search behind Russian borders.

'You come in by plane, if you're lucky,' the soldier said, much quieter. 'You do not enter Russia like this. You don't come in through this border.' There was a big pause while everyone considered their next move. It was the soldier who decided first. He poked Manjan with the end of his rifle and told him to roll over, which of course, he did.

Manjan did not recognise the soldier. The years had weathered him, as had the morning he'd just spent lying down in a trench. There were deep creases around his eyes and up his cheeks where he had grown old too quickly and each crease was full of dark mud. He looked very unhappy.

The soldier recognised Manjan though.

'The person you are looking for,' he said angrily, but with half a smile, before waving his rifle-free hand in a circle as if trying to remember something, 'you lost him in...' Manjan opened his mouth to say that he wasn't looking for a him, '... Sweden,' the soldier said. 'He's still lost? I'm sorry to hear.'

Manjan narrowed his eyes to imply a question mark

without having to ask a question.

'His name is stupid,' the soldier continued, thinking very hard, 'Oilad, no, Hylander? No. Hylad?'

Hylad turned slowly away from the hard mud and looked at the soldier, who was now looking much happier.

'This is Hylad,' Manjan said, and the previously unhappy, now happy soldier dropped his rifle and held tightly onto Hylad's thick, dirtied hand and pulled him up into an embrace.

'This is Hylad?' the soldier asked, without expectation of an answer, 'Then who are you looking for?'

'A girl,' Manjan answered, 'called Jan'. The soldier looked at him seriously.

'Jan,' he shouted as if remembering something. 'You are called Jan. There are two Jans! The girl Jan, she is in Russia?' he asked, this time expecting an answer. Manjan nodded, trying to place the unhappy and now happy soldier in his head. He had met so many people on his travels.

'Then you come with me,' he said. 'I take you across the border, you get me coffee and,' he paused as if he were thinking about something, 'and then we are even. Come. I know a place.'

Prisha the cow, now alone on the beach, settled down on the sand with the puppy cuddled into her. She was ready for the following day when she would wake up to the sunrise and eat the grass in the fields that the farmers had deserted several years earlier. The puppy let out a deep contented breath.

There really is some beauty in repetition, Prisha thought, and then she thought 'moo'.

CHAPTER 34

A RECLUSE

Russia. 1980.

The soldier told Manjan, Hylad, Micheal and Ebba how he had been forced to leave Moscow, where he had lived all his life, until three years ago. He told them how he had been 'recruited' by the Soviet Army and relocated to a town up the road from the border with only the training he'd received as a teenager to keep him safe. He told them he was lonely.

'I was married once,' he said, drinking a weak but bitter coffee and looking unhappy. 'She left me, but I waited for her, every Thursday before curfew, I waited. Outside her home. She was my angel.' Hylad looked uncomfortable and Ebba looked impressed with what she took to be the soldier's romantic dedication.

'I'm sorry to hear that,' Ebba said, with her elbows on the

table and her head in one of her hands.

'It is OK,' the unhappy man responded, looking a little happier, 'I dated her sister before I was moved. They look the same, so…' He shrugged a shrug while Hylad shifted in his seat and Ebba let out a loud laugh. The unhappy, now happy man smiled at her. 'You look a little like her too,' he said, with raised eyebrows.

Other than their little group, the coffee stand was deserted, and yet they were all huddled around one of the six tiny tables.

'This border job,' the soldier continued, 'it is a self-made job.' He waved his coffee-free hand in the air. 'I made it. I spend my time alone but away from danger.' He thought for a second. 'Away from danger, but alone.' His smile dropped again as he told them his daily routine; every day he woke up in a small hut alone, he guarded a trench for eleven hours and then he went to sleep in a small hut alone. In short, he was waiting for something to happen – for the war to end maybe? He didn't know what.

Manjan told the unhappy, then happy, now less happy man about their plan to retrace his and Ladyjan's footsteps until they found her. The man slapped his leg and laughed for the first time in a long time. 'In Russia?' he asked. 'Why would she return to Russia?'

Manjan told the soldier that he and Ladyjan had liked Russia and the soldier laughed again. 'How do you think you will all get through Russia?' he bellowed with a grin, and no one answered.

A heavy silence followed as they realised that Russia would require more planning than perhaps they had undertaken.

'Would you…' Ebba started, hoping that the open nature of her question might allow the soldier to come to his own conclusion. He looked at his green Soviet overalls with their huge, medal-less pocket on the left breast. He wouldn't be missed at the border. No one would even know he had gone. He put on his grey, once-fluffy hat, looked at Ebba and answered.

'I would,' he said, but you'll need a car.'

The only previous planning that the group had managed was to agree that, given the size of Russia, their previous zig-zag approach was probably not the most effective way to search for Ladyjan – it could take a lifetime. Although Manjan was in favour of spending his lifetime searching for Ladyjan (and indeed, in many ways he did), they agreed to simply follow the footsteps of a younger Manjan, Ladyjan, Saga and Valter. This meant hiring a car rather than travelling by train (luckily the soldier knew of a place; a place that also made coffee). Ebba offered up more of her savings to rent a modern car after hearing the story of how Ladyjan and Valter had been shot at trying to fix a tyre.

'Russia is nice,' Manjan promised Ebba, but she was having none of it. She'd never been shot at in Sweden and she'd already had one rifle pointed at her just trying to enter Russia.

Every town came with memories for Manjan, and every memory included Ladyjan. Russia was the country they'd spent the most time in together, but it was also the place where she'd first left him.

It didn't take long for them to realise that the soldier was right. Ladyjan would not be in Russia – the Soviet Union's presence was heavy, and the group were met with a cold reception every time someone noticed their foreign accents. Luckily, the now mainly happy soldier could vouch for them with his uniform.

When they eventually reached Moscow, he made a request to visit his old house.

'Are you sure?' Michael asked. 'If you're seen… I mean, we're living off the grid here. You could be…'

'I want to visit my own home,' the soldier said with a steady voice.

They waited until night (and curfew) had fallen, and drove slowly and quietly through the deserted streets to where the soldier said he had once lived. From the car, under the protection of the shadow from a large tree, the five of them looked at the large family home in which the soldier had supposedly once lived. No one admitted it, but everyone except for the soldier was surprised.

The soldier left the car and walked up to the house, but then he stopped several feet away from the front door and picked up a stone. The silence was broken.

'Oi,' he shouted, before throwing the stone at one of the upper-floor windows.

A different window the other side of the house opened, and two similar-looking women looked out. One of them put her head in her hands.

'*Vy*,' she despaired, 'you.' The other woman waved.

The soldier dropped to his knees and started singing a Russian ballad while the first woman shouted something that was presumably explicit.

Michael said his own expletive in the car and then, 'This isn't his house, it's his poxy ex-spouse's, he's going to blow our cover.' Michael, Hylad and Manjan jumped out of the car, grabbed the soldier by his arms and pulled him back.

Ebba didn't join them.

The soldier sang louder as he was pushed into the back seat of the car and the second woman started singing the same ballad, only several octaves higher, much to the annoyance of the first.

As Hylad drove away, Ebba noticed that the soldier was crying. She rubbed his shoulder.

'Sensitive soul,' she muttered, and one side of the unhappy man's mouth smiled.

'If Ladyjan is in Russia, she's somewhere here,' Manjan said when they awoke the next morning, and for that reason alone, they stayed in Moscow for four months.

Here is a list of the places in Moscow that Ladyjan wasn't:

St Basil's Cathedral
Gorky Central Park
The airport
Any of the streets
Any of the parks
Any of the museums
Anywhere.

Manjan visited St Basil's Cathedral every day. It didn't look like it should have been built on a cloud any more, as it had done when he had first visited. The green and yellow, the blue and white, the red and gold – they all looked grey to Manjan now.

Ebba and the soldier had stopped searching with Manjan, Hylad and Michael by the second month. Ebba was feeling frailer each day and the soldier had made it his duty to look after her. The five of them rented a flat on the black market under Ebba's name (which for the purposes of the rental, was Vladlena) and the soldier and Ebba stayed inside while the other three searched (Hylad in the soldier's uniform).

The flat itself was actually rather lovely and it turned out that the soldier had something of a talent for interior design. He moved the furniture around to make more space (which was ideal for the four of them sleeping on the floor) and he bought and looked after some flowers that he arranged around the flat to give it a homely feel.

Ebba, who had everyday missed Olivia for most of her life, began to feel a little less lonely.

The soldier, who everyday missed his ex-wife and her sister, also began to feel a little less lonely.

After four months had passed Ebba told Hylad, Michael and Manjan that she wouldn't be joining them on their flight to India. She wanted to stay in Russia with the soldier.

'You're not–?' Michael started to ask, but Ebba laughed and told him that no, they were not. They just found each other to be good company.

'I don't know how long I have,' she said. 'I need to slow down.'

The goodbyes were more than a little emotional. Ebba didn't know if she would see Hylad or Michael again and they didn't know if they would see her.

The soldier told them how, in his experience, people were like coils and that they always sprang back to each other, eventually.

Through their tears, everyone smiled politely.

Every other day the soldier queued for half a day to provide Ebba and himself with a small amount of food and every time Ebba left the flat she felt very closely watched by someone – she wasn't sure who, but someone. Repression filled the faces of the people they passed in the streets, and as far as the government was concerned, neither the soldier (presumed dead) nor Ebba (presumed Vladlena) existed, but finally the unhappy, happy, unhappy, then happy again, then unhappy eight years later before being happy again, then unhappy, happy, less happy, then mainly happy before being unhappy but with a smile soldier felt consistently happy with Ebba, and Ebba felt happy with him.

Neither Ebba nor the soldier's coils ever sprang back to the soldier's ex-wife, the soldier's ex-wife's sister, Manjan, Hylad or Michael again.

But that didn't make either of them unhappy.

CHAPTER 35

AN INSIGNIFICANT DOG

Goa, India. 2016.

The puppy, having been largely ignored by Prisha the cow for most of the evening, was pushing closer into her side and whimpering. It was getting cold next to the sea and he wanted comfort. An older dog might have pulled the puppy into its fur with a paw or rested its chin on the puppy's head to keep it warm but Prisha did neither of these things. Cow's legs don't lend themselves to sticking out sideways and her head was too far up from the puppy's tiny body for her to reach him, so she sat motionless.

Manjan held onto the bar with both hands to steady himself

as Shakey stood up and gestured towards the toilet.

'I'm going to the toilet,' he half-shouted, and Manjan gave a slow nod of agreement as if agreement were needed.

Shakey wasn't steady on his feet and the toilet was the other side of the dance floor. He slightly opened his mouth and started bending his knees, half in time to one group of silent disco singers and half in time to a different group of silent disco singers, but not completely in time to either. His neck attempted to bob along too but seemed to take on a completely different rhythm.

Under the influence of alcohol, Shakey tended to adopt the same technique when in transit. He focused on his destination (in this case, the toilet) and he'd blank out everything else. This, he found, was the best way to walk straight.

He ignored the group of vests to the right of him, who were all bent down low singing 'I'm so low, low, low. I need you, you, you,' with headphones in their ears.

He ignored the large group of vests to the left of him who were facing one of the DJs with their hands in the air and singing 'I've been dreaming, of a feeling, for so long that I can't remember starting'. They didn't know that the DJ they were facing was playing a song that went 'I'm so low, low, low. I need you, you, you'.

About five metres from the toilet (a wooden door with a picture of a male looking into a female toilet on it), Shakey turned his head right.

She was in a group of vests, many of which were deep into the mating ritual, and she was dancing, seemingly in slow motion – the girl from the fishing trip.

Shakey moved his left leg in the direction of his gaze and flexed his biceps. He would tell her that fishing wasn't really his thing. His right foot did not follow his left and continued walking towards the toilet, undercutting his left foot as it did.

He could tell her about the old-timer he was now friends with; that would impress her. He was a vegetarian. He could tell her that. He wouldn't tell her that he sometimes ate burgers.

His left knee buckled as his right shin hit it and his out-of-time nodding head jolted backwards, as his elbow, and then his shoulder, hit the floor.

For a couple of seconds everything seemed blurry, and when he stood up he heard the girl saying something to him, but, embarrassed, he focused again on the toilet door and allowed his feet to lead him through it without replying.

The wind hit the puppy in the face and the wet in both of his eyes and on his nose chilled him further. His whimpers grew louder and louder until they crescendoed into a series of yelps.

Prisha picked up the bulk of her weight and, without standing, re-positioned her hips and stomach, leaning towards the sea in an attempt to warm the puppy.

Prisha had ignored the puppy for most of the evening. Despite his constant jumping and barking she hadn't even looked down at him (which was a shame, because the puppy had a lot to say). Even now, as the wind picked up she didn't move her head towards him, but her small shift in weight was enough. At the same time, the puppy pushed back into Prisha, turned his head and nuzzled under the crevice between her body and the sand, and slowly the puppy's body warmed up.

In the toilet, Shakey sat on an inappropriately painted toilet seat and swore at himself.

He called himself stupid and an idiot.

He hit his leg with a clenched fist and then held his leg with his other hand because it hurt more than he expected.

He dropped his head and looked at the floor. He couldn't believe he'd fallen in front of her. Why on earth had he ignored her? He'd essentially run away, and now, to make things worse, he'd been in the toilet far too long for this to be a wee.

He stood up, re-fastened his trousers and walked out, confidently shutting the door behind him. He didn't look at the girl from the fishing trip. Instead, he focused on Manjan at the bar, blanked out everything else, and let his feet do the rest.

Later in Shakey's life, he would hear about how he had blanked the girl the second time he'd met her regularly and he would be told how arrogant that made him, but for now, he was just saving grace.

Manjan picked his hands up from the sticky bar with slightly more force than he thought would be necessary and smiled at Shakey. He didn't know who the girl was, but he'd seen the fall and he could see the embarrassment on Shakey's face.

'Shakey,' Manjan said when Shakey had reached him. Shakey just looked at him.

Manjan held onto one of Shakey's hands and shook it lightly, as a parent might do to a baby.

CHAPTER 36

A MOTH AND A LIGHT, AND A LIGHT, AND A LIGHT

India. 1981 – 1982.

Hylad and Michael looked at the old rusty door of 'The New Sunshine Hostel'. Still overlooked by four taller buildings, it didn't look like sunshine at all. Behind them, Manjan was beaming.

'It's been done up,' he told them excitedly, pushing between his two companions to open the door. The first thing Manjan noticed were the showers. They were still in the same place, but there was a clouded glass door covering them and from what he could see over the door, the showers were clean, shiny and new.

The first thing that Hylad and Michael noticed was that the desk had no one behind it and that it was covered in what appeared to be soot. The second thing they noticed was the kitchen, which was the other side of the desk to the showers, and consisted of a kettle with no lid and a toaster that had its wires hanging out. Finally, they noticed that the phone was so out of date, they both doubted it would work.

Manjan walked up to the phone and lifted the receiver.

'It's clean!' he told them happily.

'You lived…here?' Hylad asked, looking a little disgusted and Manjan nodded.

A man in a pink polo shirt and jeans walked down the stairs.

'A room?' he asked.

'God no,' Michael answered far too quickly, and then looked embarrassed.

'We're looking for Kalem,' Manjan said, 'does he still live here?' The man walked over to the desk and pulled out a large red book, flipped through the pages to a list of people beginning with K and stroked his index finger down the page.

'Kalem,' he said. 'Kalem… Nope. No Kalem here, sir.'

Manjan, Hylad, Michael and the man behind the desk were quiet for a while. Manjan felt deflated. There was no way Ladyjan would be here, and if Kalem wasn't here either, there was no need for the three of them to be in Varanasi at all.

Eventually, the man in pink broke the silence.

'I'll ask the owner if he knows a Kalem living here, sir,' he said, 'I think he would remember, he is called Kalem too!'

The group drank in the same place where Kalem and Manjan used to drink every night. Nothing had changed. There was still no front wall between the bar and the alleyway, the man behind the bar was older, but the same guy, and he was selling the same beer that he kept safe in the same box using the same rusty padlock.

'I am humbled, Jan, I am truly humbled that you would come back just to see me. You will find your Jan, I know you will. It is god's will.' Kalem still had his hand on Hylad's leg from his previous monologue about how grateful he was to Hylad and Michael for looking after Manjan.

'It's great to see you so well,' Manjan said before Kalem interrupted.

'The phone,' he urged excitedly, 'did you see the phone in Sunshine?' Manjan opened his mouth before Kalem continued, 'It's not sticky. You can pick it up now without getting sticky on your hands.'

'I saw the showers,' Manjan laughed, and Kalem explained how the showers had been his first triumph when he'd taken over the hostel.

'But my wife,' he said, 'I love her with every inch of me, but she will not bathe in the Great Mother any more. She showers in the showers now, and she washes away the dirt, yes, but does she wash away her sins? I wash in the Ganges alone every morning.' Manjan knew Kalem and he knew that this wouldn't be true. Kalem would talk to everyone within earshot at the river bank and the river bank is a busy place.

No one slept that night. No one even tried. Together, Manjan, Hylad and Michael told Kalem about their journey and the search for Ladyjan. Kalem was less than impressed to hear that Manjan was still looking for the girl who had, as far as he knew, left him in the '70s, but wished them luck nonetheless.

Kalem explained to Manjan, Hylad and Michael how he had started helping out at the desk at the Sunshine Hostel, using his fine English to stop travellers from complaining (although most stopped complaining due to his hugely friendly smile rather than his language skills). The hostel manager died two years ago. No one claimed the building and there was no will, so it was agreed that Kalem and his family could take it over.

When the sun rose at 5 am and morning prayer was called, they stood up, all a little tipsy.

'Come with me to the river,' Kalem offered, after performing a wobbly prayer, but the three of them declined.

'We need to get to Delhi,' Manjan explained. 'I want to ring a place down there first though. Can I use the phone at the Sunshine Hostel?' Kalem shook his head.

'You can pick it up,' he said smiling, 'and your hands will not get sticky on them, but it will not ring or call people. That's my next job.'

Hylad stepped onto the train, followed by Michael, followed by a moth, followed by Manjan. All but one knew they were going to Delhi and all but one were nervous about it.

Hylad and Michael had heard about Alistair, the wide-stubble-faced man who had killed Manjan's father. Hylad liked Manjan's father and he felt responsible for his fate. Had he not lost Manjan all those years ago in Sweden, Manjan would not have met Ladyjan and persuaded her to travel with him. Ladyjan wouldn't have ended up alone in Fishton, nor would she have been tangled up in the illegal lamp-transporting game (another thing that Hylad felt guilty about) and Alistair would not have come looking for a 'Jan'. But now they were travelling to Delhi and he would see, albeit from afar, the man who sold the lamps to Ladyjan to transport back to England. The thought of seeing anyone involved in Ladyjan's enslavement or Manjan's father's death made Hylad shake with anger. He just hoped he didn't do anything stupid.

Michael was nervous because he knew that Hylad blamed himself for, well, for nearly everything. Whatever happened in Delhi, Michael knew that Hylad would find it hard and a loved one's burden is also the burden of the lover.

The moth had boarded the train by following the light that someone else had installed onto the train's carriage. It did not know it was on a train, and because of that, it was not nervous.

Neither Hylad nor Michael's nerves compared to Manjan's. For thirteen hours, the entire journey from Varanasi to Delhi, Manjan tried to stop himself from shaking. They planned to watch the lamp-seller for seven weeks from a nearby building's fourth-floor window, which meant that for the next seven weeks, Manjan would dread seeing Ladyjan, and if he did see her, his whole world would fall apart. They should have gone to Delhi first.

There was no announcement that the train was pulling into Delhi and there was no warning that it would only settle there for six minutes. Many of the passengers missed their stop, but Manjan hadn't slept and had seen the sign. He woke up the other two and stepped off the train, followed by a moth, followed by Michael, followed by Hylad.

'We start tomorrow?' asked Michael, stretching his arms in a yawn. They were all only just recovering from a night spent drinking with Kalem.

'We start tonight,' both Hylad and Manjan said in unison.

Due to its own flawed navigation system, the moth followed

the light and left the station into a crowded street. The sun was nearly down but the city continued to pulse with traffic, market stalls and badly installed neon. Not able to choose its own direction, the moth fluttered towards the largest orb of light, which had been installed by someone else at the top of a pole in the middle of the only dark patch around. There it bumped into lots of other moths, then it bumped into the light, then some more moths and then the light again.

In the morning, when the sun rose, the moth found that it was in a large park surrounded by a feast of nectar. Some moths eat nectar, and that is a little-known fact about moths. It wasn't just the past two days that the moth had lived like this, it had spent its entire life just following someone else's directions, but sometimes that's all you have to do.

CHAPTER 37

AND ANOTHER POXY VEST

India. 1983-1987.

Seven weeks turned into ten, and ten turned into twenty-six. Twenty-six weeks is half a year, and then that became an actual year. It turned out that the lamp-seller only sold lamps on one day of each month, which made sense to Manjan in hindsight, as he would presumably only need to make one sale (albeit a very specific sale) a month. It took Manjan three months of waiting in a room on the fourth floor of a nearby building to work out the pattern. The group had originally planned to watch the lamp-seller for seven weeks, which is forty-nine days, which was now the equivalent of four years, and so it was. Manjan certainly didn't want to see Ladyjan meeting with the lamp-seller, but he also wanted to know that she wasn't.

Manjan, Hylad and Michael were allowed to use the room every day for free provided they cleaned it regularly so that the owner could let it out to travellers at night. They didn't tell the owner that they would also be sleeping there for the first few weeks. It was in these first few weeks that a fourth person, Jason, started watching the market with the group.

Jason and Melissa

'It's just so exciting,' Jason said on the third day of watching a market without a lamp-seller in it. Manjan, Hylad and Michael didn't agree, but all politely smiled in an attempt to imply agreement. To Jason, who had only just arrived in India, this was a real-life detective thriller. He thought that by staying in this fourth-floor room with three strangers, he was seeing the world, which Manjan and his moustache found infuriating. After a pause Manjan had an idea.

'It is exciting,' he said, 'but I can't tell whether the lamp-seller is standing around that corner.' He pointed to a street corner at the far end of the market, half a mile away. 'If you could have a...' – before Manjan finished his sentence, Jason had started putting his shoes on – '...look.'

Seven hours later, much longer than Manjan could have hoped for, Jason returned to the room with Melissa. Melissa was a traveller whom Jason had met around the corner, half a mile away from the window. He'd explained how he'd spent the last three days fighting illegal lamp-trafficking in the pursuit of someone else's true love (he'd also flexed his bicep slightly) and Melissa had been impressed. Together, they'd spent the afternoon drinking masala chai, getting to know each other and forgetting to return to the room to let Manjan know that there was not a lamp-seller around the corner half a mile away. That was the night that Manjan, Hylad and

Michael found somewhere else to sleep, so that Jason and Melissa could…well…they could… Shucks, I'm no good at talking about these things.

Eighteen years later, at a silent disco holding a plastic cup of white wine, Shakey held a hand up to a much older Manjan.

'Whoa,' he said. 'Whoa. What a coincidence. My parents are called Jason and Melissa.'

Manjan was barely watching when the lamp-seller started flinching. The four-year stint was coming to an end, Hylad and Michael had returned home to be part of a movement fighting discrimination laws in Sweden, and Manjan was tired of watching the same muscular, confident teenage boy buy the same lamp from the same seller every month. In a few months he would meet up with Hylad and Michael again, for the last part of their search tour, in Goa. Ladyjan wouldn't be there. Of course, Ladyjan wouldn't be there.

There was a break in the market crowd. Something was creating a moving hole through the masses of people. A bull, maybe? Manjan didn't know what it was but it was making a direct route to the lamp-seller, who was now looking around him in a panic as if he intended running somewhere.

A young boy in tattered shorts fell to the floor, smashing the lamp he was looking at as a small man, not much bigger than the boy, emerged from the hole in the crowd, flailing his arms to clear his path. The lamp-seller stood tall and faced forward like a soldier as the small man started to shout an onslaught of abuse at him. The young boy picked up the lamp and ran.

From his window, Manjan couldn't hear what the small man was saying but he watched as his small body became increasingly animated, and grew more menacing and imposing until the lamp-seller was reduced to phlegmy tears (made to look even more disgusting by the heat). He began begging and then dropped to the same height as the small man and held onto his clothes, but the small man hit the lamp-seller's head and pointed into a building. Slowly, the lamp-seller moved on his knees, across the filth of the market floor, in floods of his own bodily fluids – sweat, tears, phlegm. Every few metres the small man kicked him until, eventually they disappeared into the building.

Manjan scanned the market and saw that people were either oblivious to what had happened, or they were pretending it hadn't. There was no gap in the crowd and there was no one at the stall to serve the lady patiently waiting, holding a decorative green lamp while several children stole the rest of them.

'What are the…?' Manjan said to himself, before he put on his sandals and ran down the stairs, out of the door, through the crowds and up to the lamp stall (now fresh out of lamps). 'Saga?' he asked. 'Why do I always seem to find people here?!'

'You thought I'd leave him, didn't you?' Saga asked. 'Everyone assumes we're going to break up even though we've been together for nearly twenty years. I never liked him for his money.'

'Honestly, no, Saga, I just asked how he is,' Manjan smiled. He'd missed Saga.

'No, you didn't. You asked how he is, but you asked with a

tone that actually said "are you still together?". And we are.'

They had already gone through small talk on the way to Old Delhi and while ordering two masala chais.

'I'm glad you're still together. I like Valter! How is he? Is he here?'

Saga explained how she'd fallen in love with India when they had visited the first time and how she had missed it when they'd returned to Sweden. India had brought out the worst in Valter, though. He didn't like the attention Saga had got from other men and he became insanely jealous. After their second child arrived, Saga decided she would visit India alone every year, and Valter hadn't argued. He loved Saga's sense of adventure and he also loved time for just him and the children. The mention of children made something inside Manjan hurt.

Every year Saga flew to Delhi and then visited a different city or town.

'Last year I visited Varanasi again,' she told Manjan. 'It made me think of you.'

'The last place I saw you,' Manjan responded thoughtfully. 'I was in a bad way then.' There was an uncomfortable silence as this sank in.

'Well,' Saga continued, 'I met this fascinating man in Varanasi who spoke incredibly good English. I could tell he was good at English anyway, but he also made a point of telling me quite a lot. He was so grateful for everything, he thanked god for most things, but nothing was taken for granted. It was because of him that I actually swam in the Ganges! You could have taken some tips from him back then.'

Manjan confirmed that he probably had.

After another chai, Saga finally asked Manjan what he was doing in Delhi and Manjan told her.

'You're still looking for Jan?'

'No, I'm looking for Jan, again.'

'Oh. She's in Goa. At least, she was last month.'

Manjan's eyes opened wide and stared at Saga. His heart pounded at his ribcage and the streets of Old Delhi stood quiet around them. He heard his own voice, several octaves lower and in slow motion.

'Shee's iinn Gooaa?'

And then he heard Saga's voice, in the same fashion, say something about Palolem and giving up stealing. Manjan's heart was louder than the next thing Saga said, but when it calmed down again, he made out the words 'one', 'last' and 'job'.

CHAPTER 38

ONE LAST JOB

Goa, India. 2016.

'She was here,' Shakey said, sat up straight and with his eyes wide open. All of a sudden, he felt like he might turn around and see Ladyjan right behind him, but, as I'm sure you know by now, Shakey wasn't that clever.

'I don't see her,' Manjan said sarcastically, looking around the silent disco. His belief that Ladyjan would turn up at Palolem had never really wavered over the past thirty years, but he was fairly certain that when she did return, she wouldn't be at a silent disco.

'I carried on searching. I spent the rest of my life searching.' Manjan looked at his empty plastic cup and tilted it. 'I travelled all over Europe, Australasia, Asia, the Americas, each time coming back to Palolem. Just making myself available to fate, really. Five years ago, I decided to stay here and let the universe take over.'

Shakey looked right and then he looked left. Ladyjan probably wasn't there.

'So, you never saw her again?' he asked.

'The last I knew of her whereabouts was from Saga. She was here thirty years ago, and she'd given up stealing.' The crowd behind them cheered, but for a different reason. 'Oh, and something about one last job, but I don't know what that was.'

One last job. Fishton. 1986.

Since the day she'd left Manjan in their tiny Stockholm apartment in 1978, Ladyjan had become somewhat settled. She'd remained in Sollefteå, a small riverside town in the middle of Sweden, and lived with the same friend who had picked her up eight years ago and taken her there.

Ladyjan had spent her first few evenings in Sollefteå down at the river, taking what she could from unsuspecting strangers' back-pockets, but the town was small and most of the population knew most of the population. It wasn't long before she knew the people she was stealing from, and that made it harder to not get caught.

It was Ladyjan's friend who told her about the job going at the local fishing school, boxing up the fish that the students had caught so they could take them home to cook. A steady income, a sociable job and an all-round pleasant way to live. You'd be surprised at the number of people who enjoy living as a box-packaging specialist and technician.

Something was missing though.

'He'll never find you in Sollefteå,' Ladyjan's friend said quietly over dinner. 'If you love him, you need to look for him.' Ladyjan didn't respond, so her friend continued. She told Ladyjan a story about a girl called Olivia who had moved to Sollefteå years ago because people thought she was mentally ill. The girl had lived in Sollefteå most of her life, seemingly happy, but there was a part of her that was missing – a girlfriend whom she'd left in Stockholm. I know that you know the rest of this story, but it was the first time Ladyjan had heard it and the ending, along with a profound emptiness somewhere near her heart, made her cry.

'But I don't even know where he is,' she said.

Fishton in 1986 was the same as the Fishton that Manjan knew when he was a child back in 1965. It was also very similar to Fishton today. Fishton rarely changes.

As Ladyjan drove, in full disguise, down the only road in and out of Fishton, she began to shake. She didn't know the exact reason for the shaking. Fear? Sadness? Anger? Whatever the reason, she would use it.

She parked outside the house where Manjan had grown up, tied up a stranger and ultimately lost a child. For Ladyjan this house held only bad memories, but if Manjan was in Fishton, this was where he would be.

At 3.30 pm she watched two children run into the house, pushing each other and laughing. At 4.07 pm she watched the same children come back outside again and kick a ball to each other in the freshly cut, no-longer-overgrown front garden. At 4.11 pm she watched one of them fall over and bleed from the knee and at 5.16 pm she watched a man in a stained t-shirt step outside the front door and kiss a woman walking in through the garden with a briefcase. The children followed.

Ladyjan daydreamed about living like the people who were living in Manjan's old house long after that day, but on that particular day she didn't. Instead, at 5.49 pm, she started up her car and drove down to the harbour.

The doors to the factory were wide open and the noise of manual workers and machinery poured into the car park, over the bank of grass and to the spot in the trees where Ladyjan was hiding. If it were nice weather the sun would be setting, but it wasn't, and instead the rain just grew darker. Eventually the workers started leaving, none of them dressed for the weather and several holding their hands over their heads for shelter.

The doors remained open. After an hour of waiting, a soaking Ladyjan considered crossing the car park and entering the building, but as soon as she'd plucked up the courage, a muscular teenager and a short man (who made Ladyjan shudder) walked out, sheltered under an umbrella. The short repugnant man locked the doors with a large chain as the muscular teenager took an inordinate amount of money out of his raincoat pocket and laughed. They stood together discussing something by the doors before they both got into a sports car and left.

Ladyjan waited shivering for one more hour before she cranked open a window with a car jack and slipped inside. The fish factory, like Fishton itself, hadn't changed, except for one thing; it used to be a large warehouse full of industrial machinery and buttons that Ladyjan was scared to touch, but now it was a large warehouse full of industrial machinery and buttons that Ladyjan was not scared to touch. She planned to touch the hell out of them, in fact.

As soon as she pressed the first button (the one on the forklift truck that she'd just climbed up on) an alarm sounded through the factory.

Determined and cool, Ladyjan drove across the factory floor and through the short man's office door, smashing it down as she did. The short man's desk fell to pieces as the truck slowly reversed out of the office which had once served as a prison to Ladyjan and many others. Hurried but focused, she jumped out of the forklift, found a key in the rubble and then reversed the forklift again, back through the factory to the garage door (which crumpled under the force of two iron forks).

The rain felt even heavier now but the wind cooled her down from the frantic adrenaline. As she drove away from the factory and closer to the water, the alarm grew quieter.

She fumbled as she crammed the key into each of the soulless cement prefab lock-ups which stood along the waterfront, to find the right one, repeatedly looking back to the factory, knowing that she was on a deadline.

After the fourth unopenable lock-up she started to shout expletives into the rain. She looked back to the factory. A light went on. Another expletive.

The fifth lock-up, a green door, KEEP OUT painted on the top. Ladyjan recognised the paint. She pushed the key in and turned it while whispering a thank you to no one. A man's voice shouted something from the factory, although what he was shouting didn't seem directed at anyone in particular.

'He hasn't seen me,' Ladyjan repeated to herself, 'he hasn't seen me.'

When she turned the forklift back on, he saw her. She

drove the forklift into the green lock-up, picked up ten crates, reversed, moved the handle forward, jumped off the moving truck and ran.

'#$@&%!' the man shouted angrily as he pushed her to the wet, concrete harbour floor. 'Who are you?' he screamed, towering above her. It was the muscular teenager from the car park.

Ladyjan managed to utter the name of the lamp-seller in Delhi, but she didn't know why. Then she said something about Manjan's father. People say some strange things under pressure. The teenager wasn't listening anyway. Ladyjan looked up for a second, expecting to see the last thing she would ever see, but instead she saw the boy holding his head with both hands and noiselessly screaming into the sea. The forklift and its ten crates rolled into the sea.

It wasn't until the sound of it sinking had subsided that Ladyjan could hear the teenager's muted scream break into an agonising cry.

'Lamps! He's going to kill me!'

Luckily, by the time Ladyjan did hear this, she was hidden by the trees.

'What do you think it was?' Shakey asked Manjan loudly over the cheering 'silent' disco.

'Probably nothing,' Manjan replied equally loudly, and then as the cheering died down, he shouted, 'stealing cash, maybe someone's passport,' and the two people next to him at the bar moved to a different chair.

CHAPTER 39

A CRAB, A COW, A PUPPY, A MOUSTACHE AND A VEST

Goa, India. 2016.

The earth shook. The beach became full of commotion as it moved this way and that. People came running out of their beach huts, all with questions but none with answers. The waves in the sea had started hitting each other and breaking both towards the sea and towards the land simultaneously, and occasionally, one of the beach huts that had been badly built on top of stilts, fell to the ground.

The crabs stopped rolling their tiny balls of sand and disappeared below the cracks in the beach, the puppy whined a high-pitched whine and the cow attempted to wobble towards it to offer protection.

Eventually, after two tremors, the earth stood still again.

The lady who sold melons said something to the man who worked at one of the bars, who in turn opened the hatch on his drinks cabinet. Those who could return to their huts, did, and those who couldn't, settled their nerves with a drink. Many slept on the beach.

Manjan snored through the earthquake. At one point he muttered something to the moving earth about leaving him alone, and during the second tremor he turned over with a low grunt.

Shakey also slept through the earthquake, his head bobbing along to the bed's movement with his mouth slightly open, completely unaware of how vigorously his body was being thrust about the room.

If Shakey didn't notice the earthquake, there was no chance that he would notice his top lip as it quivered and pushed through a single ginger hair.

PART SIX

PART SIX

CHAPTER 40

A FLY

Goa, India. 2016.

Manjan stepped outside, holding his head in one of his hands. It pounded, but it often pounded.

The people who had slept on the beach had moved out of the way for the sunbathers. Manjan looked to his right. A French couple were rolling out their towels and unpacking various beach objects from an oversized floral bag while a cow looked out to sea.

Then Manjan looked to his left. He could see the rocks where the beach ended. The COCK-tail sign had fallen to the floor and had been buried slightly by the sand. Manjan couldn't help but show a little smile. A bit further down the beach an Indian family were playing in the water – the adults fully clothed, and the children fully not.

There was no sign of Ladyjan.

He looked right again. There was a pile of wood behind the French couple that wasn't normally there, and the cow was jolting her head down and then up again, seemingly distressed. Something wasn't right. A puppy ran in circles excitedly next to the cow.

Manjan looked to his left. He strained his eyes as hard as he could, but still he couldn't see her. It was no good. She wasn't there. Just like she hadn't been there the day before, or the day before that. He always looked anyway, just in case, because probably, one day, Ladyjan would be there, and he'd hate to miss it.

It wasn't until after a spot of yoga, when he was ordering his usual fruit salad in the nearby health restaurant that someone mentioned an earthquake to him. He hadn't registered the missing beach huts or the hum of discussion between those who had woken up. 'What else hadn't he registered?' he wondered, rubbing his forehead.

Then he looked right again and then he looked left again.

Manjan continued the rest of his day as he always did. He chatted with the melon-selling lady for a while, before going to the same health restaurant for lunch (this time ordering a masala dosa). Then he scanned the beach for Ladyjan.

In the evening, after scanning the beach for Jan, Manjan sat in the same bar that he had sat in the night before with a glass of red wine. He half-expected Shakey to come and sit next to him, but he didn't. Instead, Manjan sat alone with his thoughts and memories until sundown, when he had a quick look around in case Ladyjan had turned up before he made his way to bed.

Shakey did not step outside that morning. He spent his morning binge-watching a TV programme that he had downloaded before his flight to India. He didn't understand how his not-unpacked but open backpack had moved from one side of the room to the other, but he had probably done it when he'd come in the night before. Probably.

By the time the fourth episode was playing, Shakey realised that he hadn't been paying attention to his laptop and he started the series again. He paid even less attention the second time and he didn't even look at the screen the third.

Shakey never saw the morning beach clean-up operation, in which both tourists and locals worked together to move the broken huts, even though it was just outside his door, but travelling can be like that sometimes. He did spend some time lying on his bed watching a fly move from the bedside table to the window ledge and then back again repeatedly. It was one of those large black flies that make a lot of noise when they fly and it was that noise that sent Shakey to sleep.

For lunch, Shakey ate a packet of crisps and three chocolate bars from his backpack. He felt terrible and couldn't face the outside world, so he didn't see the fishermen bring in their catch (hundreds of freshly caught fish, a few crabs and a starfish) and he didn't see the group of sunbathers walk over to watch and congratulate them. He did see the fly land on his head, though, and that made him hit himself, which in turn reminded him of how much his head still hurt from the combination of vodka and Red Bull buckets and wine. That afternoon Shakey had another nap.

He woke up again at 5 pm, but he didn't leave his room until six. Instead, he put on the first episode of the series he hadn't really been watching again, and didn't really watch it again. As his laptop played, Shakey watched the fly attempt to find a way out of the now stuffy and smelly room.

Had Shakey left his room at 5pm, he'd have seen the girl from the fishing trip order a small plastic bucket of vodka and Red Bull at the bar next to his room. She sat down for about thirty minutes, but after fending off some unwanted attention from two male vests who had arrived at the beach that day, she left. When Shakey left his room, she had gone.

After sweating his way through a chicken vindaloo by himself, Shakey went back to his room. He opened the door and pulled his laptop onto his knees, searched through his emails and found one with the subject: 'Your trip'. What was it that the old man had said yesterday? Something about seeing the world properly?

The fly sat on the windowsill, unaware that Shakey had left the door open. Then it moved to the bedside table.

As Shakey hovered his arrow over a button that read 'change your flights' and held his breath, the fly found its way to the doorframe. Shakey clicked, exhaled and then stared at the screen for several minutes.

He didn't notice the fly move back to the bedside table and he didn't notice the fly go past the doorframe, leave Shakey's stuffy and smelly room and enter the vastness of the entire world.

CHAPTER 41

A FAMILY MEMBER

Cambodia and Thailand. 2016-2017.

When Norman first visited Kampot in Cambodia, he had expected to visit the secret lake (which was conveniently highlighted on a map in the *High-Tide Travel Guide*) and then leave the next day. But, when he arrived, a coconut fell from a tree next to Norman's head. He picked it up and took it to the hostel bar.

'This could've killed me,' he said, but in a much calmer way than you probably read it. The man behind the bar smiled and then laughed.

'But it didn't,' he said. 'Here.' He took the coconut from Norman, plunged a hole in it with a corkscrew and then turned towards the back wall of the bar. When he passed the coconut back to Norman it had a straw sticking out of the top.

That night was hazy. From what he remembered, Norman made good friends with the barman and they might have created new lyrics to some old '80s hits together. Unsurprisingly, Norman did not make it to the secret lake that day. He'd go tomorrow.

The next day, Norman asked the barman how to find the secret lake (it was signposted) and the barman went into some depth, before he noticed a girl standing behind Norman.

'Can I help?' the barman smiled, looking around Norman's head.

'A room for the night?' the girl asked as she dumped her backpack on the ground. 'I want to see the secret lake.'

'I'm off to the secret lake too,' Norman said, by way of an offer.

The girl sat with Norman and listened to the barman explain in detail how to get to the secret lake (it was down the road, on the left). Then she ordered a vodka and Red Bull and Norman ordered a rum.

That night was also hazy. Norman thinks that he, the barman and the girl had played crazy golf very badly and lost all five of the hostel's golf balls. Neither Norman nor the girl made it to the secret lake the next day. They'd go tomorrow.

The next evening, having slept through sunrise and sunset (which is of course, the best time to see the secret lake), Norman, the girl and the barman discussed the possibility of Norman working as a barman at the hostel. Norman was more than a little keen.

'I reckon I could do it,' he said, determined, even though neither the barman nor the girl had any doubt that he could – after all, the job seemed mainly to involve drinking with the guests. The hostel gate creaked, and Norman jumped behind the bar. 'Trial run,' he explained.

A ginger boy in a luminous vest came in. His mouth was slightly open and his head was bobbing in time to the bar's music.

'Shakey?' Norman asked.

'Mad Norman!' Shakey replied, with his mouth slightly more open than before. And then he saw the girl next to Mad Norman and slyly flexed his bicep.

'Hi,' he said, but he fumbled the 'h' sound a bit, so everyone thought he was just clearing his throat. Smiling, the girl waited for Shakey to say something, but he didn't.

He's so mysterious, she thought.

Shakey knew that Mad Norman was in Kampot, due to Mad Norman's extensive online bragging, but he hadn't gone looking for him. Since deciding that maybe he hadn't found himself in the sand in Goa, Shakey was now trying to learn more about who he was. So far, he'd learnt that he was incredibly nervous every time he saw one particular girl and he'd also learnt that he was a little scared of elephants. Both were disappointing things to learn.

'You were amazing on that fishing boat,' the girl said. Shakey looked pensive, which was very attractive, but was actually a result of tensing his bicep for too long. He laughed unnaturally.

'Have you seen the secret lake?' he blurted.

'Not yet,' the girl responded, with an implication in her tone. There was a long pause in which, feeling uncomfortable, Norman offered them both a drink.

'Shall we go today?' Shakey asked with a slight croak in his voice, and the girl nodded with a large smile spreading from her lips to her cheeks and then to her eyes.

'I'm Moira,' the girl said with her hand firmly extended.

'Moira,' Shakey repeated.

'Wow, what a coincidence,' Moira said, 'we have the same name!'

'Sorry, no, I'm Shakey,' Shakey said, and then he held Moira's hand and shook it lightly, like a parent might do to a baby.

'Oh,' Moira said, 'I get it!'

Shakey and Moira both stayed in Kampot longer than they expected to. They talked, they listened, they drank and at one point they kissed. Moira was from a town called Fishton, which Shakey was sure he'd heard of before, but he couldn't work out why. When they did eventually make it to the secret lake, it turned out to be a very busy secret, so the next day they explored further and found a cave together (which was so secret that it didn't even have a name) and then spent a whole day in it.

Shakey and Moira travelled across Cambodia together and then into Thailand, by which point they had become more than friends.

When they got to Bangkok, Moira told Shakey that she had to fly back to Goa to meet her parents before she could carry on with the rest of her trip. Did Shakey want to join her?

'I'm trying to learn more about myself,' Shakey told Moira in a worldly way that Moira admired, 'and what I learnt in Goa was that I needed to leave Goa.'

The night of her flight, Shakey and Moira watched the sunset over Wat Arun from the river. When it was dark Moira called a taxi, kissed Shakey softly and then set off to the airport.

The sunset really can be spectacular.

Mad Norman stayed in Kampot and worked as a barman, with the barman, for the next three years. It turned out the barman was his second cousin and through each other they learnt more about their respective extended families, and in turn, about themselves, than either had ever imagined possible.

During the second year in Kampot, Norman and the barman compiled a family tree together and spoke to their respective extended families on the phone.

'Wait,' said Norman, holding his hand flat on the page where the barman had just entered a name, 'how do you know my great grandfather was called that?'

'Your dad told me,' the barman replied, picking up a coconut from the ground and reaching for his corkscrew.

'Mr N Hemming,' Norman said to himself. 'Aka Mad Norman.'

CHAPTER 42

A RAT

Australia and Fiji. 2017-2018

Shakey may have felt as if he'd had an 'awakening' when he changed his flights after his night with Manjan, but a vest does not simply just stop being a vest. On the Great Ocean Road, Shakey 'found himself' in some sand again and, in Sydney, he thought he'd had a genuine 'home visit' with someone local. This was only true if, after you say 'local', you also say 'to London, England'.

He'd been travelling for two years now and it had been over a year ago that he and Moira had shared their last sunset. He had considered going home three times since they'd parted, but he hadn't. Something wasn't complete.

It was in one of Sydney's many vest-frequented clubs, while accidentally taking part in a mating ritual, that Shakey realised once and for all that it was over. He had to go home. He was talking to a girl in a luminous green vest which advertised a local beer, and she was pretty, but Shakey wasn't flexing his bicep. What was the point?

'Do you want a drink?' Shakey shouted, interrupting the girl mid-sentence. She laughed and then she nodded. Glumly, Shakey pushed his way through the crowd. He would buy the girl a drink, but then he would go back to his hostel room and book flights back to England.

'What did you say?' shouted the barman over the music, even though Shakey hadn't said anything yet.

'A bucket,' Shakey replied quietly.

'What?' the barman shouted again. Shakey didn't reply. The door behind the barman opened and a wave of steam from the overworked dishwasher poured out. Shakey watched as a hand waved its way through the steam, held on to the bar and then...

'Moira?' Shakey shouted above the music.

'What?' shouted the barman.

They sat in the club car park with two cars, a large blue and black bin and a rat.

'My parents cut me off,' Moira said. 'After I met them in Goa they told me that they'd pay for my flights, but I have to pay for the rest. After Australia, it's Fiji and then home for me.' Shakey said he was sorry and Moira laughed at him. 'They paid for my flights,' she said. 'That's still pretty good.'

The rat shuffled about in some newspaper deciding what to eat next. He'd just finished a pizza crust and wanted something to follow it up with, maybe a cinnamon swirl. The rat visited the same blue and black bin at the same time every night – around the time that the kitchen threw out the waste.

'I'm going home,' Shakey said eventually, although he was less convinced that he was now. 'I'm done travelling I think. I miss my parents.'

'You said,' Moira paused, remembering something Shakey had told her a year ago, 'you said that your parents are your best friends. That's sweet.'

It was 3 am and the other barman had left. The night was warm, the moon was full and neither Shakey nor Moira were looking at each other.

'Full moon,' Shakey said uselessly, and then silence.

Moira shuffled her trainers in the gravel and the rat looked up. He'd heard a noise and that normally meant trouble. Rats are clever animals; they learn from past mistakes. Moira turned quickly towards Shakey as the rat scurried away to hide.

'Come to Perth,' she said, 'that's where I'm going next. Come to Perth and don't go home, not yet.'

Fiji

Shakey's plane landed in Fiji after eight insanely happy weeks in Perth. Once again, Shakey had changed his flights, this time so that he could join Moira in Fiji. He hadn't been able to book the same flight as Moira, though, so he decided not to tell her that he was coming. It would be a romantic surprise.

On his first day in Fiji, Shakey visited Sri Siva Subramaniya Temple.

He looked to his right.

He looked to his left.

Then he looked to his right again.

Then he looked to his left again. Moira wasn't there.

On his second day in Fiji, Shakey visited Denarau Island. Again, Shakey looked to his right, and then again, he looked to his left. The island was beautiful; dark green tropical plants, long stretches of white beaches and crystal-clear sea. Only one thing was missing. Moira.

Moira had visited Denarau Island yesterday, but today she was visiting a local eco park.

On his third day in Fiji, Shakey visited a local eco park. He looked to his right. Moira was not there. He looked to his left. Moira was not there either. Not today. He looked in front of him and he looked behind him. He looked around every tree and across every bridge, but Moira was not there. Moira was visiting the Sri Siva Subramaniya Temple that day, but Shakey had already looked there…

On his fourth day in Fiji, Shakey didn't leave his hostel room at all. He thought about Manjan, the lonely moustache he'd met in Goa. He knew that Manjan would still be sitting on Palolem beach by himself. Ladyjan wouldn't be there. Of course Ladyjan wouldn't be there.

But that was Manjan. Shakey pulled his laptop out from his backpack, sat on the edge of his bed, and paid for one last flight.

CHAPTER 43

A FISH

Fishton. 2019.

Professional fishermen never look at their fish. Not properly. They might pick out some seaweed or categorise the catch for selling, but a cod is a cod and a plaice is a plaice.

In Fishton, when the fishermen come in, tourists gather to watch. They look at the haul and they discuss the boats, but, like the fishermen, very few tourists will think beyond the weight of a halibut to consider how the halibut's day has been.

Shakey watched a large net being lifted off the boat and onto Fishton's cold, hard paving slabs. His mouth was slightly open and, although he didn't realise it, his head was bobbing slightly to the sound of a seagull's rhythmic call.

'Caaa.'

He marvelled at the sheer amount of fish – so many more fish were caught in Fishton than in Palolem.

Shakey didn't notice the small, ageing grey haddock that had flopped down on top of seven other younger fish. This was fair, though, as the haddock had spent its eight-year life not noticing anyone. It had never been caught before and even now, surrounded by humans, it chose not to notice them. In fact, the haddock had only ever had one relationship at all and that wasn't by choice.

When it was five years old (which is not young for a haddock), the haddock had swum under a rock, turned around and looked out from under the rock before swimming away again. It did this most days, but on this particular day, it had noticed another haddock copying it. It wasn't mating season and the haddock didn't have any interest in forming any other kind of relationship (few haddocks do), but no matter where the haddock went that day, the other haddock followed.

And the next day.

After a few days of being followed, the haddock had stopped even noticing the other haddock. It wasn't so much that one was following the other, but instead, they simply swam together. As far as both haddocks were concerned, that's how it had always been.

Shakey watched the mass of grounded fish all hitting into each other with expressionless faces. He watched, but didn't see, the small ageing grey haddock move through the mass of fish to the other side of the net and, because of their expressionless faces, Shakey did not notice the two haddocks find each other. Neither Shakey, nor the fishermen and certainly none of the other tourists cared that the two haddocks had managed to flap about next to each other for the last few minutes of their conjoined lives on the pavement.

But then, the haddocks didn't see Shakey either. They didn't see the fishermen and they didn't see the tourists. They didn't know that Shakey was waiting in Fishton for a girl called Moira, they would never find out that the smallest fisherman on the boat always struggled when making small talk with girls, and they didn't care about any of the hundreds of stories that the tourists kept within them.

And that's a shame really, if you think about it.

Shakey wasn't sure what to do with his time in Fishton. He knew that Moira would be there when she returned from Fiji, but he didn't know when that would be, and he didn't know where her parents lived.

Most days, he had watched the fishermen bring the fish in and then queued with the rest of the tourists at one of the fish shops. He'd enjoyed a game of pirate-themed mini-golf (he was only human) and chatted to several people with bells around their ankles about music.

He'd walked past the old fish factory to find that the building was empty and unused. He didn't fully remember the old moustache's story but seeing the building derelict made Shakey smile an insanely wide smile for some reason.

One night, in one of Fishton's darkened pubs, Shakey had spoken to an old man wearing an England football shirt and large leather boots. The man told him several stories from his fishing days. There were stories of treacherous storms and of sea creatures that nearly sank one of the many boats he had captained. He told Shakey about impressive hauls and underhand deals with restaurants and shops that he was proud of. Before Shakey left the pub, the man with the England shirt boasted about the time he'd caught a stowaway on his boat and heroically handed him in to the police, but, as I'm sure you can tell, the man's stories were not completely accurate.

By the end of spring, Shakey felt at home in Fishton. He loved the quaint cobbled streets, the sign that pointed to the only road in and out of town and the fun names that the fish shops had. Fishton truly was 'A Plaice to Remember', but no matter how much Shakey roamed the streets in the day and the pubs in the evening, he was yet to see Moira.

In an attempt to increase his search, Shakey started to participate in some of the town's summer street folk dances so he could get a good look at who was in the crowds (or, at least, that's what he told himself), and he applied to go to every single town hall social group, just in case. Moira wasn't at the knitting group and she wasn't at the scarecrow-making group. It was when Shakey sat down to discuss a fear of dust, which he didn't actually have, to a group of impeccably clean men and women, that he realised his search was getting desperate.

The following day, Shakey decided to stop trying. He would stay in Fishton and at some point, Moira would turn up, but until then, he would relax. He rang his parents and asked if they wanted to visit him in the next couple of months (they did) and he packed a small bag with a towel, sunglasses and some headphones. He walked out of his room, down the pebbled steps into town, around the corner, past the pirate-themed mini-golf and down the slipway onto Fishton beach. He unrolled his towel onto the sand, put his headphones in and looked out to sea.

Shakey wondered what country he'd get to if he travelled

directly across the North Sea from where he was sitting. Probably Norway, he thought. Maybe Sweden. He put his elbows on the sand, leaned his head back, relaxed and finally he fell asleep.

The beach was crowded when Shakey woke up. A group of gulls were circling above him in the sky and a small boy ran past him, scattering sand on his chest. Shakey stood up, dusted the sand off him and walked to the water's edge to cool down.

The beach was alive with crowds of people sunbathing and enjoying the sea. A lady was playfully splashing her young son while he giggled and unsuccessfully tried to push the water back at her. A large woman rubbed sun-tan lotion onto her equally large husband's hairy shoulders and then pulled a hair out from her fingers. A teenage couple sat on the beach wall eating fish and chips together, and a million stories went unnoticed by a million others.

On his way back to his towel, Shakey noticed a lady dressed in colourful baggy trousers, a white shirt, sunglasses and a wide-rimmed straw hat, standing up straight at the back of the beach. One of her hands was held up to her forehead as if she was searching for something. Then she looked to her right. After a minute or two she looked down to the floor.

Then she looked to her left. Shakey watched the lady scan the beach two more times as he walked past his towel and through the crowd of people. He passed a hundred different lives and a million unique stories as he walked to the back of the beach.

'Um,' Shakey started as he approached, 'Jan?'

CHAPTER 44

A SMALL QUAIL WHO RE-OCCUPIED THE TREE

Sweden. 1979.

With two quails to the right of her and one on the left, the quail who used to occupy the tree listened to the same deafening noises of the garage that she had listened to every day for the past year.

Noise is good, she chirped to herself, as she did every day. Noise is forgetting.

Some days aren't like every other day though. Some days change everything.

The raised hood above her head shook and the engine she was sitting on jolted. That had never happened before. Over the past month, the quail had watched the garage slowly empty. She'd watched as men had taken down a sign outside the garage door, and she'd noticed fewer people come into the garage every day. She had never expected them to clear out her home.

The wheels started rolling, and she saw that the three quails she shared an engine with (but had still never acknowledged) looked just as panicked as she did. As they rolled onto the street and across the road, the hood dropped and the four of them were plunged into total blackness.

A year ago, this would have been perfect. A year ago, the quail would have appreciated blackness, but today she was scared.

She could hear faint noises from outside but nothing distinguishable over the loud roar of the old, previously unused car engine. After what had felt like hours in the dark, the engine stopped.

'I reckon there's something jammed in there,' a man's voice called to another man in the car, although the quail didn't understand. 'I'll have a look.'

The boot popped open and the engine was flooded with light. The four quails all jumped out, a little blinded and a little clumsy.

As her eyes adjusted to the light, the quail began to make out where she was. It was St. Djurgården, her old home. Her thoughts and her memories flooded back to her in the quiet of the park, but she found that she didn't want darkness and she didn't long for noise.

'Chirp,' said another quail. It was one of the quails from the engine.

In the noise of the garage, she'd never heard him chirp. She looked back at him.

'Chirp,' said the quail.

ACKNOWLEDGEMENTS

We Are Animals was originally released as an ebook exclusive in March 2020 or, as pretty much everyone in the UK considers it now, the month that the pubs closed. As it happens, I was more concerned about the closure of trampoline parks, but hey, in the words of High School Musical, we're all in this together. I sang that song *a lot* in 2020.

This book has received a great deal of support over the past year, and the fact that it now exists in paperback is thanks to the tremendous support of early readers, bookstagrammers, bloggers, my fellow debut authors and a whole mass of people with nothing better to do than watch me make an idiot of myself nightly on Twitter.

I should probably explain the Twitter thing…

To get myself through lockdown, I started to upload a different reading from *We Are Animals* every night, each one in the style of someone different (including Eminem, Celine Dion and the cast of Hawaii Five-O). The fact that this ridiculous idea carried on for as long as it did is testament to the amount of people willing to support it. The internet is full of astounding, fascinating and clever content. I'm aware that the decision to watch me pretend to be Mr Tumble was an act of kindness, and I am very grateful for that.

We Are Animals took around four years to write, but it was not a lonely experience. I had a lot of help. In particular, I want to thank Gemma Tordoff, Hannah and Harry Parkin and Beth Geere for going through the chapters for me, editing them, and letting me know what you liked and what you didn't. You have all been invaluable.

My wife, Gemma, didn't only help to edit the book, but she also pointed out, around four chapters in, that I'd forgotten to add a plot. This book may literally never have ended, or indeed begun, without her. Thanks, Gemma, not just for that, but for everything. I also want to thank my son, Indy. I can't honestly say that he helped me write the book. The truth is that there were probably times when he hindered it (Gemma could tell which chapters I'd written on only three hours sleep), but thank you anyway, Indy, for being the perfect son that you are.

Thank you to everyone at Lightning Books, not only for choosing to publish *We Are Animals*, but for making the journey such a collaborative and enjoyable one. Thanks, in particular to Dan, Simon, and Clio for all of your time, effort and hard work, and to Ifan Bates for creating the stunning cover. I see it every day (yep, I'm *that* guy) and I still love it.

I'm grateful to my employers for allowing me to book a meeting room every day in my lunch breaks to write. That's basically moonlighting when I could have been putting in the extra hours. So, um…let's not dwell on that, and thanks.

Thanks also to Mum and Dad, John Howell, Paula Ewins,

my sister Katie Ewins, Mark Smith, Ann Trotter, Debbie and Matt Hepworth, the Giles family, Becky O'Neill, Chris Coomber, Craig Evans, Sue and Ade Clark, Emily and Luke Sessions-Glenn, Chris Pavey, Jake Cooper, Dan Hiles, Greg Cox, Lucie Ellrich, Ali Castriotis, Michelle Pavey, Sara Mather and Tim Blowers. You have all changed the book in some way. Just to clarify, your changes made it better.

Luther, you're my favourite animal. Good dog.

And finally, a massive thank *you* for reading. I hope you enjoyed it. And well done for reading to the end of the acknowledgements; I'd have probably given up during that long list of names.

Oh, and if watching authors pretend to be someone else while reading from their book is your thing, you can do that here: **https://www.eye-books.com/post/tim-ewins-the-author-of-many-voices**

If you have enjoyed *We Are Animals*, do please help us spread the word – by posting a review on Amazon (you don't need to have bought the book there) or Goodreads; by posting something on social media; or in the old-fashioned way by simply telling your friends or family about it.

Book publishing is a very competitive business these days, in a saturated market, and small independent publishers such as ourselves are often crowded out by the big houses. Support from readers like you can make all the difference to a book's success.

Many thanks.

Dan Hiscocks
Publisher
Lightning Books

⚡ New Voices from Lightning

WE NEED TO TALK

Jonathan Crane

It's 2019 in Sudleigh, a market town not far from the south coast. It's not a bad place to live, provided the new housing development doesn't ruin it, but most residents are too caught up in their own grudges, sores and struggles to notice.

Gap-year Tom is cleaning toilets but finding unexpected solace in his Chinese house-share. Former lounge musician Frank wants to pass his carpet business to his nephew Josh, killing the boy's dream to become a chef. Sharp-elbowed phone-sex operator Heather will stop at nothing to become manager of the golf club. Miss Bennett keeps putting her house on the market when she doesn't want to move.

Do they all know how their lives are linked? And will creative writing tutor Tony, hard at work on his ironic pseudo-children's book, *The Jazz Cats*, ever pluck up the courage to leave his unappreciative girlfriend Lydia?

Meticulously observed, with flashes of wicked comedy, *We Need to Talk* offers a jigsaw puzzle of unwitting connections for the reader to assemble. The finished picture is an unflinchingly honest portrait of multi-jobbing, gig-economy Middle England on the eve of Covid.

A hymn to the mundane, as intricately crafted as an Ayckbourn play. A brilliant first novel – Ailsa Cox

THE GIRL FROM THE HERMITAGE

Molly Gartland

It is December 1941, and eight-year-old Galina and her friend Vera are caught in the siege of Leningrad, eating wallpaper soup and dead rats. Galina's artist father Mikhail has been kept away from the front to help save the treasures of the Hermitage. Its cellars could provide a safe haven, as long as Mikhail can survive the perils of a commission from one of Stalin's colonels.

Three decades on, Galina is a teacher at the Leningrad Art Institute. What ought to be a celebratory weekend at her forest dacha turns sour when she makes an unwelcome discovery. The painting she starts that day will hold a grim significance for the rest of her life, as the old Soviet Union makes way for the new Russia and her world changes out of all recognition.

Warm, wise and utterly enthralling, Molly Gartland's debut novel guides us from the old communist era, with its obvious terrors and its more surprising comforts, into the bling of 21st-century St Petersburg. Galina's story is an insightful meditation on ageing and nostalgia as well as a compelling page-turner.

Compelling and enthralling...a convincingly authentic story, as well as a moving and thought-provoking one – NB Magazine

Stunning... Here is human survival in every form. An extraordinarily well-written book for a debut – Historical Novels Reviews

Elegantly written, convincing...an enthralling read –Yorkshire Times

Shortlisted for the Impress Prize; longlisted for the Bath Novel Award